DOCTOR WHO

RAGS

MICK LEWIS

BBC

Published by BBC Worldwide Ltd,
Woodlands, 80 Wood Lane
London W12 0TT

First published 2001
Copyright © Mick Lewis 2001
The moral right of the author has been asserted

Original series broadcast on the BBC
Format © BBC 1963
Doctor Who and TARDIS are trademarks of the BBC

ISBN 0 563 53826 0
Imaging by Black Sheep, copyright © BBC 2001

Printed and bound in Great Britain by Mackays of
Chatham
Cover printed by Belmont Press Ltd, Northampton

Luckily, the books he wanted were on the bottom shelf.

He pulled out *Dracula* first, a thick book with a purple cover as large as his head. He nearly dropped it, it was so heavy. He flicked through the yellow, well-thumbed pages in search of the scary bits. The bloody bits. His eyes bugged when he found them.

Next he dragged down *Dr Jekyll and Mr Hyde*. The text was dense and long-winded, but he still managed to find passages that excited him. Utterson's bones jumping on the street under the blows from Hyde's cane. He memorised the powerful words of violence, and then he reached for a third book.

This one was bound in an ancient plastic cover that depicted a monstrous figure peering between the curtains of a four-poster bed at a terrified man.

'What do you *think* you're doing?' The shrill voice cut through his secret pleasure. The librarian with her bird-like features and pointed, no-nonsense spectacles was behind him, staring down at him in rather the same awful manner as the monster on the cover.

He glanced back at the book in his hands. It was obvious what he was doing. The librarian snatched *Frankenstein* from him, holding it out so that she could examine the cover. She slammed it back into its slot on the shelf and seized hold of his right hand, pulling him up from his cosy squatting position on the parquet flooring. The rubber soles of his shoes squealed on the wood as he struggled.

'You're far too young to be reading these,' the woman barked at him, dragging the eight-year-old boy away from the adult section of the library. She didn't notice him snatch *Dracula* and slide it under his jumper. He hugged the book close as she dumped him in the children's corner.

'Does your mother know you're reading this sort of thing? I don't think she would be very pleased. Although, then again, maybe *she* wouldn't care. Where *is* Mrs Sawyer?' The librarian glanced around peevishly. Although only in her thirties, the severe bun of hair and vicious glasses transformed her into a middle-aged spinster. Her brow crimped with displeasure as she realised the

1

boy's mother wasn't in the library. She crossed to the check-in desk and reached for the telephone.

The boy slumped down on a window seat in the children's corner, flicking desultorily through *The Sleep Book* and *The Sneetches*, comforted by the feel of the thick book under his jumper and the naughty thrills it would deliver later when he got home.

He glanced over his shoulder as he pulled more children's books down from the shelves. Mrs Nasty Specs was wittering away into the telephone. He hated her. Ugly witch. She was like all of them, treating him like some kind of weirdo. At school they still made him read Janet and John. He'd been reading proper books without pictures in them for about three months now at home, although his mother didn't approve. She'd clouted him once when she'd caught him with a book of horror stories by Poo. He sniggered. Not Poo: Poe. They'd been pissin' good. And he could swear like a grown-up too – especially when his mother took Poe off him; she was just like his teachers at school who thought he was stupid, just like Nasty Specs. They all *wanted* him to be stupid. But he wasn't. He'd show the pissin' lot.

His investigating fingers found a large hardback stuffed behind the leaning books, hidden like a guilty secret. Dust puffed at him as he pulled it free. He glanced at the cover, wondering idly when his mother would come and get him. And then he forgot his mother, the librarian, even the book shoved behind his jumper. Suddenly he felt very cold, even beneath the hot strip-lighting of the library.

A claw raked at his guts as he stared at the chilling illustration. Foreboding thick as lukewarm soup clogged inside him. Without knowing why he did it, only knowing that it really would be better for his peace of mind if he *didn't* do it, he opened the book and began leafing through the large illustrated pages.

Dust billowed up with each turn of the page, like kisses from the dead. And with each page, his fear grew. Not conventional homely fear that eight-year-olds could understand: not fear of the

2

dark or something under the bed. This was top-gear terror that squeezed his mind black. He was crying softly to himself after the first six pages, his little pudgy hands trembling pathetically as he held the book. His embryonic sense of self shattered. The library with its ordinary everyday walls, its Tintin posters, orderly bookcases and quiet readers seated at tables was gone. He was lost. Horror stalked him, like the grim, awful thing it truly was. The pictures in the book, luridly drawn, possessed a life of their own; they seemed to reach for him, to shriek for him, although of course he knew they didn't. They *couldn't*. And still he read, and stared, and cried.

Finally he dropped the book and staggered to his feet. The library was back around him, but it didn't feel safe and ordinary any more. And he knew it never would again. He made for the exit, tears streaming from his wide, wide eyes. Then he was outside, almost fainting, and the air was good and clean and…

He didn't even notice *Dracula* fall from under his jumper to lie forgotten on the road.

Side One

'We've been crying now for much too long...'

Chapter One

It had been a lousy gig. Doc realised they should have known better than to play a sheep-pen like St Columb, population twenty-three and a half. Nobody had even applauded, let alone danced to their racket. But then where else could they get to play? The answer was only too painfully obvious. They were hardly The Rollin' Bleedin' Stones. More like The Sex Pistols if Malcolm McLaren had decided not to choose the yob with the meningitis stare as his singer. They were nothing. They were shit.

Next to Doc in the passenger seat of the Bedford van, Animal was dozing fitfully, despite the roar of Slaughter and the Dogs playing on the dashboard stereo. A half-empty bottle of Newcastle Brown Ale was balanced on one knee. Doc glanced at the hedgehog-haired singer in irritation as he guided the van along the twisting moor road. The dozy pillock was still wearing his shades, for Christ's sake. Doc could hardly see where he was driving what with the rain and the dark, and that tosser was still hiding behind his wraparounds. Sham. Like the band. Sham soddin' '79. As he threw the van angrily round a sharp bend, the equipment slid across the back. Winston the skinhead cursed as the amp toppled on him for the umpteenth time. Nobody laughed.

A tor reared up in the headlights ahead, bleak and ominous. Doc suddenly drew the van to a halt alongside it, jerking the handbrake on roughly.

Animal stirred. 'Whass 'appenin'?' he mumbled, beer bleeding from the bottle tilted on his knee. Doc ignored him, pushing the driver's door open against the force of the wind. He needed to take a leak, but more than that, he needed air. Fresh air that didn't stink of his smelly friends, of beer, cigarettes and failure.

Rain pattered on his head and slicked down his face, and the cold blasted at him from across the moors as he made his way over to the jumble of rocks beside the road. But it felt good. It felt real. It was the beginning of May; yet out here on Dartmoor, it could have been November.

He paused before the rock pile that littered the base of the tor, his back to the dazzling headlights. Black snakes uncoiled and crawled amongst the boulders. His chest tightened in sudden panic; then he relaxed as he realised they were just the shadows cast by his long, straggly hair.

This was a wild place. He felt at home here, without really understanding why. This barren beauty, this emptiness. Here there was no sham. No laws. No rich, no poor. Here a king could be a clown, a prince a pauper. Doc was as good as them all here, with the wind roaring; and the rain, the wonderful rain, falling…

The Range Rover was doing at least sixty. And on these roads, in these conditions, at this hour, that was hardly a good idea. Or a sober idea, for that matter. But then, not one of the singing, roaring, joking young men in the vehicle *was* sober. They were returning from the University Spring Ball in Exeter, they were wearing tuxedos, and they were wired. Roger Browne was the first to see the shabby Bedford van parked awkwardly at the side of the road. But then he should have been, as he was the driver. He slammed on the brakes, yanking down hard right on the steering wheel and for a moment it looked like they might just make it. Then the wheels slipped on the wet road, the rear of the Range Rover backswiped the Bedford and the vehicle was rolling, the laughs and jokes turning to screams.

Animal was smashed sideways against the driver's seat at the impact. His beer flew from his hand. The passenger window shattered, the door bulging inwards as if a giant had punched it. The whole van rocked and slid across the road. The singer looked up to see the Range Rover rolling to a standstill on its side, and then he was climbing out through the driver's door, and doing what came naturally to him: shouting obscenities.

'You crazy bastard! Whassamatter wiv ya? Got hay for brains?' He stood in the road, staring at the overturned vehicle, waiting for someone to make a move from inside, making no effort to step forward to help. Eventually a head *did* pop out of a buckled door. And when Animal saw the well-groomed, callow face, when he saw the *tux*; when he heard the young man's cultured and indignant voice return his obscenities as he fell out on to the road, Animal began to see red.

Doc heard the rending of metal and shattering of glass as he urinated into the wind. He was about to turn to investigate when he spotted something glinting, half-buried beneath the rocks in front of him. He paused. He could hear Animal shouting now, which meant at least he wasn't hurt. He realised with a dreamy languor that he really didn't care either way. He glanced again at the glinting object and, responding to some impulse that was beyond his ken, he crouched down and tugged at it. It was a handle fashioned from some sort of bone and it resisted his efforts, so he tugged with all his weight.

Animal had the beer in him, and the fury too. If there was one thing in all this world he hated, more than coppers, more than bosses, more than *anything*, it was toffs. They made him just lose it. He'd done six months for ABH once when a toff in a pub spilled beer on him. Animal wouldn't have given a toss if anyone else had spilled beer on him, shit he did it to himself all the time. But a toff…

He had the toff by his stoopid bow tie before the bleeder could even begin to wonder if maybe he'd made a mistake climbing out of his overturned Range Rover. Animal began shaking him, speechless with rage. 'Look what you done,' he growled into the wind as rain streamed over his shades. 'Look what you soddin' *done*.' Behind him, Winston the drummer and Alf the bass player had also got out of the van. They stood in the rain looking at the dent in the driver's door like they were slowly and stupidly trying to work out how it got there.

Animal threw the toff down. The young man looked terrified.

He lay spread-eagled in the road, rain pooling under him. Animal spat on him, and lurched over to the Range Rover, yanking at the stiff passenger door, his rage only just starting.

Roger lay frozen for a moment, the expensive tuxedo sticking wetly to his back, his trousers soggy. He had been sure the punk with the shades was going to kill him. When he looked up and saw the other two lumbering towards him through the rain, all ripped leather and big boots, he began to feel *really* afraid. He rolled to his feet and dashed off into the night, towards the tor.

Doc was waiting for him in the shadow of the rocks. The ancient dagger, crumbling with rust, was held stiffly in his hand. A strange glee danced inside him as he listened to the voice telling him just what he should do. Do it now, the voice seemed to whisper. Or was it the wind, was it the rain? *Do it now.*

Roger huddled amongst the rocks, watching the punk with the shades dragging his friends, yelling and squawking, from the Range Rover one by one. He saw the boots go in, the shrieks of pain. He didn't notice the punk standing right behind him in the dark, rain pouring from his leather jacket, his eyes black with hate, the knife raised over his head.

Animal was laughing. One of the toffs had pulled a tyre iron from the Range Rover. Yeah right. Let's see ya use it, rich boy. The toff began to back away from him, across the road towards the tor.

Doc stood over the corpse, wiping the blade on the bloody tux. Blood glistened in the grass at his feet, dripped down the partially buried boulder over which the body was draped. He considered dropping the knife, then the rage swept him again and he hacked some more. He'd done it. Just like he was supposed to. The wind laughed in his head, and at last he stopped his carnage. He tottered away from the blood, his mouth wide, the knife clasped firmly in his hand. He didn't see the rock behind him begin to flicker, begin to pulse with a sickly red glow.

'Let's see ya use it, rich boy!' Animal was roaring now, the rage inside him stronger than anything he'd ever felt. *'Come oonnn!!!'*

The rich boy used the tyre iron. A glint came into his eye, and for one uncertain moment Animal recognised what it was. Hate. He could understand that; yeah, he could appreciate that. He knew it was in his own eyes. And then, the rich boy used it. He brought the tyre iron down on Animal's head with everything he could put into it.

Alf and Winston saw their mate drop to the grass like a slaughtered heifer. They had been standing around uncertainly, fearing Animal might just go too far this time. They hadn't expected this. The other toffs were leaning against the Range Rover, clutching their bruised ribs where Animal had kicked them. They looked uncertain too. The sight of Animal's blood trickling from his head, running with the sluice of rain, seemed to make them come to some sort of decision. At the same time Alf and Winston began to understand what *they* should do; especially when they saw Doc come stumbling out of the night, a gory knife clutched in one hand, grinning like Boris Karloff. The toffs threw themselves on Alf. One of them had a corkscrew in his hand, and he seemed to know what to do with it. Alf was screaming on the ground, and now Doc was slashing at the toffs. Winston would have laughed. It was all too crazy. He would have laughed...

But he was crazy too.

Rain. Rain and wind and darkness.

And death.

It stretched. Lifting from its bed of rock like mist rising from a lake at dawn. Mist solidifying, soaking up the blood that layered the rock, gathering form. Sniffing the air, sniffing the violence. Two remained alive beside the wrecked vehicle now. The thing from the rock felt the rage of the two, and the rage was good. He wanted more. More of this. With sinews that had once been stone, the creature raised its arms. And the two men became one.

Became none.

Chapter Two

If the Brigadier came in the lab just one more time 'to see what on earth he was up to,' the Doctor was sure he would have to kill him. He loved the man dearly, of course – although he would never have admitted it – but there were limits to any Time Lord's patience. Jo was bad enough, knocking over his instruments and bumbling around in general, but at least she giggled her way out of his bad books. The Brig, bless him, just became bluff and flustery if he ruined one of the Doctor's experiments with his clumsy curiosity: red in the face, and acting as though it was the Doctor's fault for having the blasted delicate instruments in his way in the first place.

But right now, at least, peace reigned in the UNIT laboratory. The Brigadier had been absent for a good half-hour and Jo had retired to bed. This was the best time for endless experiments with the ineffable mysteries of the dematerialisation process – embodied in the infernally prosaic form of the circuit now cradled between two sensors on his desk. This was when he could really concentrate, could strain his consciousness, and indeed his subconsciousness, for the slightest trace of meaning; for the faintest of clues, remembered or only imagined.

And always the clues were there, and always they remained just beyond his grasp.

It was as the Doctor was reaching an almost trance-like state of mind with the spark of knowledge just beginning to glow in the darkness of his amnesia, that the Brigadier chose to visit the lab again.

For once he didn't come out with some inane comment, but merely stood just inside the doorway, swagger stick tucked importantly under one arm, hands crossed behind his back. The Doctor tried his utmost to block the intruding presence from his mind, turning his back obstinately towards his guest and bending over the dematerialisation circuit. It was too late, of course: the firefly glow of incipient knowledge had winked out again. Gone. Maybe for ever. The Doctor closed his eyes and sighed heavily, as if all the woes of the universe were upon him – which of course they were, and now he had the burden of the Brigadier to add to them.

'I take it you're bored, Lethbridge-Stewart?' the Doctor said resignedly.

The Brigadier took this as his cue to advance into the room, like a vampire receiving a welcome invitation. 'I'm too busy to be bored, Doctor. On the contrary, there seem to be a million and one things demanding my attention.'

The Doctor turned to him, his face stern and unaccommodating. 'Then why in the blazes don't you treat one of them to a little bit of that attention, instead of continually barging in here pestering *me*?'

The Brigadier tried his best to look unfazed by this rebuke, only the merest hitching of his moustache betraying his irritation at being so directly challenged.

'May I remind you, Doctor, that this laboratory remains under my authority and that I am responsible for everything that –'

'What are you frightened of, Brigadier? D'you think I'm going to try to sneak off in the TARDIS as soon as your back's turned, like an errant schoolboy playing truant?'

The Brigadier's eyes twinkled with victory. He knew he had won this little argument. 'It wouldn't be the first time, would it Doctor?'

The Doctor surveyed him gravely for an instant. Then his irritation subsided a little. He had the grace to realise when he had been outmanoeuvred. He allowed his friend a little smile and turned back to his desk. 'Yes, well, you really have no need for concern on that score. I'm not going anywhere.'

The Brigadier strode up to the circuit that was perched like a metallic sausage on a barbecue-spit between the two sensor probes, and said, 'What on earth are you up to, anyway?'

The Doctor's smile vanished. He was about to lose his

graciousness altogether when the circuit suddenly emitted a harsh buzz, flipped into the air – narrowly missing the astonished Brigadier's head – and clattered to the floor a good ten yards away from the table. The Brigadier followed its trajectory, a look of buffoonish incredulity on his face. The Doctor was more interested in the sensor probes. They were twin cones of alloy cannibalised from the guts of the TARDIS console, and were connected to the ship by leads straggling away from the desk between the blue double doors. Now they were flashing manically and urgently and, for some reason he couldn't fathom exactly but suspected must be due to the sensors being linked to the very core of the TARDIS, their epileptic activity filled him with instant dread.

Out in the howling Dartmoor night something was moving. A large and filthy cattle truck was pulling up next to a tor on a road obstructed by two broken vehicles. The engine growled for a moment like a grumpy beast, then cut out.

The creature from the rock watched three men descend from the cab and approach the tor. These were bad men; the creature knew that from the ease with which they had been summoned. They were bad, and they were vicious. They were hungry for darkness and sin.

They would do.

She was standing outside the railway station and she couldn't remember why. Was she supposed to be meeting someone? For that matter, which station was it? The taxis parked in ranks didn't give her any clue, nor did the grimly modern buildings across the busy square. Somewhere European, she guessed. Amsterdam? Then that would be the Centraal Station behind her, and she would recognise it when she turned round to look at it. For some unaccountable and disturbing reason, she couldn't turn round. But she knew it wasn't Amsterdam. More like Eastern Europe, judging from the architecture. And now a boy was beckoning to her, so it must be him she was supposed to be meeting. He was standing beside a taxi, and he was smiling. Face a little pale, but his eyes were honest, and he was dressed well. And… and for some reason she knew she had to follow him. So she did, and it must have been something to do with her distracted state of mind, because it hardly seemed to take any time to leave the large square and to find herself in a narrow passageway hemmed in by buildings that must once have been picturesque and Gothic but were now grimy and somehow… *shamed* – as if they had for too long witnessed events that had marked them with guilt.

The boy was standing at the end of the passageway, and he was still smiling, still beckoning, and the sun was going down behind him, which was strange because she had the distinct impression it had been broad daylight when she had been waiting outside the station. Now the alley was a trench of shadows, and the boy looked drabber, dirtier, his smile not so welcoming and innocent. More guileful, desperate.

Charmagne began to feel pricked with dread. She should turn round, she knew and leave this lonely place, so near and yet so far from the busy square. She should leave. But again, it was impossible to turn. And now something was happening in front of her. A grinding sound dragged her attention to another, even smaller, alleyway branching off to the right. In the shadows she could just make out a round metallic object sliding across the paving. A hand was emerging from a hole darker than the shadows, like a pale, dirty rat questing for food. An arm followed, begrimed and sleeved in tatters. A small arm. Now a head, the head of a child, raised itself from the hole; and the face was staring at her with all the loneliness and desperation and hate that should never be in the face of a child. A boy, no more than nine, popped out of the sewer and stood there before her in his rags. Hand outstretched.

'Nu Mama,' he said. 'Nu Papa,' and Charmagne saw his broken teeth. The first boy – the one she had followed into this gloomy place and who she now realised was as ragged as the second –

had approached her now, and was pointing at the boy in front of her, at the hole behind him, which was emitting another child. A girl this time: pretty, yet somehow made wicked by her poverty, by the stained shreds of clothes which covered her gaunt body; most of all, by the absence of anything in her eyes.

'Nu Mama, Nu Papa,' they said, as they came out of the sewer.

Filthy children: so many, so many. All advancing on her with their rags and their chant and their outstretched hands, and Charmagne Peters was afraid of them, of their rat-like agility, and of their utter apathy.

They don't care, she told herself, as she backed away up the alley. They don't care, because nobody has ever cared for them.

Nu Mama, Nu Papa. *Nu Mama, Nu Papa.* NU MAMA, NU PAPA…

They don't belong, because they have no status. They have no worth, so they should not be. They should not be!

She was mouthing the words in the dark, in her bedroom. The church over by Plymouth Hoe was striking two in the morning, and her cheeks were wet with tears.

Chapter Three

There wasn't much to see except the moor and the prison, but Nick felt like staring anyway. There wasn't much else for him to do. Behind him, the muted babble of lunch-time drinkers inside the Devil's Elbow lulled his senses. Sleep dragged at him. As the sun pressed down on his eyelids he wondered idly how long Sin would take with the drinks.

'Lazy dole-scroungin' scum!'

Nick's eyes flew open, maybe expecting to see some excitement. It was only Jimmy, wearing his ever-present American Civil War Confederate cap. The wild-eyed, leather-jacketed scourge of Princetown settled down comfortably on the bench next to his friend.

'Said the kettle to the pot,' Nick murmured sleepily.

'Uh?'

'Nothing, just an obscure cliché. Don't know what it means exactly. Don't make me think about it for any longer than I have to.'

'Then don't use it. It's annoying.'

Nick accepted a cigarette off Jimmy and gazed over at the dour Victorian prison half a mile up the high street of the little town. 'And to think we stay here by choice,' he said ruminatively.

'You telling me you don't like it here?' Jimmy quipped humourlessly. It was a very old and worn joke. 'Where's Psycho Sin?'

Nick jerked his thumb behind him, indicating the pub. As if on cue she appeared in the doorway, a small, pretty Chinese girl in her early twenties, her eyes maybe a little wary, her sensuous lips pursed and stubborn. Her eyes looked even more wary when she saw Jimmy perched next to Nick. She plonked two pints down on the wooden table and sat opposite the two men.

Jimmy looked up in mock dismay. 'You didn't buy me one.'

'There's a man in there who stands behind a bar waiting to

serve people. Why don't you make his day?' Sin Yen wasn't in the mood for Jimmy.

'The Beast? He doesn't like me.'

'He's not alone then.'

Jimmy did his best Johnny Rotten sneer and sauntered off reluctantly into the pub.

'What's that bonehead doing here?' Sin asked as soon as he was gone. Her skin was translucent in the sunlight. It really was a beautiful day, Nick thought as he pulled on his cigarette. And Sin had never looked more beautiful, with her shoulder-length black hair and mahogany eyes. Yet this dismayed him oddly, as if maybe that beauty was there just to torment him. Suddenly he knew they wouldn't be together much longer. He shrugged away the fear the thought brought with it and concentrated on being his usual laid-back self.

'Hmm? Oh, just biding his time. Just like the rest of us. Killing the days.'

'Can't you get shot of him? You know he gets on my nerves.'

'We've got to stick together, Sin. It's an uncaring world out there and we need all the friends we can get.'

'He's a waster.' She sipped her pint moodily.

'Ain't we all? The only difference between us and Jimmy is he wastes his time on drugs and we waste our time brooding about being wasters. At least he's happy.'

'I just wish he'd be happy somewhere else.' It came again, with no warning: *gonna lose her*. It was like a shotgun blast cutting his soul in half, and yet there was no foundation for the thought. He turned his face towards the sun, closing his eyes; maybe the brightness would chase it away, like the shadow it was.

Jimmy reappeared, brandishing a pint of Old Peculiar.

'The Beast served you then?' Nick asked unnecessarily.

Jimmy grinned happily. This was all he expected of life: to sit in the sun with some mates and a decent pint. Nick envied him. He swigged at his beer. It might be an old Princetown joke but he really did feel like one of the prisoners. He was going nowhere: a reject in a society that only respected money. Where opportunity never knocked, only the bailiffs. Lighten up you old bastard, he scolded himself.

'Hey, lighten up you old bastard,' Jimmy scolded him. Nick realised he was looking even more po-faced than usual, and gave his friend two fingers and a reluctant grin.

Sin suddenly sat forward, squinting across the moor. 'What's that?'

They followed her gaze, screwing up their eyes against the blaze of the sun. To the north, the rugged folds of the moor, stretched to the horizon studded with rocks and tors. Half a mile from the edge of the town sunlight glinted on metal. A truck. A cattle truck, bouncing carelessly over the uneven grass.

'They'll screw up their suspension,' muttered Jimmy. Nick was more curious as to what the truck was doing driving cross-country towards Princetown. Wasn't the road good enough? Soon they could hear the growl of a diesel engine and see the thick mud caked on the corrugated flanks of the vehicle. It pulled up a hundred yards short of the low stone wall that guarded the community of Princetown from the wilderness of the moor. The growl died and for a moment nothing happened.

The windows of the cab were dark, grimy with mud. Nick, Sin and Jimmy waited.

Dartmoor prison. Thirty-two acres of grim Victorian repression crystallised in stone. A more forbidding and depressing collection of buildings it would have been difficult to imagine. The main prison block squatted on the moor like a satanic mill worked by men of shame. Hewn from the dour indigenous rock, the barracks embodied the desolation that surrounded it.

For the men who lived there, unable even to see the hundreds of miles of freedom represented by the moor because of the intentionally high positioning of the cell windows, Dartmoor prison was a hulk of human despair. The bricks, the walls, the courtyards – all were as grey as their thoughts, their dreams. The only respite from the bleak monotony that was their lives was the weekly visit to the work-farm outside the sprawling complex, when some of the men would get a snatch, however brief, of life beyond the walls of repression.

For Pemo Grimes that time was now, and he intended to make the most of it. Trudging over the moor with ten fellow cons, he decided he wasn't going to overdo things today. It was far too warm to be overly energetic in his digging and planting, despite it only being early May. Sunlight cast a golden mantle over the moors. It lifted Grimes's heart to see the usually dismal setting smiling for once. It inspired optimism, an emotion habitually alien to the long-term con. It made the remaining seven years of his sentence seem not quite as unbearable as they had the night before as he lay on his bunk, listening to the rain and the porcine snoring of his cell-mate. Shit, even the screws looked almost human today. There were three of them escorting the party that morning. There should have been more but staffing difficulties were bedevilling the prison. Nothing new there. Who the hell in their right mind would want to work in a place like this? Being a screw here, you really did share the sentence with the cons, something Grimes always derived a gritty satisfaction from. He could almost feel sorry for the bastards. They *chose* this. It didn't say much for them. You had to have real personality problems to end up being a screw. What was the difference between a con and a screw? A few bars, and a uniform.

The work party had left the circular complex some distance behind now. Grimes turned to savour the view of Princetown. He could just make out the Devil's Elbow and promised himself again that the day they let him out of the gates for good, he'd walk slowly – not rush, but walk *slowly* – to the pub, relishing every step. Once inside, he'd drink till he fell over; pick himself up, and do the same again. All the time staring out of the window at the prison, and telling himself he'd *never* go back. Still, that was for another day.

As he turned away from the view of the pub, Grimes's attention was distracted by a flurry of activity over to the north of the town, just beyond the grey wall that marked its boundary.

Three figures were bustling around a large, rusting cattle truck parked on a slight rise of ground. Sunlight reflected off something metallic; straining his eyes, Grimes made out a squat amplifier. Guitars and amps were being lugged out of the back of the truck and dumped on the grass, wires and cables were unravelled carefully. He would have put it down to some sort of spring fête if it hadn't been for the shabby and disreputable appearance of the three men.

He frowned. It was the first time he'd ever seen a band rehearse on the bloody moor. Several other cons were staring at the distant spectacle as well, and raucous laughter arose as one of them cracked a joke about the scruffy roadies and the filth coating the cattle truck.

Grimes noticed Eddie Price staring intently at the truck. Eddie was a lifer without the slightest trace of a sense of humour, and as he was in charge of the wheelbarrow full of gardening implements Officer Evans nudged him to continue walking. Price didn't respond.

'Get your big hulk moving, Price,' the prison officer barked, shoving him a little more firmly.

Price continued to stare at the distant truck, mesmerised. His lumpen features were quivering as if some great emotion were tearing through him. His eyes were stark. Grimes could see the lifer's soul bare and wild in those eyes. A killer's soul. He turned away, a cold pool collecting in the small of his back.

Across the moor, the roadies were almost ready.

Rod was waiting by the wall along with a crowd of curious onlookers; a mixture of locals and tourists, all gathering to watch the band.

Jimmy, Nick and Sin joined their friend as the band climbed from the back of the truck and strolled casually to pick up their instruments.

'Bloody hell,' Jimmy said. Rod said nothing. His usually glazed eyes were curiously alert now, although with his scruffy beard, long unkempt hair and torn dinner jacket he looked as dilapidated as ever. Nick stood next to him, his attention fixed solely on the band.

He'd never seen anything like this.

Someone was joking. They had to be. The four musicians were a pick 'n' mix mess. A motley nightmare of clashing clothing and clashing periods. They were festooned with bright tatters like seventeenth-century mummers, and their hair was dyed and spiked with punk malevolence. The singer's hair was grass-green, his trousers rags of paper stitched over hose. A torn leather jacket and wraparound shades completed the confused picture. The guitarist wore a top hat with its circular crown hanging down like a hinged lid – a cartoon tramp with minstrel trousers, leather waistcoat and spiked codpiece. The drummer was a skinhead adorned with coloured rags, tattoos and a bullet belt. The bass player was a skeletal ogre with a motley tunic, big boots and a Sid Vicious haircut.

'What's this, The Morris Pistols?' Sin said in an attempt to lighten the inexplicable unease Nick was sure she must be feeling. He was sure because he was feeling it himself, and he didn't quite know why. The sun was hot, and he was sweating inside his leather jacket. But he felt cold.

'I know the roadies,' Jimmy said as the three denim- and leather-clad men leant back against the truck to watch, their work over for now.

'Sick bastards,' Rod muttered. 'From Tavistock,' he added, as if there was a natural connection. 'Seen 'em in the Bull there. Tend to keep to themselves.' Rod knew all the seedy haunts. He'd spent his adolescence discovering them and had realised, too late, that *they* had discovered *him* and made him their own. It was no longer any good trying to escape them now. Slow, creeping alcoholism had him in its horny grasp.

'They're sick all right,' Jimmy agreed as the band tuned up, shivers of electric sound skidding across the moors. 'Been linked with most of the bad shit that goes on around here. Evil stuff, you know? Devil worship, child murder. You name it, the Old Bill's tried to pin it on 'em.'

'So where did these nutters come from?' Sin wanted to know, nodding at the musicians. Nobody answered. Nobody knew. The crowd were muttering, the way crowds do. Local Princetonians, people from neighbouring villages, strangers. But as yet, not a sign of the village bobby.

Just then, the band began to play.

'There's a good pub in Princetown,' the Doctor assured Jo as Bessie swept them along the moorland road. 'They serve a wonderful breakfast as I remember.'

'At two o'clock in the afternoon?' Jo grinned at him, her hair whipping across her pixie-like features.

'Yes, well, I had to do a bit of engineering before we could set off, if you remember.' The Doctor nodded at the device attached to the dashboard of the motorcar, a smaller version of the sensor probes that had so suddenly been activated the night before and which had since become dormant. 'And I'm sure they'll still be serving breakfast at the Devil's Elbow. The landlord's a bit of a character, mind you.'

'You really are amazing Doctor. You've dined in all the most exotic restaurants in the universe, and here you are looking forward to sausage and eggs at a pub in the middle of nowhere.'

The Doctor returned her grin fondly, his white bouffant hair barely perturbed by the slipstream. He steered Bessie deftly round the tortuous bends, past tors that had lost some of their grim aspect in the sunshine, past sheep mulling blankly over the stretches of moorland.

'The middle of nowhere is sometimes the most rewarding place to be, Jo,' he said, in his familiar mock-patronising tone. 'And sausage and eggs take some beating.'

As soon as they had reached the beginning of the moor Jo had noticed that the Doctor's eyes were continually straying towards the probe on the dashboard. They did so now, and she realised that despite his playful tone he was really rather worried about something. When she had inquired about the reason for this sudden trip to the extreme reaches of the Southwest, he had fobbed her off with some story about research. She had sensed that wasn't true then, and she was certain of it now. But for once she wasn't going to pry. If he wanted to keep things close to his chest he must have his reasons, and she wouldn't irritate him by pressing for them. A first for her, she thought, and smiled to herself proudly. She really *was* growing up quickly with the Doctor for a companion. But then that was hardly surprising was it, considering some of the things she'd been through with him.

The Doctor saw her smiling and obviously thought his attempt at obfuscating the real issue with trivial nonsense was working because his grin widened. Pompous old devil, she thought affectionately, and gazed out across the bleak but beautiful moorland sweeping past them. Despite her concern, the fresh smell of the heath was invigorating and her spirits rose defiantly.

They were nearing the town now. Outlying cottages huddled behind stone walls for protection against the encroaching bleakness. Whitewashed walls and gardens bursting with spring flowers marked a determined effort to shrug off the all-pervading mood of the moor.

They passed the houses and turned a corner to find themselves in the high street. There was the pub, over to the left; there was the prison looming in the distance; and there was the band playing on the moor beyond the town.

'Oh great, there's a fair on!' Jo chirped delightedly. The Doctor swung Bessie into the kerb beside the pub and sat for a moment with the engine running, staring in the direction Jo was pointing.

'That's no spring fair,' he said gravely. The tone of his voice made Jo turn. He looked suddenly very old. When the device on the dashboard began to glow, ever so slightly, the lines on his face deepened with his frown.

Jo forgot about her hard-won maturity. 'What *is* that thing for, Doctor?'

'It's a tracking sensor, Jo. And it means we've come to the right place.' He was dropping his avuncular attempts at protecting her from the truth and, rather than making her afraid, this only made her feel relieved. She wasn't easily fooled, despite her innocent, goofy, surface act, and maybe he was beginning to realise that. The Doctor transferred his gaze from the fluttering glow within the translucent sensor column to the band. He switched the engine off, and they could hear the music.

The music rose into the spring air with a lazy gusto that belied its vehemence. A breezy but sinister crunch of guitar, bass and drums married to the uncompromising growls of the singer. The four musicians looked like fancy-dress trolls gatecrashing an Old England fête.

'Scum,' belched the singer. 'The scum of the earth. Scum, scum, scum of the earth.'

Nick gaped. Sin stared. Rod and Jimmy began to feel like smiling, but couldn't quite do it. There was something too unwholesome about the lurching stride of the anti-tunes, the latent viciousness of the musicians. This band dealt out attitude like an axe in the face. And yet, somehow, it felt *right*. Rod and Jimmy started to let themselves go, release tensions and resentments that had been folded away inside. Let go.

Nick felt the same liberation blast through him. It was simultaneously breathtaking and terrifying. The lyrics spoke to him, the *music* spoke to him, in a cacophony that spat on melody while also courting it; a murder of song that paradoxically threw out hooks of harmony at once irresistible and repulsive.

And the band played on.

The Doctor was watching the musicians play. He and Jo stood on the fringe of the crowd, beside the wall. Jo was staring, and she was sweating. Something yawned in her, a gulf opening wide. She didn't feel the Doctor's hand as he touched her arm. She had forgotten he existed.

The Doctor withdrew his hand. Jo was trembling, and even though she was dressed as usual in a skimpy miniskirt and impractical trendy top, he knew it was nothing to do with the cold. He glanced round at the rest of the crowd. Tension, fear and excitement were jolting through them like electricity. He could taste the unease like bitter wine.

The band finished a song. A death rattle of evil guitar vibes, then silence. The green-haired singer sent a missile of phlegm into the crowd. Nobody offered a protest.

'It's time,' the singer rasped, 'for the scum… to inherit…'

The band blasted into another number.

Prison Officer Evans seized hold of Eddie Price's shoulder. 'Did you hear what I said? Move it!'

Eddie didn't blink an eyelid. Pemo Grimes was rigid beside him. The ten cons were watching the band: the music carried easily across the moor, a tremble of subversion in the sunshine.

Officer Evans had reached the limit of his patience. He whipped out his stick and brandished it before Eddie's eyes. 'You got a choice, Price. You move, or you do a month in the hole.'

'Join the Unwashed,' the singer called to them. *'Join the Unforgiving. Join the Ragged, for we are the way.'*

Price chose to move.

He stooped to pull something from the wheelbarrow in front of him, swung it upwards glinting in the sunlight, slammed one end of the pickaxe blade through Officer Evans' chin. The PO went down squawking, dragging the implement with him.

The two remaining POs watched the bloody event with a surreal lack of understanding.

Pemo Grimes moved next. He threw one thick arm around PO Jellard's throat and held him fast, choking him. PO Samuels tried to bolt for it. Three cons grabbed him, and hauled his arms behind his back.

'Join us,' the band called. *'Join the Unwashed, and the Unforgiving.'*

The riot hit the prison at forty-three minutes after two in the afternoon. All morning everything had been quiet within the complex.

Then... Bedlam.

Cons smashed everything they could get their hands on: chairs, crockery, windows, screws. The officers retreated before the onslaught, locking the doors to the main containment halls of the wings, effectively sealing off the cons' exit from the blocks but leaving them in control of large sections of the complex. The governor called an emergency meeting in his office after alerting police task-forces from Exeter and Plymouth. He listened to the bloodthirsty chanting coming from the blocks, and seriously wished he had chosen to be a baker, like his old dad.

The two guards were dragged across the moor towards the band. They tried to argue, to reason with their captors, but the cons remained eerily silent as they tramped over the heather.

The band continued to play as the prisoners approached, welcoming their new audience. Constable Jervis saw them too, as he pushed his way through the crowd, and all thoughts of simply pulling the plug on the raucous band left him immediately. He hurriedly turned back towards his car to radio for help. The crowd held him firm in their embrace. The music, the ferocious music, pummelled at his brain.

Pemo Grimes pushed Officer Jellard before him as he moved to stand between the band and the stone wall. Tom Ellis and Sparky Peters clung on to Officer Samuels, who was still attempting to appeal to their common sense, his pleas lost under the music. Eddie Price lowered his wheelbarrow.

The band finished another song. Silence. The crowd shifted

uneasily. A few uncertain cries went up. Some people began to break away. Most simply froze, waiting.

They didn't have to wait long. Constable Jervis had nearly made it out of the crowd when the band began their final number. Something made him twist his head to stare backwards. He saw the cons force the two screws down on their knees in the grass. He saw the singer chuckle lewdly into the mike. The guitarist slammed chords like pike thrusts through the audience. The bass player let loose low notes kicked out of hell. The drums exploded into a crescendo.

'We... will never... forgive.' The singer chanted the words, shaking his head slowly, grinning.

Pemo Grimes pushed Officer Jellard face down in the grass and took a shovel from Eddie's wheelbarrow. He turned the blade on its side and swung it down brutally. Once.

'We...'

Twice.

'Will never...'

Three times.

'Forgive.'

Officer Jellard's head leaked blood into the grass. Officer Samuels stopped his pleading. He gaped up into the faces of the cons, into the faces of the band.

'We will NEVER forgive.'

A pair of garden shears opened. Closed. More blood.

The four musicians killed their music and flung their instruments into the grass beside the two corpses. They turned as one and strolled slowly towards the back of the cattle truck. The cons watched them go; the roadies began to gather up the gear. The crowd began to scream.

The prison riot stopped as abruptly as it started. The cons returned to their cells like sheep, vacant and subdued, and waited for the screws.

Constable Jervis had not made it to his car. He lay three yards from it, his helmet smashed, his head smashed. Nick had seen him go under as the crowd began to panic, and now he dragged Sin away from the stampede, pulled her towards the haven of the Devil's Elbow.

The pub was deserted. Even the Beast had gone. Nick and Sin stood inside the doorway and watched the turmoil on the streets of Princetown.

After a while the Beast turned up, looking guilty and confused. Nick ordered two pints, the coins shaking in his hand, and waited for Rod and Jimmy.

And after a while, they came.

Chapter Four

Jo watched the police take the cons away. The prisoners looked dazed and confused, like they'd just woken up from the wildest party of their lives and knew they'd done something bad, but couldn't remember quite what it was. Jo was shaking. Their bewilderment scared her almost as much as their former violence. The Doctor watched them too, his eyes narrowed. Jo saw him glance at the cattle truck still waiting beside the wall. The roadies were sitting in the dark cab, smoking. The police had questioned them briefly, perfunctorily – or so it seemed to Jo. They hadn't even gone to the back of the truck to speak to the musicians.

And what were the musicians doing in the back of the truck anyway? Why didn't THEY sit in the cab?

The thought was gone almost as soon as it entered Jo's head. She frowned, but couldn't remember what she had been thinking about. The police were going; the cons were back in safe hands. The crowd was dissipating. Most of the townsfolk were silent, stunned, returning to their homes as though they too weren't sure about what had just happened. Jo could hear the jukebox playing in the Devil's Elbow. 'Black Sabbath'. It was filling up quite nicely in there, she thought, and the idea of a drink was suddenly *very* appealing. She shook herself slightly. She was acting like nothing had happened. Was she shocked too? Just like everyone else around her? Everyone except…

She hadn't said a word to the Doctor since the murders. She looked at him now, and he was still watching the truck. Her turned to her suddenly, as if she'd spoken.

'Are you all right, Jo?' He put a hand on her arm.

'I'd like a drink.' It came out abruptly, making her sound like a spoilt child.

'Of course. Go on inside, I'll join you shortly.'

'Why, what are you going to do?'

He was ushering her towards the pub, deliberately not answering her question. 'Be careful who you mix with,' he said. 'There are some decidedly odd people about.'

She was about to walk away, then stopped. She felt drugged. The whole situation was surreal. The Doctor hadn't mentioned the murders either. She could see the barman serving drinks through the open pub door, business as usual. Had the whole world tipped upside down? Had she slipped a sanity gear?

'Doctor, those prison officers – they've just been murdered. Horribly. And no one really seems to have noticed.'

The Doctor looked at her closely, the cracks around his eyes deepening as he frowned. 'You took your time, too, Jo.'

What the hell did he mean by that? She felt indignant and annoyed and was about to give him a curt answer, when he smiled compassionately at her.

'Go and have that drink, Jo.' He waited, hands on hips; a dramatic figure, cloak blowing slightly in the late afternoon breeze from the moors. She nodded and left him.

'You're that newswoman, aren't you?

Charmagne looked up from her glass of red wine. The hippie she'd been interviewing at the pub table looked up too. For a bizarre second, she thought she had found fame and fortune at last. Of course, though, the biker who had asked the question wasn't directing it at her, but rather at the BBC anchor girl who had just entered the pub along with a rotund cameraman. She felt an irrational jealousy prick her. This was *her* story. They had no right.

She frowned at herself. What the hell did she mean by that? An hour and a half ago she'd been in Plymouth, writing reports on neighbour from hell feuds and parrots sucked up by vacuum cleaners. This wasn't her usual sort of scoop. And why did she have such a personal interest in it? Her editor hadn't been convinced she should cover it, but she had practically hauled him up against the wall. She remembered the startled expression in the tubby little prat's eyes. *I'm doing this*, her tight lips and narrowed eyes had told him, without her having to say another word.

Of course he'd let her. She'd have bloody gutted him if he hadn't.

She turned back to the hippie opposite. He was scanning the TV girl's arse with more than casual interest.

'You were saying about the band?' she prompted with some impatience.

'Uh?' The hippie dragged his gaze away from the glamour girl and blinked at Charmagne. 'Any chance of another of these, love?' He held up his near-empty pint and dragged on his cigarette, squinting at her.

'You said you saw them arrive?' she insisted. He'd get another pint, but only after she'd got the whole gruesome story out of him.

'Never seen nuthin' like it. Thought this lot were crazy bastards…' He gestured at the jukebox. *What is this that stands before me? Figure in black which points at me*, the singer was droning. 'But this bunch just…' Yeah, you're lost for words, aren't you mate, Charmagne thought. Full of admiration: I can see it in your eyes. They just instigated a mini-massacre and you're *proud* of them.

'S' like all this punk shit, that's coming out now. I expect you've 'eard it. I mean, it was like them, but it wasn't. Know what I'm sayin'?'

Actually, no. That's why I'm buying you a drink, so you can tell me. She bit back her frustration. She concentrated on scribbling down some of his words, vague as they were. But there was something else fuelling her frustration – the biggest burst of excitement she had felt for a *long* time. This *was* big. Not just the murders, but something else behind them; maybe something to do with this band that played a gig, watched people die to their music and then simply strolled away. *That* was what excited her. And this long-hair was alluding to that big thing without being eloquent or intelligent enough to nail it. And that frustrated her immensely. Maybe she should talk to someone else. And then she knew she didn't need to.

A mummer had entered the pub.

The Beast had never seen the Elbow so busy. Even if it *was* full of scruffy-looking bastards he'd never seen before. He wished the town could see in a few more riots and murders, just to help his trade along a bit, you understand. He grinned as he collected empty glasses from a table and awarded himself a glance at the TV chick's legs. Mmmm. Can't beat the odd atrocity for bringin' out the talent. Yeah, he was a Beast, and he knew it. Admitted it to himself. But he had a heart of gold, y'understand.

Heart of bleeding Gold…

'That's right, my girl,' he winked at the TV girl, er, whassername… Truly Goodlegs, or somethin'. 'You tell all the good folks out there in TV land what's been goin' on. I can fit 'em all in here, see.'

She looked at him doubtfully. Like he was some sort of dog splat on her shoe. Just buy some more G&T's, ya bitch. Let my good old till chime. Anyroad, what right had she to give him a look like that when there was *this* dodgy crowd in here. Jeeeee-sus. Look at 'em. He would have refused to serve the whole bleedin' lot of 'em 'cept for the fact that he had a heart of gold.

Then the ugliest bleeder he'd ever clapped eyes on entered the pub.

Jo was sipping her half of bitter nervously. In fact, she didn't think she'd ever sipped a beer *more* nervously than she was now. Thanks, Doctor. Thanks for bringing me to the most threatening-looking place I've ever been to. Ogrons, Axons, Daleks: they were nothing compared to these freaks and villains. She'd never really adjusted to punk. Too violent, too nihilistic. The flower child in her would take some banishing. But, looking around her, she realised this crowd could kick it out of her in seconds.

Spiked hair; multicoloured hair; leather. Spiked belts. Big boots.

Most of them hadn't been here at the start of the gig, she realised. They'd just sort of materialised as the day wore on. Drawn here, like the TV crew and the Doctor. *And herself*. Still, there were a lot of hippies about too, and bikers. They seemed almost conservative now, or at least conventional, and wasn't that strange? The jukebox hadn't acclimatised to the change in the musical environment either: Hawkwind was blasting out right now, and some of the punks didn't look too amused by that. One of them spat on the floor next to her at the bar. She turned away, her anxiety deepening. She wished the Doctor would hurry up. It had been a good thirty minutes since she'd left him.

And yet, strangely enough, part of her didn't want to leave.

You're a mixed up girl, Jo, she told herself and smiled wryly. Someone next to her turned to her and smiled wryly back. Not the punk who'd spat, but a young man with a black mohair jumper and dark jeans. His eyes were a little lost-looking, his face thin but friendly. Of course, his hair was a little too spiky for Jo's tastes, but he was kind of sexy. Then a cute little Chinese girl came up behind him, close enough for Jo to get the hint they were an item, and she smiled again, this time a little wistfully.

'You all right?' the young man asked her, and Jo wondered how many more people were going to say that to her tonight.

'Well, considering I've just seen two men brutally murdered, I think I'm not shaping up too badly.'

'You saw it too, then? Thought you might be a TV person.'

The Chinese girl was frowning at her as the young man spoke. Her eyes were quite cold, and Jo imagined she could have an evil temper on her.

'No, I'm just... just a traveller,' she said and sipped her beer. Where was the Doctor?

'You don't look like a traveller.' The Chinese girl's voice was accusatory.

'I'm Nick,' the young man said a little too quickly, and grinned sheepishly at her. 'This is Sin. And going out with her *is* one, believe me.'

'You're such a corny bastard, it's embarrassing.' Sin grimaced and fired up a cigarette, grudgingly offering one to Jo. Jo shook her head and smiled her friendliest smile.

She was struck again by the unreality of the situation. Here were these two, having a domestic in front of her. She glanced around at the rest of the pub clientele. The mood was losing its initial tenseness. Boozy banter was replacing the stone-wall antipathy she'd met upon entering the Devil's Elbow. People had even stopped discussing the incident – and then it struck her. *Stopped? They'd never started!* Apart from Nick, she hadn't heard a single other person mention the band or the murders. She glanced at Nick again, and maybe recognised the same confusion in his eyes.

Just then the mummer walked in and everyone... *Everyone* went silent.

'What the hell...' said Jimmy, moving up alongside Sin and Nick at the bar, '... is *that?*' Then even he apparently forgot how to speak.

Rod was also staring at the bizarre figure. Of course he was, the whole damn pub was staring. The mummer didn't even seem to notice the effect he had made on the pub crowd. Jimmy wasn't sure if it was the clothes (and, after all, they weren't any odder than those worn by the band) or the face, or something about the weird *aura* of the character that demanded everyone's attention.

The face was certainly powerful enough. The nose was hooked, the jaw long like a wolf's. A profusion of dandelion-coloured hair sprouted from under the tilted minstrel's cap. The mouth was too large for the face, voluptuous and cruel, like a hedonistic shark's. Jimmy gazed into the man's eyes.

Rod took in the tatterdemalion clothes, bright rags stitched together over shards of leather. The gloves, old leather again, the fingers gnawed away by the elements. The boots, split and caked with the dried mud of centuries. The mummer looked like he'd just strolled down a summer lane that stretched back to the seventeenth century, maybe casually deadheading daisies along the way, nonchalantly playing his lute.

He was playing his lute now. Rod looked up, into the man's eyes.

And he knew the pint of beer clutched in his fist just wasn't strong enough.

He was playing a merry air, and his eyes were fixed on Sin. He saw past the pout, he saw past the paranoia. He saw the child within, reading Moomin books beside a muttering stream as evening stained the sky. She looked up at him with a welcoming smile, and stretched out a ten-year-old hand. The stream changed tune, and it was only the mummer-minstrel's lute, a quiet trickle of olde melody that was yet as loud as a waterfall in the silent pub. The jukebox had shut up too, almost as soon as the mummer entered, but Sin barely registered that. Her hand was still reaching out for the figure with the childhood-restoring eyes, and now he had stopped playing, was reaching inside his tatters and pulling something out to give to her.

Charmagne saw the pretty Chinese reach for the paper the mummer held out, and the spell she was under broke. She reached past the girl like a jealous child snatching a sweet from a favourite uncle and held the square of paper tight, as if her life depended on it. Maybe her career *did* depend on it, a voice told her – the inner voice of compulsion, which had carried her this far on a whim and would carry her so much further because of this day, because of this character. She knew this, and read the flyer.

The Chinese girl snapped out of her bewilderment and snatched the paper back. By then Charmagne had read it, memorised it, no longer needed it. She looked up at the mummer and he was smiling at her with eyes that were the colour of treacle.

'Welcome to the Beginning,' he said to Charmagne, in a voice that danced like the notes trickling again from his lute. 'And welcome to the End.'

Then he turned, and she was shut off from him, left with the memory of his words and the endless space of those eyes.

Jo looked over Sin's shoulder and read the flyer. The Chinese girl read it aloud for the benefit of Nick, Jimmy and Rod. The mummer was busy distributing more flyers around the pub, and Jo could see that everyone was taking them.

The flyer said:

THE UNWASHED AND UNFORGIVING TOUR. JOIN THE RAGGED ARMY. HATE IS THE SWORD OF US ALL.

Underneath the bold red capitals was the venue: The Oblong Box Inn, Postgate, Dartmoor. Tuesday, 10th May.

'Two days,' said Sin, and Jo met her eyes. The Chinese girl's expression was as ominous as her words. Sin looked away, resuming her icy guard.

'What's the story here, then?' asked Jimmy, scratching his hair through the worn Confederate cap. 'Some sort of crusade?' Nick shrugged, but looked wary.

Sin sniffed. 'Might be a laugh.'

Might be a laugh. Again the words sounded hollow to Jo. She followed the progress of the mummer as he finished doling out flyers to punks, hippies, bikers and anyone who looked interested – *anyone who looked hungry, or desperate for something*, she realised. The mummer had plugged into something and the air was electric with raw need. She took a step towards the door, hoping the Doctor would flounce in and chase away the cold that had suddenly filled the pub, and noticed with a deeper coldness that it was pitch-black outside. The night had caught them all unawares.

She smelt him before she noticed he was near her. A barn smell, a fog smell, a compost smell. A hand like a mottled turkey's claw settled on *her* hand. She had brushed it off before she could stop herself and the revulsion tugged at her mouth.

He was grinning at her, and the row of teeth in his upper jaw were whiter than snow-capped Alps; the bottom row held only the graves of teeth – grey and worn. She sucked in a scream and a laugh fell out instead, a shocked, terrified laugh, because his eyes were like muddy tarns, with no whites and no irises, and of course that was ridiculous, just a trick of the failing light and where...

She had to learn to stand on her own two feet – learn to stop always needing the bloody Doctor!

Was that her own voice in her head? It really hadn't sounded like it, and oh God she might be going mad, and now he was leaving, yes he was leaving the pub and the jukebox was playing again and she had never felt so alone and miserable in all her life.

The Doctor had been watching the cattle truck for some time. The police had long gone, and even the reporters and news crew whom he had seen arriving a good hour or so before had apparently exhausted their avenues of interrogation and left after greedily snatching all the footage they could get. Patience was certainly not one of his virtues and, after walking up the road to take a curious look at the prison and then returning to his vigil at the wall, he began to wonder if his time wouldn't be better spent with Jo in the pub. All the while the roadies sat in the cab smoking, and swigging from bottles of whisky. They seemed in no hurry to leave. When the dusk came down like a lid closing over the world, the Doctor felt it was finally time to move, and if he was surprised at the unnatural rapidity with which the night had arrived, he gave no sign of it.

He vaulted nimbly over the stone wall and on to the springy turf of the moor. Behind him, the pub was silent. And he gave no sign that he had noticed that either, so intent was he on watching the truck. The village was quiet too. Not even a passing car disturbed the spring evening. A sprinkling of stars was flung against the blackness and the moon's blind eye peeped at him from above the humped metal back of the truck as he strode through the heather towards it. Wind brushed his hair, stroked his cheeks. It was cold. Colder than it should be for this time of year on the moor. It was as though the cold was creeping from the blank, dirty sides of the truck.

The Doctor made his way to the back doors of the vehicle and paused, studying the rusty padlocks that secured them. The stink made him pull away as if he'd been slapped. It was shambles smell, blood and farmyard and rottenness combined. He steeled his sensitive nostrils and leant closer to the left-hand door, where he could make out a hole, bored by rust, that was just about the size of a man's eye.

Then he was being lifted into the air like a stuffed teddy bear held aloft by a disgruntled child, and the double doors came a little *too* close as his face was pressed against the corrugated metal.

'You wanna look inside?' The voice was husky with threat and whisky. 'Wanna look inside, Mr Ruffles?'

The Doctor considered struggling, but the grip holding him showcased the power of a bull elephant. 'That was admittedly the intention,' he quipped, twisting his head to get away from the dried filth on the doors and to try to catch a glimpse of his assailant. The hands pushed his face harder against the cold metal. The Doctor felt his generous-sized nose flatten, and indignation betrayed itself in his shout. 'But I've since come to the conclusion that *it wasn't such a good idea*!'

To his relief, the man – for it was obviously a man – laughed, and lowered the Time Lord to the grass. 'Got that right, Mr Ruffles.'

The Doctor was free, and able to turn and face his companion. He recognised him immediately. One of the roadies, and he guessed the head one, judging by the way this man had co-ordinated the clearing away of the band's equipment. He was big all right. Big and shoulder-chip mean. His head was like an anvil, a solid wedge of bone with a shaven head and a great spade of beard. His arms, the width of beech trunks, were etched with old tattoos.

'Was that really necessary?' The Doctor straightened his finery with as much dignity as someone who has just been tossed around like a rag doll could muster.

'You got a *biiig* nose, Mr Ruffles. You poke it too close to my truck again, I'll make sure you don't damn find it again in a hurry. Whaddayer say to that?'

'Only that I prefer to keep my nose where it is, thank you very much.' The Doctor smiled wryly at the giant. 'Well, if this little interview is over, I have some rather pressing business to attend to.'

'I'm sure you do, Mr Ruffles.' The giant placed a hand the size of a baseball glove on the Doctor's cheek. 'But if I find you here again...' He patted the Doctor's face twice, then stroked one finger suggestively down the Doctor's nose. 'You get me?'

'Yes, well, I wish I could say it had been a pleasure, Mr er...'

'Good night, Mr Ruffles.' The giant waited until the Doctor had returned to the wall and vaulted over it. From the other side, the Time Lord waved cheekily at him. The roadie remained where he was, arms folded.

'Doctor, where have -' Jo's face collapsed with relief when she saw the Doctor enter the pub. The mummer had walked out and, shortly after, the Doctor walked in. Nature abhors a vacuum, so they say, and why was she thinking such absurd things anyway?

The Doctor let her hug him, then held her at arm's length. 'What's been going on?' he asked, picking up a flyer from a beer-puddled table. The pub was noisy again, faces flushed and voices swollen with alcohol.

He read the flyer, then looked up at Jo. His eyes were grave. She was about to ask him what was wrong when Jimmy came over, obviously well on his way to being drunk. 'What's John bleedin' Gielgud doin' in 'ere?'

'Down, Jimmy,' Nick said and stared at the Doctor with a level, inquiring gaze. The Doctor returned it, then smiled benevolently at the four young people standing around Jo. He screwed the flyer up into a ball. 'I'm glad to see you've made some friends, Jo. *Very* glad indeed.'

He turned and glanced back out of the open door of the pub.

He could just make out the silhouette of the truck, like the dark back of a slumbering dinosaur, against the paler gloom of the moor.

'Now then, where's the landlord? I think it might be an idea if we had a room for the night, don't you? Or maybe we should make that two nights?' He beamed even more expansively and threw the ball of paper into an ashtray.

Chapter Five

The police were laughing at him. He'd wasted their money, time and resources and they were bloody well laughing at *him*! Pole dragged furiously on his cigarette and spat on the roadway.

'OK, you've had your fun,' the sergeant was smirking into his megaphone, 'now go home in a quiet and orderly fashion.' The cordon of police officers buckled in the centre, allowing passageway for the fifty or so cold and bored protesters who, after having been hemmed into a disused cul-de-sac for the last two hours by skilful police manipulation, were only too glad to be allowed to disperse sheepishly and head for the nearest pubs and takeaways. A few half-heartedly stuck some fingers up at the police as they passed or mouthed nearly inaudible profanities – mostly on a porcine theme – just to show that they had won the day *really*.

Derek Pole couldn't believe their passivity. One arrest for drunken and disorderly behaviour, and a few jeering anti-police songs. That was hardly the anarchy he was trying to instigate, was it? He climbed on to a low wall that ran alongside the cul-de-sac and waved his arms at the dispersing crowd.

'This ain't over yet! Don't let them corral you like bloody sheep! Remember, today the streets were *ours*, and not the council's! We had a major victory and we can do more!'

A protester with green spiked hair and Machine Gun Etiquette painted on his leather jacket turned and stared at the protest organiser. 'A *cul-de-sac* was ours, today, Derek. A cul-de-sac that no one ever uses. They herded us in here like schoolboys at assembly time, and you know it.'

Pole snarled at the protester. 'Yeah, and you let 'em! All of ya! We could have sealed off the city centre. We could have stopped traffic for a whole bloody day if you had just listened to me; if you hadn't all been so apathetic.'

'Do yourself a favour and go home, Derek. We did our best.' The punk turned his back and headed off with the rest of the

45

protesters. Derek stood on the wall like a failed general haranguing a deserting army, and saw that the police were climbing into their riot vans, having decided there was going to be no more disturbance here today. The final insult. They weren't even waiting for *him* to leave!

Derek climbed down from the wall, conscious that his face was burning, and threw his cigarette stub after the departing Machine Gun Etiquette jacket. Bastards! Trying to muster as much dignity as he could, he strode towards the mouth of the cul-de-sac, past the few remaining police officers who were putting away emergency traffic cones and cracking jokes about the unconventional dress of the Streets Are Ours activists. He spotted a telephone box across the main road leading to New Street Station – the protesters' intended target for isolation – and trotted over to it.

He thumbed in some coins and dialled. It was not a call he was looking forward to. Somebody was going to be decidedly unhappy with today's lacklustre results. The protest had hardly brought one of the busiest zones of Birmingham city centre to a standstill as had been the desired intention. He was going to look like a right prat. And, unlike the police, somebody was not going to be in the mood for laughing.

'Here's to you all then,' Kane said, raising his pint and toasting the lunch-time drinkers. 'Here's to every last miserable, spineless one of ya!' He grinned wolfishly and glared round defiantly as he leant against the bar of the Falcon. His long dark hair framed an angular face coarsened by stubble and bad humour. He had their attention, all right, and he was ready to take on anyone who dared give him any lip back. Not cos he was particularly hard, but because he was particularly drunk. A few of the drinkers pretended to ignore him, but he heard Buster Egan, a meathead who – so the village gossip went – was knocking off a fourteen-year-old schoolgirl, call him a 'tosser', and that just made him grin even more.

'You and me both, Buster, old chap,' he called back. He gulped at his Old Peculiar and waited for the big man to come for him. Jimmy Turrock held Buster back, muttering something in his ear.

'I think you've had enough, Kane.' Trevor the landlord was looming above him, head just shy of the rafters he was that tall.

'Do you, Trevor?' Kane put his beer down. He dragged a cigarette from its pack with his teeth, lit it and blew smoke at the publican. 'Funny how two people can disagree so wildly over something, ain't it? Cos I don't think I've had *nearly* enough.'

'Drink up and go home.' Trevor looked as impassive as ever, but he was blinking a little too quickly, and Kane knew that was a sign the giant was becoming annoyed.

'Let me tell you about the day I've had, Trevor, and then we'll see if you still want me to go.'

'Oh believe you me, Kane, I'll want you to go even *more*.'

Kane wasn't listening. 'The bastard sacked me, Trevor. Sacked! For what?'

'Falling asleep on the job, from what I heard. Being a lazy, no-good git, from what I heard.'

Kane whirled round to face this new challenge. And his grin grew wider. Cassandra King had entered the bar from the lounge. She might have been nearly thirty, but she still had a waist you could easily strangle, a chest you could lose yourself in and eyes wild, green and dancing. Her hair was teased into a semblance of punky disorder without being too prominently spiked. Cassandra was following fashion, not politics.

'Well, hello,' Kane drooled. 'Condescended to come in the bar with all the scum, huh?'

'I only see one piece of scum round here, Kane.' But she said it with a smile that pushed him off the bar and brought him a step closer to her, close enough to lick her. So of course she stepped back to compensate, as if she was frightened he was going to do *just* that.

'I only had a little kip, rich bitch,' he threw at her. 'Hardly a reason to sack a bloke.' He had been assigned a road to dig, along

47

with Andy the Letch, his groundwork mate, and had got bored riding the jackhammer. So he'd snuck off into a newly constructed house to see if he could get some shuteye, which had seemed perfectly reasonable to him on account of the fact he had a bitch of a hangover and so should hardly be expected to do *too* much work. The ganger had disagreed with that philosophy and sacked him on the spot.

'How old are you, Kane? Thirty? Thirty-one? You're no longer a teenager. You don't have to keep playing the rebel. No one cares any more. Isn't it about time you started using your brain for once?' She stared up at him with those dazzling green eyes. 'You have got one, haven't you?'

Kane scooped his half-empty pint off the bar counter just as Trevor made to snatch it away. 'I ain't allowed to use it, am I? I've been branded a waster ever since I was a kid…' He belched for emphasis. 'So I might as well stick to what I do best. Two questions for you, Cassandra: one, do you get off on playing all concerned when we both know you don't give a damn…' He paused and sucked his cigarette, still grinning like the wolf he always wanted to be.

'And two?' She folded her arms over her breasts, and she was smiling too.

'Aren't you supposed to contradict me before we get to two?'

'And two,' she repeated, still smiling.

'Two's obvious; d'you wanna come back to my place?'

That got a laugh from some of the drinkers, who until this point had been pretending not to listen to the conversation.

Cassandra sighed. 'I've got something for you. You might find it interesting.' She held out a square of yellow paper. A flyer. He let her wait there with it in her hand while he took his time finishing his pint, and then he plucked it off her.

'What's this shit?' He studied it, and then he felt the blood fill his face, felt a fist clench inside his gut. The flyer said:

SIMON KING PROUDLY PRESENTS;
THE EPIC OF GILGAMESH,

A MORALITY PLAY OVER TWO THOUSAND YEARS OLD
CIRBURY VILLAGE HALL 19TH & 20TH JUNE

Kane scrumpled the flyer into a ball and tossed it into his empty glass on the bar counter. His grin had gone. He turned and left the pub without a final line.

Cassandra came out into the street after him and caught hold of his elbow. Sunlight made him squint. He tried to shake her off. 'If you ain't gonna bed me, do me a favour and get lost,' he snapped.

'You can't hate him for ever, Kane,' she said, tightening her grip. He turned and lunged at her before she could move. He pinned her up against the outside wall of the Falcon and had thrust his tongue between her lips before she could do anything more than utter a muffled squeal. Then, just as suddenly, he shoved her from him and strode off up the street. She came after him again.

He kept walking, up the long incline of the high street. 'Want some more?' he said without turning.

'You're a pig, Kane.'

'So they tell me. I'm no good, good for nothing, fit for nowt, a bum, loser, long-haired hippie. You can't come up with any insults I ain't heard from this town a hundred times.'

'What about a coward?' She had to hurry to keep pace with him.

'Yeah, why not? I'm not John Wayne, you know. Calling me a coward's not gonna make me turn round, squint and say "The hell I am!" I don't give a damn. But just for the record, what am I supposed to be scared of? Not that I'm really interested.' He sneered at a middle-aged housewife doing her afternoon shopping who was watching him with a frown, her head tied up in a silk cravat like a wrinkled, disapproving package.

'You're scared of my brother. Of the fact that he's achieved something and you haven't, and never will.'

Kane snorted. 'Any tosser with a silver spoon wedged up their hole can *achieve*. You try underachieving, like me. That takes real hard work.'

'So I take it you won't be going to see his play then?'

Kane stopped outside Merretts greengrocer's, plucked an apple from the display box outside, took a big bite and replaced it. He carried on walking. 'Is he gonna be in it, or is he going to be *producing* it?' He sneered the word. He sneered a lot of words these days. His whole life had become a sneer, and that was fine by him. That was his guard against the world, against the bastards who were out to prove he was nothing.

'He's starring in it.'

'Then I'll definitely be going. Me and a couple of tins of rice pudding. Opened of course, with a spoon for flicking.'

'It's a special occasion for him, Kane. Don't spoil it.'

'That's what this is all about, isn't it?' Kane stopped again and faced her, deliberately blocking the path of Sergeant Sallis, the village bobby, who had to step around him on the narrow pavement shaking his head with contempt.

'Yes, that's what this is all about. I wanted to ask you, as a favour to me, not to do anything nasty.'

Kane laughed harshly. 'Nasty! Hell, your brother knows all about nasty. I could tell you some things would make your eyebrows stand on end.' He paused thoughtfully. 'Anyway, why's he doing this play here, in this one-hog place, if he's such a big-shot producer at the BBC?'

'It's going to be filmed for television when he performs it at the Edinburgh Festival. This is a dry run in front of the people he knows best. A sort of thank you to his roots.' Cassandra bit her lip. He could tell even *she* knew how crap that sounded. He resisted the urge to pull her apart. Or almost.

'He's coming back to remind us how great he is,' he spat finally. 'And to let us know how privileged we are to have known him. *That's* why he's coming back.'

She frowned, her eyes angry now.

'Are you going to cause any trouble? Yes or no?'

'Are you going to sleep with me? Yes or no?' When she didn't answer he laughed. And belched.

'Don't worry, Cassandra. *Of course* I'm going to cause trouble.

I'm going to make this homecoming very special indeed.'

He blew her a kiss and disappeared inside the Co-op to get some more fags.

Chapter Six

The last hunt of the season had ended in failure. The horns were silent now, their jubilant cries scorned. With dusk spilling across the Dartmoor landscape and the twilight mourning of a blackbird trickling in their ears, the three riders decided to split off from the rest of the hunt in search of some much-needed cheer.

They had almost had the fox at one point; the hounds streaming after the streak of russet cunning, the cream of Devonian aristocracy pounding along behind. Through a knot of larch trees they had galloped, thorns and brambles tearing skin and blood-red livery, and then out into the open again; and there was the pack, milling confusedly at the edge of a brook where an old stone bridge crouched protectively over the laughing water. They had scanned the moorland – tors, heather, sheep. Of the fox, nothing could be seen.

Edward Mortimer had pushed his animal forward on to the road and over the weed-pierced bridge, towards a mulberry-coloured VW Beetle parked carelessly on the other side. Penelope followed obediently, admiring the straight sweep of her lover's back, cocksure in red. She would have followed him to hell and back, twice over, but then Penelope Fitzgerald was not the sharpest tool in the box; Edward had been cheating on her with her best friend Edith for the last six months, and had no intention of stopping. It was his sport, like shredding foxes.

As they approached the car, a gaunt-faced man wound down the window, his skull earring and menacing eyes not promising much of a welcome.

'Fox?' was all he said.

Edward nodded. The man, in his thirties, had pointed across the moor to a tor shaped like a witch's profile on the horizon. Edward had looked at the others, clearly not trusting the stranger. But what choice did they have? The hounds weren't helping any.

So they had taken the trail, and of course it *had* been false. After an hour of fruitless searching, with tempers fraying by the minute, the hunt had dispersed leaving Edward, Penelope and Henry Patton-Wilde to ride alone in search of comfort.

The Oblong Box would provide it, only a mile away across the moor.

Nick, Sin, Jimmy and Rod were among a growing crowd of restless, curious spectators watching the roadies preparing the equipment in a grassy hollow in front of the Oblong Box. Towering speakers, two guitars, mike stand and a gleaming drum kit contrasted oddly with the bleak sweep of the moor.

The nearest village was a good two miles south, invisible in the gathering dusk, trees hiding any lights that might be blooming. Despite the seclusion of the pub, which looked defiant and entrenched as if from years of shrugging into itself against the loneliness of the spot, a sizeable audience had already gathered. Nick estimated about 150, maybe double the number who had witnessed the Princetown gig. And still nobody knew the name of the band, or the purpose of their tour. No money had changed hands, no tickets were on sale.

Most of the crowd were young, and dishevelled. But there was also a healthy contingent of older, shabbier characters shuffling and scowling amongst the younger breed. Nick found it hard to believe they had come to watch a band. Their interests seemed to lie in other directions. Perhaps they hoped for an encore of the violence the first gig had brought.

He sincerely hoped they would be disappointed.

Some of the crowd were obviously having difficulty understanding what they were doing there themselves; their frames twitched and shuddered with obvious cold turkey, their faces were sucked dry of vitality. Others sported countenances so ugly with misanthropic hate that Nick began to wonder if the riot at Dartmoor prison had not been more successful than had been reported. He took shameful satisfaction in the presence of a token police force positioned around the pub.

On the fringe of the crowd he could see the eccentric form of the white-headed man with his pretty companion, Jo. What had brought them back for more? He knew they had been staying at the Devil's Elbow, but had not seen them since meeting them in the pub. They were an odd couple too, that was for sure. It was like the band attracted nature's strange.

'I'm surprised old Fossil Farris allowed this shenanigan outside his pub,' Jimmy said, complacently sparking up a joint.

'What, with the crock o' gold he'll get from all the ale sold tonight? He knows a good thing when he smells it,' Rod said, eyeing the joint eagerly.

'Well, he obviously didn't smell this lot first, did he? He might have changed his mind.' The dried blood on Jimmy's grey Confederate cap reminded Nick of the Princetown gig and unease slipped into him, like a ghost. The blood had been there for over a year, from the time Jimmy was evicted from a Tavistock pub by a bouncer who objected to his dubious state of drunkenness. Jimmy had promptly come straight back in, through the feature window, a spectacular entry riding a cloudburst of shattered glass. He'd cut his fingers on his way in, and the blood had somehow found its way on to the cap. The bouncers had chased him back out of the pub again, aided by some locals enraged at having their peaceful evening so violently shattered along with the picture window.

Blood. Dried blood. Nick hoped it wasn't a sign.

'One, two,' barked the head roadie into the microphone. 'One, one…' He coughed into the metallic throat and then shuffled away from the natural stage towards the cattle truck parked further down the incline.

Edward reined in his horse as they came over the rise. 'What the bloody hell…?'

They hadn't expected this: people crowded around the usually quiet pub – and he used the word 'people' rather loosely. Oiks from hell, more like. He didn't like the look of them at all. Mutants.

Those disgusting punk types, and worse, much much worse. Lord, it was a veritable freak show.

'I think we should ride on by, Edward,' Henry piped up from behind. Edward could hear the fear in his companion's weak voice.

'What, and let the oiks scare us away from a good whisky? I think not.' He straightened demonstratively in his saddle and kicked off towards the pub, leaving his two anxious companions to trail behind.

The closer he got, the less sure of his convictions he became. This really *was* a scary-looking bunch. He pulled up just short of the dirty crowd that spilled out like a stain over the moor around the pub, conscious of the jeering looks he was attracting. His horse skittered nervously. He was aware of Penelope and Henry directly behind him, and really didn't want to look indecisive now.

'Edward, I don't like this...' Penelope trilled. Just then one of the oiks slung a bottle in their direction. It struck Olivier, Penelope's stallion, and the horse reared, flinging its owner from the saddle. She landed on the hard turf with a whump! and Edward flinched at the sound. He dismounted rapidly and moved to her aid.

She was nursing her back. Bloody woman. Why hadn't he brought Edith along instead; she was better in the saddle in both respects.

'Are you all right, darling?' he forced himself to ask. A loud cheer had erupted from the crowd at her fall, and he felt anger blending with his frustration.

He made a brusque examination of his fiancée while Henry sat rather helplessly on his horse. 'You'll live,' Edward told her shortly, and helped her to her feet. 'It looks like you've stunned your spine, that's all.' Anger blared through him. 'Dammit woman, can't you be more careful?'

He sensed her imminent tears and cursed even more, this time silently. 'Come on, we'll have to get you inside and telephone an ambulance.'

Henry stared at Edward as if his friend had lost leave of his senses. 'In there?'

Penelope began to cry then, just as Edward had known she would. Bloody, *bloody* woman! Instead of answering Henry, he threw Olivier's reins to his friend, and began leading his own horse towards the pub. What a nightmare the day had turned into.

He tied the horse to a wooden rail that ran around the side of the pub, where the crowd was thinnest. He was only too aware of the hostility he was evoking from the undesirables surrounding them.

'You wait here with the horses, Henry,' he ordered, and helped the hobbling Penelope towards the door.

A man in a long green mac with a head bald as a mushroom blocked their way. *Here we go*, thought Edward, and he felt Penelope tense beside him.

Just then the band began to play.

They ambled slowly across the grass from the cattle truck. Jo had seen them leap down from the back doors and had felt a sudden lurch of excitement. The crowd whistled and cheered. Dusk fell, the horizon purple above dark moor. She could feel the emotion emanating from the people around her; its intensity scared her.

She had once seen a film called *The Wild Bunch*. At the climax, the four surviving outlaws walked down the main street of a Mexican town side by side, towards their own extinction. It had moved her in a way she had never been able to understand. Until now. Here was the same stroll towards doom, she sensed; the four musicians moving to take up their places with an inevitable finality that punched her soul. What was she talking about? No one was going to die here. There would be no repetition of the other day. They were merely going to play some…

… Songs?

'Scum, scum, scum,' the singer spat into the microphone as the tramp-hatted guitarist struck up chords Jo could almost *smell*, they were so rotten. A spotlight winked on like a crimson, evil eye, and the band exploded into action.

'Scum we are, and scum we'll stay,' the garish singer growled and swore, and if it was a song, it was the vilest Jo had ever heard. 'Scum, scum, scum, the scum of the earth.' The bass player moved towards the crowd which stood paralysed in front of the band, and Jo saw Sin, the attractive Chinese girl, standing next to Nick and gazing at the band with a kind of rapt horror. The bass player, a mummer-punk troll with hair sticking up into the evening air like black straw poking out of a scarecrow's head, stepped on top of a rock for better elevation and bullied his instrument, the sunglasses that he and his three fellow band members were still wearing throwing off red glare from the spotlight. The notes rumbled into the night like dinosaurs venting their spleen. Sin was directly below him as he stood on the rock, the electric lead trailing back to the generator behind him. Jo sensed what was coming and moved forward, although the action was futile, separated as she was from the girl by the heaving crowd.

'And we shall inherit,' barked the singer, and the bass player smiled, and spewed a green waterfall of puke down into Sin's upturned face.

The crowd went mad.

Join the Unwashed. Join the Unforgiving.

They were preaching to the converted.

The band was in full fury; Sin was staggering back, her hands clawing at her face. She opened her mouth to scream and it was clogged. She couldn't see. But she could hear. The ecstasy of the crowd, an ecstasy of horror and revulsion and *delight*, and she empathised with those feelings because they were her own too. The man had sicked up on her, and the stinking slime was still all over her, and yet she was consumed with excitement as she mopped at herself. As Nick helped her, his face torn with disgust, she could only feel the pride, the *honour* of being chosen. It was a kind of madness, she knew that. Yet no one else had been singled out. She was grinning through the bile.

They had come for her, and she was going to leave this banality behind – this sickening boredom that was her life.

So she grinned at Nick and at the mummers from hell as they pranced and prowled around their grassy stage, and then she began to dance, the ecstasy pulling at her as if she were on strings, and she was laughing, laughing…

The bald man blocked Edward's way.

'Excuse me…' the aristocrat offered feebly. The man stared, a wax statue, eyes barely blinking. He reminded Edward of something: a grotesque character from a comic he'd read as a child. Grimly… Grimly Fiendish, that was it. The bald man in the long shiny mac looked just like Grimly Fiendish.

The band had begun to play, a fearsome din that convinced Edward he and his friends might just possibly have taken the wrong path out on the moor and ended up in some parallel hell.

The bald man bowed mockingly, stepped aside and ushered Edward and Penelope inside the pub. As they squeezed past him, Edward glanced at his face. The whites of the man's eyes were invisible, squeezed out by black gobstopper pupils.

Inside the pub, the lounge was surprisingly empty but for two men leaning against the oak bar. Edward seated Penelope at a corner table and made for the public telephone box in the passageway leading to the toilets.

Penelope was alone with the two men. Three men: the bald man had decided to come in too and stood in the middle of the room, watching her.

She would ignore him. Even though she felt his stare like a live shock all through her. She gazed around the lounge to take her mind off him, at the familiar oak wainscoting; the cosy, though unlit fireplace; the ancient animal traps rusting on the walls; the stuffed bear's head that had seen better days. One of the bear's glass eyes had fallen out, giving her the impression the creature was winking at her. The other eye reminded her of the bald man's stare. *Hurry up Edward!*

* * *

'Come away, Jo.' The Doctor had to pull his companion from the crowd, so reluctant was she to miss the spectacle.

She gazed round at him blankly, and he shook her. 'Jo!'

Her eyes swam back into focus. Alarm filled them. He drew her away from the fringe of the crowd and sat her down on one of the picnic benches beside the road.

'You've got to remain alert, Jo,' he told her sternly.

She nodded, not understanding what had happened to her, what was still happening to the rest of the audience, only knowing that something *had*. She felt weak, a headache nagged behind her eyes. The band continued to play, swinging their instruments dangerously, careless of any member of the audience who might venture too near.

'Wait here,' the Doctor instructed her and, before she could protest, he was hurrying up the lane to where Bessie was parked a hundred yards away from the pub.

Jo felt unclean. She remembered the unnatural green sick that had struck Sin and felt like throwing up herself. The music bulldozed the crowd, repelling them, inciting them.

Nick was holding Sin's hand, and he was no longer angry at her violation. The music soothed and aroused, scared and exhilarated. It spoke in a language they could understand. The whole crowd understood. The songs encouraged Nick to free resentments and prejudices long buried. All around the homeless, the loveless, the hopeless were reacting to the vibe; there was horror, and there was hate. In time there would be much more, *and it would be oh so good*!

The Doctor didn't need to look inside Bessie to check on the sensor probe. He could hear it emitting its eerie bleat from yards away. He reached in and deftly detached the instrument from the dashboard. It positively rocked in his hand. A cold finger prodded his soul. It was far more active than at Princetown. On impulse, he moved away from the car, trudging across the open moorland to where the cattle truck loomed beyond the band and the enraptured crowd.

As he had sensed it would, the energy indicator all but burned in his hand the nearer he got to the filthy vehicle. And there, like a statue in the dark, the roadie waited, guarding the back doors with massive arms patiently folded. The Doctor backed up, hiding the indicator inside his cloak, unsure if the giant had seen him.

In the natural hollow, the band reached a climax of obnoxious sound.

The man must be on drugs, Penelope decided. His bulbous eyes didn't shift from her, and his mouth was working silently.

At the bar, the other two men had turned to face her. One of them was wearing a blue anorak over a white tunic of some sort, and was fiddling with the zipper, his black lank hair falling over his wide eyes.

Ziiiiiiip. Ziiiiiiiiiiiiip.

The noise played on her nerves. The other man was short, fat and bearded like an oversized garden gnome, without cap or fishing rod but just as malevolently odd. He pulled something from his trouser pocket and slipped it over his head – a balaclava. He was squinting at her, his face squashed inside the woollen opening.

Ziiiiiiiiiiiiiiiiiiiiiiiiiiiiiiiip.

She would scream. If Edward didn't come back soon –

Edward appeared. He was looking harassed and grumpy but she had never been so happy to see him.

Unfortunately, the bald man chose that moment to interfere.

He seized Edward's arm and swung him round. Penelope stood up quickly. She could see John Farris, the landlord, peering out from behind a hanging row of crisp packets, and he also looked scared.

'Do you mind?' Edward shook himself free. His voice was full of outrage, but Penelope could hear the quaver of fear there too. She looked up into Farris's eyes. And it was then she knew.

It happened very quickly, like a circus act on fast forward.

The bald man grinned, and it was a grin wider than any Penelope had ever seen, and his eyes popped madly from his face as he seized Edward again and threw him against the wall.

'Yes I do mind, sir,' he said with a quaint country accent that was soft and sinister all at once. 'I *do* mind, sir. And so do my friends here.' He reached above Edward's head and unhitched a long metal object from a hook. An animal leg-trap. Now he was clamping the sharp metal jaws around Edward's neck, and handsome, brave Edward was screaming, and blood was squelching down on to the red of his livery and dousing the bald man as he wrestled the hideous contraption tighter round Edward's throat.

The other two men peeled away from the bar, taking their cue. The man with the balaclava waited beside the door, as if he had sensed Henry was about to spill through all whey-faced and spineless. The zipper man came for Penelope. But not all at once. He took time to take his instrument of choice – a long viciously hooked gaffe – down from the wall, and displayed it for her with relish, like a shopkeeper demonstrating his wares, as the music burst into brutal orgasm beyond the pub walls and Penelope screamed and screamed and…

She saw the bear winking at her, just before her world went red, and then black.

Chapter Seven

Dawn broke stiffly over the Oblong Box.

The crowd was still there. The police had been unable to move them, and had settled for clearing them away from the immediate vicinity of the pub. An ambulance, now loaded with three corpses, trundled almost sheepishly away from the scene of the butchery.

Jo watched another vehicle, this one black, turn on the narrow road and lurch off after its white companion. In the back window a face stared out at her, eyes wide as inkwells, head bald as the mad moon.

She shuddered and leant closer to the Doctor. Throughout the night, long after the band had ceased playing and retreated into their cattle truck like motley clockwork figures, the people had continued to arrive. In beat-up VW campers, in decrepit buses, in cars of all makes and descriptions but all sharing a similar state of shabbiness.

'What I'm going to ask you to do now is probably the hardest thing I've ever expected of you, Jo.' The Doctor was sitting with her on the bench, sipping a mug of tea from the pub. 'And probably one of the most dangerous.'

She didn't like the sound of that at all. She tried to ask him what he meant, but her voice was a croak. She thought of the three men who had been led out of the pub by the police, docile as kittens, blood patterning them like the daubings of a mad artist.

'From Coney Hill,' someone from the crowd had told her. The words had meant nothing until Nick, who had been standing nearby with Sin, filled in the blanks.

'A local asylum,' he had said gravely. But it had seemed to Jo that Sin was smiling. Or was that just shock?

The Doctor was talking again, the morning breeze stroking his hair. 'I'm going to have to leave you for a while.' He put a finger to his lips as she opened her mouth to protest again. 'Let me finish:

this is vitally important. I need you to stay here, with your new friends.' He indicated Nick and Sin who had now been joined by Rod. Jimmy was sitting in the driver's seat of his purple camper van which was parked ten yards up the road, sucking on a joint. All of them, apart from Sin, looked detached and stunned but were unable for some reason to leave the scene. 'I'm sure they'll take care of you.' Jo thought he looked rather doubtfully at Sin for a second; the Chinese girl's eyes were shining, her lips were full and pouting. Then he went on.

'I want you to follow this tour wherever it may go. I have a feeling your young friends won't want to miss out on anything either. And I'm sure the tour has a destination of some sort or other, just as I'm sure it's an important one. I need you to stick close and find out what it is. But remember one thing...' He leant closer, and his eyes were deadly serious. 'Whatever you do, stay away from that truck.' He gestured briefly out across the moor to where the metal vehicle waited, apart from the encampment like a filthy outcast. 'And if you discover anything unusual, let the Brigadier know at once.'

He stood up. Was that it? Was he just going to leave her here with near strangers and no explanation? But instead of questioning him further, she merely nodded. She felt lonely and excited at the same time. Something was definitely... *happening*...

The Doctor smiled fondly at her. 'Well goodbye, Jo. I'll see you at the other side.' And he was gone.

The other side? The other side of what? She realised Sin was staring at her intently, still smiling that fragile, offbeat smile. *The other side of the tour of course*, the eyes seemed to be telling her. *Come along, it's gonna be one hell of a time...*

Jeremy Willis flicked the channel button on his remote and the news footage of the Oblong Box was immediately replaced by Terry Wogan hosting a game show. He hit the off-button angrily.

'Can't we watch *Blankety-Blank*?' Celia whined, as he'd

expected her to. He ignored her and reached for the telephone beside the leather settee.

He was a tall thin man, impeccably dressed, even now while he was supposedly relaxing. The open top button and the absence of a tie were the only signs that marked him out as enjoying leisure time. He was even still wearing his jacket. His hair was sliced neatly by a conservative side-parting, his tidy moustache was only slightly touched with grey. His companion was big-breasted, brunette and eighteen years old. She looked well under half the age of the proud but haughty-looking woman in the photograph tilted next to the phone that Willis was now using.

Willis was decidedly not pleased with the man on the other end of the line. When Celia's hand slipped suggestively on to his knee he transferred that ire to her. 'Will you leave me alone for just a *moment*?' he barked. She pulled away and moved across the settee, a dumb look of hurt on her callow features. 'No, I mean *really* leave me alone. This is an important call. Go and talk to the neighbours for five minutes.' He was slipping. He had become so inured to her lack of character that he'd almost forgotten she was there at all. He should be more careful, especially when talking to the man who was on the line right now.

'We don't have any neighbours,' Celia whined. That was certainly true: the nearest house was half a mile down the road.

'Well, go out and talk to the bloody squirrels then; they might enjoy your conversational skills.'

Celia got up, close to tears, and left the room. When he was sure she was out of earshot he returned his attention to the man on the phone.

'Listen: if you want the princess then you're going to have to work a lot harder for your money. Perhaps I should have some escaped lunatics on my payroll, they seem to be doing a better job than you at kicking up a stink.'

He listened for a moment, then cut in abruptly: 'I don't want to hear your excuses. I just want some results.' He dropped the receiver in its cradle and picked up the remote thoughtfully.

'*Blankety-Blank*'s on, darling,' he called and hit the on-button.

Of course, when Jimmy heard the encampment was preparing to follow the cattle truck on the next leg of its tour, he was the first to suggest they should also follow it. Sin leapt at the idea eagerly. Rod leant against Jimmy's camper van, saying nothing. Nick looked at Jo, who had joined them an hour before.

'What do you think?'

'What are you asking *her* for?' Sin blurted, jumping down from her seat on the camper's step.

'I'm asking everyone.' Nick touched Sin's shoulder placatingly. She shook him off, still glaring at Jo.

Jo attempted a smile. 'I really don't mind,' she stammered. 'But I think it might be fun.'

Nick walked away from the van, smoking a cigarette. The Damned's latest album was playing on the van's dashboard stereo: their best one yet, according to Jimmy. The music was fresh, fast and exciting; it smacked of spring-sunshine anarchy and drunken chaos. Yet the song playing now seemed like a warning – 'I Just Can't Be Happy Today'. Why did Nick feel he should heed it?

Wasn't that a stupid question, anyway? Of course he should be careful about what they did next. Three more people had just been murdered. And now that the band were tucked away again in their filthy truck, like children's toys discarded for the day, he had lost some of the wild enthusiasm of the previous night. He looked at Sin. She looked sexier than he'd ever seen her: pert, sensuous, lascivious even. As if the events of the last few days had broken her free of her previous uptight inhibitions.

The priests hang on hooks; the radio's on ice, the telly's been banned. The army's in power; the Devil commands!

'I say we go,' Jimmy shouted over Dave Vanian's croak.

All around them, the dilapidated vehicles that had arrived throughout the night and much of the day were grumbling into life. The cattle truck had crawled on to the road, where it lurked, engine idling, waiting.

Waiting for them, Nick knew.

'Let's go then,' he said, and flicked his cigarette away.

Nobody noticed Charmagne as she wandered among the crowd of people who were now breaking camp and spilling into whatever vehicles would accept them. Why should they? Even though she didn't exactly look part of the scene with her refined features and clean blonde hair, she wasn't making any undue efforts to draw attention to herself. The only person she'd spoken to was Farris, the shaken landlord of the Oblong Box, and he'd told her all she needed to know. She didn't need to bother any of the punks and hippies and general disenchanted youth who clung to the pub as if they were searching for some kind of meaning.

She watched as the encampment broke up, turning into a convoy, and realised with a shock that she was shaking. Not with fear, but with the purest excitement she had ever known.

It was only three in the afternoon, yet Kane was already in the gutter.

He woke up with the sun blazing on his face and rolled on to his side, groaning. A beer can crumpled under his weight. He shoved it away, causing a hollow rattle like metal bones.

He sat up. He was still too pissed to have cultivated a hangover. The church tower swung into his line of vision, rocking like a fat mast. He tried to focus on it, wondering what he was doing lying outside the churchyard. Ten pence rolled out of his pocket as he struggled to his feet, but nothing more. He looked at the squashed litter of cans around where he had crashed and grinned ruefully.

'Sod 'em,' he said to no one in particular. 'Sod 'em all.' He stumbled towards the gate that led into the small village churchyard. If they wanted to treat him like the scourge of Cirbury, he'd bloody give 'em the real thing… He picked the grave with the biggest bunch of flowers nestling on top of its mound and unzipped. He etched a pattern of piss over the engraving on the headstone, sniggering as he did so. His snigger died when

Simon King's face popped into his head for no good reason whatsoever. His stream of urine died too, choked by memories.

Worms. Worms and slugs and spiders.

He walked away from the desecrated grave, fumbling for cigarettes in his denim-jacket pockets and finding none. He swore.

He could still taste the worms.

He could still feel the weight of Simon's gang holding him down in the school playing-field on a warm spring afternoon very much like this one. The other boys had marvelled at Simon's inventiveness, but then all boys loved cruelty.

Slugs.

In his mouth, bitter and slimy on his tongue.

When he had cried himself to silence, choking on his own vomit and a mouthful of wriggling things, the boys had begun to lose the taste for their work. Simon had spurred them on. He could do that easily, with the power he – and his family – wielded over the village. The boys' dads liked their labourer jobs, didn't they? Wouldn't want to lose them. After all, Simon's father owned the biggest land development company in Wiltshire.

Kane stooped and picked up a stone vase laden with tulips. He aimed it at the nearest stained-glass window, then stopped when he saw the cleaning lady watching him from the church door. She was smiling almost conspiratorially. He dropped the urn.

But he didn't forget the sensation of spiders crawling across his tongue. Of worms slipping between his lips, fed from a filthy jar by the hands of a vicious fourteen-year-old.

All the way back to UNIT HQ, the Doctor worried about whether he had done the right thing. The sensor, back in its sheath in Bessie's dashboard, was silent now, at peace.

As he opened the door to the Brigadier's office the Doctor had almost made up his mind to ask his old friend to authorise a ban on the tour, to impound the cattle truck, like the glorified policeman that he was. But one look at the Brigadier's complacent air of self-importance brought him up short. He didn't know why what he saw should reaffirm his initial conviction that the tour should be allowed a free head of steam, but somehow it did.

The Brigadier cocked an eyebrow at him from behind his desk. A mug of coffee steamed in the sunlight from the window. Official files were positioned neatly next to the fountain pen which was set down exactly parallel to the blotter pad. It was a picture of order and convention.

'Dartmoor, Doctor,' the Brigadier said gravely. It wasn't quite a question, more an understated demand for some kind of report or explanation. It could remain understated as far as the Doctor was concerned; understated to the point of being completely ignorable. However, he was far too concerned about recent events to be irritated.

'I need your best man, Brigadier,' the Doctor said, leaning over the desk and confronting the military man in the no-nonsense fashion he always adopted when he wanted to cut through small talk and other nonessentials.

The Brigadier sat back, lifting the mug to his lips. He was waiting for the Doctor to elaborate. And for once UNIT's scientific adviser was happy to oblige.

'There's something very wrong afoot in the Southwest, Brigadier. Something I can't yet identify or understand, which is why I've returned here. I'm going to need complete peace and quiet while I do a detailed analysis on some readings I've received – and that means under no circumstances am I to be disturbed...' He gave the Brigadier a meaningful look. 'Frankly, it's going to take all the facilities my lab has to offer. But in the meantime, I need your help.'

'And Miss Grant?' The Brigadier had an irritating knack of always putting his finger clumsily but unerringly on the most sensitive area. It was one of his more endearing traits. 'I couldn't help noticing you arrived alone.'

The Doctor straightened up defensively. 'Yes, well, that's exactly why I need your assistance. You've no doubt heard about the large gathering in Dartmoor associated with the murders? I've left Jo there to keep an eye on things… but well, I'm a little concerned.'

'Quite rightly so, Doctor.'

The Doctor gave him a guilty frown. 'I'd like you to send someone else there to keep an eye on *her*. An undercover agent, if you like. Someone who can slip into the crowd incognito, without arousing suspicion, who can also protect Jo from any possible danger.'

The Brigadier looked at him quizzically. 'You want one of my men to pretend to be a long-haired hippie?'

The Doctor frowned even more deeply, and his voice was angry. 'Yes, that's exactly what I want, Brigadier. Now, do you think you are capable of providing me with one?'

Sin.

Sin Yen.

SIN!!!!!!!!!!!!!!!!!!!!

Nick woke. And Sin was still there. She was sitting next to him on the seat of Jimmy's camper, with Jo behind and Rod across the narrow aisle. The Dead Boys were blaring from the stereo. Perhaps that had woken him, and not the fact that he was screaming Sin's name. Apparently he hadn't made a sound, because nobody was looking at him. Outside it was dark and misty. The camper had been following the other vehicles for three hours. The convoy was moving very slowly, creeping through the countryside like a battered metal snake. They had left Dartmoor behind and were winding through north Devon. Just after the fog had come down to seal the convoy off from the rest of the world, Nick had fallen asleep.

In his dream, Sin had gone. She had turned cold and hard, like a woman made out of a gravestone, and then she was gone.

And then she was dead.

He put a hand on her knee and she turned to him, smoking a joint, her unfathomable black eyes that could sometimes show such passion now just empty holes. He gave her a smile to coax a response from her and she didn't return it. Then part of his dream had come true already.

From the corner of his eye he saw Jo gazing out at the fog and the night. Exhibiting a patience normally alien to him, Jimmy was singing along to the music as they crawled after the rusting Bedford truck in front, doing barely twenty miles an hour.

'So where do you think we'll end up?'

Nick turned to face Jo, who had asked the question that was, of course, on all their minds but which, strangely, no one had voiced aloud until now.

He took his time answering, looking at her well-cut and obviously expensive clothes and wondering what she would look like with a punk haircut. She had the air of someone who had been away for a while, someone who was normally in tune with the times and liked to be as trendy as possible but had recently been whisked off somewhere that fashions didn't or couldn't reach. She was strange all right: a bit of an enigma with her eccentric uncle or whatever he was – and again, no one had even asked her about him, as if their curiosity had been switched off like a tap. There was something in her young, yet experienced eyes, in her innocent yet haunted expression, that hinted at a lifestyle that went far beyond 'alternative'. He must talk to her properly, and find out more about her.

He took so long answering, that Sin got there first.

'The edge,' she said without even turning.

Jo frowned, and Nick felt a coldness that could have emanated from Sin.

'The edge of what?' Jo asked before he could.

'The edge of everything.'

'Don't be so bloody melodramatic!' Nick snapped. He wanted to shake Sin. Hold her tight until he could feel her warmth again instead of this creeping cold.

She ignored him, merely blew smoke from her sensuous lips. *Forget her lips, you fool. She's leaving you. You've lost her, and now there's nothing. Just a hole. A big, empty hole. Dead to you. Dead.*

Jo cut through his misery: 'I think we should all keep our eyes open.'

That made Sin swivel round to give the blonde girl a hostile stare. 'I don't need anyone to think for me.'

'But doesn't it strike you that this whole tour is a bit sinister? Several deaths already and the band don't seem bothered at all. In fact who *are* the band? Does anyone even know their name?'

'Do they need a name?' Sin was definitely on the defensive and Nick wondered just why she should be taking this so personally. Maybe it was to do with Jo. A mad hope darted through him that it might be jealousy. Could she be worried that Jo might be trying to take him away from her? But looking at Sin's impassive features, the hope curdled. Her thoughts were far beyond *him*. She was in a world he couldn't reach, and she had been ever since the day of the Princetown gig. The day before that she had lain in his bed and told him how much she cared for him. The day of the gig – *while the cattle truck was bouncing its way across the moor towards them even* – she had changed. She had just… switched off.

And it felt like there was nothing he could do.

'The band with no name.' This came from Rod, who had been listening to the conversation in his usual thoughtful way, sad and withdrawn, a loner even when amongst friends. He took a swig from his bottle of Jack Daniels, and fixed them with a calm stare.

'They're the band that doesn't need a name,' he continued, 'but I bet everyone in this convoy knows why they're here.'

Nick frowned. He felt like maybe he was missing out on something here, because Sin was smiling in conspiratorial approval of Rod's words.

'Well I for one would like someone to tell *me*,' Jo said, and Nick warmed to her, feeling a kinship for all of five seconds until Sin turned those beautiful, depthless eyes on him and froze it out of him. He snatched the joint from her hands and her tight smile became a sneer.

'Do you love me?' she said and laughed. It was the cruellest laugh he had ever heard.

Rod went back to his Jack Daniels and Jo returned her gaze to the dark fog outside.

So there they all were: Nick, Sin, Rod, Jimmy and The Dead Boys. *Ain't it fun...*

And maybe Nick had a hint of what Rod had been driving at; but, if he did, it only made him feel colder than ever. Rod was implying the band had come to make a stand for people like them: rejects, misfits, dreamers who had forgotten how to dream; people from the dog-end of society. With the help of the band they were going to fight back. After all, that was what Nick himself had felt on the two nights the band had played to its ragamuffin audience. Yes, maybe he could see what had enthused Jimmy and Sin and all the rest of them, all the ragged heroes driving to nowhere in the foggy night. Maybe he could see that. Or maybe he just felt scared, and maybe he just felt cold.

And Stiv Bators sang.

And Jimmy drove.

Ain't it fun... When you know that you're gonna die young.

Chapter Eight

Two signals.

That complicated things, of course. But maybe it made a little sense too. One pulse emanating from the cattle truck, intensifying whenever the band played – *whenever carnage was unleashed* – and otherwise practically dormant, only detectable under the amplification of the TARDIS's booster circuits rigged up on the cluttered lab desk.

And the other signal? That was the mystery. And pointed the way to the answer too. All he need do was identify where that other signal – so much weaker than the first, like a faint heartbeat slowly waking – was coming from.

It was an aural shadow of the first pulse. It shouldn't be such a huge task for the Doctor to isolate it.

Simple. Then why, despite all the technology his lab had to offer, was it taking such an interminably long time to do that one simple thing?

The Doctor straightened up from his desk. His thoughts kept straying from the task in hand, from the taunting elusiveness of the signal source, to the subject that worried him even more. He strolled to the window overlooking the canal, stroking the underside of his nose pensively.

Jo.

The fool on the hill.

Jimmy sat with his back against the Glastonbury tor and looked out on the world spread below him. Fool? He was a sodding king up here, surveying his kingdom. That kingdom was a flat green carpet cut by straight dikes and winding lanes. I can see for sodding miles and miles and… In a field at the foot of the hill the encampment was a disordered junkyard of almost certainly illegal vehicles. Jimmy marvelled at how large the convoy had become since the Oblong Box. Cars, buses, campers and motorcycles had just tagged on to the end of the metal snake as it slithered through England's green and pleasant land as if it were growing a new but decidedly tatty tail.

To the south, Glastonbury was a sprawl of elegant masonry laden with windows reflecting a golden sky, dominated by the skeletal abbey, a haven for romantics. There'd be no one from the convoy visiting that relic, Jimmy thought. Hippies were dead, and their Meccas were crumbling. The travellers were on to something new and dangerous and exciting... He dabbed his tongue into the little plastic bag and rubbed the white powder across his teeth. Jimmy was nobody's fool. He knew it was down to him that they were here, on the tour to end all tours; the magical mystery tour to heaven, or maybe just to hell. Whichever, did he care? Princetown was a hell, and he'd got out of there. At least he'd have a laugh looking for the next one. At least he'd go out kicking against the pricks.

Yeah, they'd all wanted out of Princetown for ages, but it took something like the band to make them get up off their arses and do it. They'd all silently and unanimously agreed that this was something better than they had going for them in Princetown, which was nothing. But Jimmy had been the deciding factor; he had the camper, and it was down to him.

They'd thank him for it one day.

He took another dab of speed and snorted as his roving gaze fell on the two police-cars parked at the foot of the steep hill. They'd trailed the convoy all the way from Dartmoor. What did they think was gonna happen anyway? Maybe the end of society as they knew it?

Why not? Might be a laugh.

He hated pigs. *Hated* 'em. But if anyone had ever thought to ask him why, he would have been stumped for an honest answer. It was just the way he felt. They got in his way. Stopped him doing what he wanted. Was that good enough? It would have to do, ladies and gentlemen.

Jimmy sat on the hill in the brilliant afternoon sunlight and waited for the speed to kick in.

Sin watched the band climb the hill. They were wearing their shades and carrying their instruments. Different instruments, she realised, as they threaded their way through the travellers thronging the crest of the hill. The guitarist and bass player each clutched an acoustic guitar. The drummer jingled a tambourine as he strode towards the stone tower, the childish instrument incongruous in such brutal hands. The singer carried nothing and ignored anyone who tried to talk to him. Once somebody was foolish enough to pluck at the multicoloured but grubby tatters of paper that adorned his frame. The singer dealt with this intrusion into his privacy by kicking the offender squarely in the face. No one else tried to slow his progress.

Sin glanced at Jo sitting a little to the left of Nick, on the brow of the hill. What did she want with them? She was from a different world, Sin could sense that. There was something very odd about the girl, and it troubled her. Jo had got quite friendly with Nick. That didn't bother Sin at all, and she wondered why. Perhaps because she didn't care any more.

Didn't care about anything.

Was that true?

The band moved inside the ancient tower. Anyone already inside promptly moved out.

Sin had a good view of the tor, sitting as she was barely ten yards away. She picked a daisy and crushed it in her fist as the band began to play.

This was a different kind of gig. Gone was all the manic energy and electric violence that had characterised the earlier performances. Sin sat up straight. The singer was crooning, leaning in the entrance of the tower with a sneer on his gaunt face, his voice amplified by the natural acoustics of the hollow monument. His companions stood beside him, strumming lazily, contemptuously. The cheeky jingle of the tambourine was a piss-take.

77

The music was quieter, obviously, but still trembling with a skeletal attitude. The melodies were stripped raw and bleeding; chilly bones of sound in the radiant daylight. Sin felt dirty fingers slip into her soul, caress it untenderly. Perverse passions awoke in her, passions for things unhallowed, a desire to embrace the unknown and the shunned. And she found that she *did* care after all.

She lay back amongst the daisies, let the music wash over her. She felt it carry her away on a breeze of ecstasy that swept her over the edge of the hill, floating in a dream, her body throbbing with sexuality. She stretched, every tendon and nerve languorous and teased by delight. Her veins ran with pleasure. Her body arched on the grass, daisies pricking her cheek as she turned her head to one side, moaning. Her tongue moistened her lips and her fingers played through her gorgeous dark hair, then crept down her body.

Night at the camp, and the fires played against the silhouette of the hill. Jo huddled beside Jimmy listening to his constant stream of bravado and nonsense and wondered, not for the first time, if the Doctor had not taken the easier option by heading off in Bessie, probably back to the comforts of UNIT HQ, and leaving her here with these good-for-nothings.

That was uncharitable. They weren't good-for-nothings. They just hadn't learnt how to fit in. She could understand how that felt. By God she could. But this whole set-up freaked her in a way she could not explain. Perhaps numerous gory deaths had something to do with it, she mused ruefully. But then, she was used to death, thanks to her unconventional companion. No, this special foreboding of hers ran deeper. Hadn't the Doctor told her to keep away from the band and to be extra careful? But what was she supposed to look out for?

Jimmy was obviously wired on some drug or other; he wouldn't keep still for a moment. One of the tin rifles that crossed on his cap was bent outwards, rather comically. It was a pointless detail that she would remember long afterwards, and for no good reason – or perhaps because it was one of the last things to occupy her mind before the mummer appeared and stole all her rational thoughts away.

She didn't see where he came from; he was just there, strutting amongst the travellers hunched round their various camp fires, lute in hand. She watched him chatting animatedly to some punks nearby, but couldn't hear a word of what was said. She noticed that the attention of the entire encampment was riveted on the bizarre figure. Just like in the the Devil's Elbow, all other conversations ceased. And suddenly it was their turn.

He was striding towards them, slightly hunchbacked, his face threatening yet jovial all at once. The shark grin glinted in the firelight as he stopped beside Jimmy. He spoke.

And Jo didn't hear a word. He was barely four feet away and she saw his mouth move and Jimmy's head nodding frantically in response. She could see Sin smiling like a cat on the other side of the fire, pert with satisfaction. And Nick…

Nick was frowning.

Jo promptly forgot about Nick and leant closer to the singer in an effort to hear what was said.

And suddenly, as if a dial had been turned up inside her head, the words were clear as daylight.

His eyes wide and moist with intense fear, Rod stared at the wall, scarcely breathing, until he realised where he was.

'Murder!' he hissed, his voice clogged with ruined sleep. The moon threw a creamy blanket of light over the interior of the camper van. Snores grumbled up from Sin and Jimmy, sprawled in sleeping bags on the seats nearby. No one had heard him. His hair was slick with sweat. The nightmare that had woken him was gone, not a fragment remaining; but he knew it was a real *horror*. His insides were curdling, his brain seething like it was boiling with maggots. He had to get out, suck in fresh air.

He wriggled out of his smelly sleeping bag and lurched across the cold floor towards the door, careful not to wake Jo who was tucked in near the driver's seat. He pulled his leather jacket and jeans down from the baggage rack and quietly hefted the door open.

The moon was waiting for him outside, full and inherently evil; it painted the encampment with weird light, casting a surreal pall over everything. Above him the hill rose like a silver cone, topped with its strange tor. He sat on the runner and struggled into his army boots.

Murder. Prison officers kneeling in the grass at Princetown, three body bags carried out of the Oblong Box. What was he doing on this mad tour? What were they *all* doing? He remembered the front-page headline in a copy of the *Sun*, tattered and smeared with mud, lying in a thistle bed in a lay-by en route to Glastonbury. He remembered the headline clearly, because he had pissed on it: WORLD'S MOST EVIL BAND PLAYS ANOTHER DEATH GIG. That was pretty strong stuff. How could he have forgotten it till now?

He leant against the side of the camper van, suddenly dizzy. The moon watched him coldly, a ghost eye gloating over his horror. The passion he had felt earlier for the band was... dead? He remembered the mummer talking, talking, and it had all made such perfect sense. Something about taking them all on a journey to a new society, where everyone would be equal: that was it. He had felt inflated with euphoria, and he was sure everyone else had felt the same.

Something made him look up at the tor just then. Call it fate – and if that was what it was, then it was an evil fate that had no time for a loner like Rod; because what he saw marked the end of the road for the good-natured bum from Tavistock.

A figure was moving up on the hillside. A stooped, ragged silhouette – he could discern the trailing tatters even from this distance. The mummer? For a moment, Rod was sure it was... but no, this figure was dressed differently, was somehow more twisted, like an old and stunted tree. It wasn't a particularly cold night, but Rod's skin felt suddenly coated with frost. Yet despite his unease, he really wanted to see that figure more closely. Hesitating, he looked back once, and only once, at the camper. Through the smeared windows he could see Nick's head cosied into his sleeping bag, Sin sleeping beside him. A yearning to be back with them hit him like a stake through the heart. My friends: my only friends. Never had anything else but them. Why was he saying his goodbyes – because that's what it felt like. His eyes moistened. This was ridiculous. He needed a drink, not a trek up the hill at – he looked at his watch – three-thirty in the morning. He glanced around the encampment. Uncannily, everyone was asleep. Not a sound. On other nights at least some of the travellers had stayed up until morning, smoking and drinking and listening to music. But not tonight.

His mind made up, Rod moved slowly through the rusty vehicles towards the stile at the edge of the field. He climbed over on to the path that led up the hill.

The hunched, spindly figure was still there, and whatever it was doing Rod was sure it was unhealthy work. He didn't recognise it, but somehow he knew it was someone he should investigate. Why? *Murder!* Because Rod had woken up, and he suddenly knew the others wouldn't, or couldn't.

With every step he took up the winding path, his thoughts ran clearer, gathering momentum. He knew what the figure was. It was the reason for the tour, the philosophy behind the band, and he knew this because every nerve in his body wriggled with terror as he got nearer the crest of the hill. *This* was what they were all following.

MURDER!

He stopped on the path, tears of utter terror trickling down his cheeks. He would piss himself in a moment. Go back you old bastard – go back to your friends. Get back in your sleeping bag and pretend you never saw this hunched spectre on the hill.

And now he could no longer see it as the gradient of the hill obscured the monument. The grass was silver beneath his feet, sweating dew. Above him the moon hung, a glowing, dead face. As lonely as him, but tonight it was a dreadful thing.

It was just the moon, for God's sake!

He reached the brow of the hill and the tor reared into view. The figure was gone. Rod slowed his pace, treading softly towards the tower. His tired eyes left it, roved across the world stretching all around him. Looking out over the patchwork nightland he could make out objects that he knew had not been there in the day; there was one in the field below the hill – a wooden pole with a cage at the top. A black gibbet with a corpse manacled inside rusting metal ribs, its eyes stolen by crows. And there, beside a dike running with moonlight, a gallows with its highwayman trophy swinging in the breeze – Rod could hear the creak. The body swung more violently and the rope broke. Other, more distant figures tumbled from their hanging poles like rotten fruit and began to totter on long-disused legs. Some wore tricorn hats and clutched flintlock pistols in their bone hands. All of them were converging on the tor, seemingly from across the land.

Unreality rushed him: this was a trip and nothing more. Jimmy must've slipped him some acid, the bastard. He tilted his head up to the sly old moon, sucking in cold air, and then looked down again. The ghostly robbers of the rich had vanished but now the countryside below had been transformed, grass seared to grey dust, trees deformed and leafless in the middle of summer. A spiteful land of ash and decay – and where Glastonbury should be there were just black remnants, bones of houses. The dikes that sliced the land were no longer filled with water, but were choked with bodies: trenches of gnarled, brittle human ruin, dead wood cast aside. Thousands and thousands and…

Rod screamed, and twisted round to face the tor again.

The figure was waiting for him, stepping out from the shadows of the tower.

A shredded cloak hung from its body, stirring idly in the night breeze. Rod was shaking and crying aloud because he knew that in a moment he would have to look at the face he had climbed all the way up here to see – and that now he would do anything, *anything*, not to see it.

And so they stood together for a timeless moment or two. Then one of them made a gesture and the other stopped crying.

Stopped everything.

Stopped…

And at the bottom of the hill PCs Roebuck and Williams were being relieved by their colleagues PCs Luton and Smith. Roebuck and Williams had been sitting in their squad car for the last five hours, watching and waiting for something to happen; and, as it had turned out, without anything to report. Now they could go home, and home for both of them was only a few miles away in Wells. They were both looking forward to a good sleep and maybe a cuddle with their respective wives. Upon reaching their houses, however, they chose to do something rather significantly different instead. They woke their wives with a detached precision, stared at them for a moment ignoring all puzzled inquiries, and then set about systematically slaughtering them. In PC Williams' case, there was a particularly troublesome teenage daughter to be dismembered too. He did that after bludgeoning his wife's brains all over the bedroom wallpaper with a golf club. The screams would stay with both constables for the rest of their lives. From the moment they left Glastonbury, picking up their own cars from the station, to the time they were led from their homes sleeved in blood a mere two hours later, they uttered not a single word.

In PC Williams' bedroom the words ARE WE FORGIVEN? were written in his wife's blood in big spiky letters on the wall.

Chapter Nine

'I've got just the man for you, Doctor.'

The Doctor looked up from his interminable study of the sensor probe. It was now lashed to a device resembling a dentist's drill which the Brigadier was sure could serve no earthly purpose whatsoever apart from being there just to baffle him... like just about everything else in the Doctor's lab, come to that.

'Oh, really?' The Doctor looked drawn and tired. His investigations must be leading him up a blind alley then, the Brigadier thought with a mixture of smugness and impatience. Couldn't the damned fellow do something more positive instead of continually poking at that infernal object? Five days he'd been buried in his lab now. Maybe this news would spur him on to some action.

'And who might that be?' the Doctor asked, blinking sleepily. Obviously been tinkering around the clock, to boot, by the look of him. Wouldn't he ever learn that a disciplined mind resulted from a disciplined lifestyle? A good night's sleep was essential for rational thought and decision. The Doctor looked crabby and haggard.

The Brigadier told him the name of the agent he was sending in and the Doctor looked suitably relieved, as well he might. Then he told him about the Prime Minister's decision to replace the police with UNIT as the force to shadow the convoy and, as he had expected, this item of news was not received quite as well as the first one.

'What the devil does he want to go and do a foolhardy thing like that for?' The Doctor was blustering with righteous rage. 'The whole point of letting the tour go ahead is so that we can monitor it covertly and hopefully discover what their intention is. We're not going to be able to do that with your clodhopping army boys stepping on their heels! Not only will it stop whatever is behind this endeavour from showing its hand, it might even exacerbate the situation and cause more trouble. Has your blessed Prime Minister stopped to consider that? Well, has he?'

The Brigadier braved this storm without batting a military eyelid, and then replied calmly: 'The Prime Minister is in an untenable situation; he is being forced to bow to pressure from the Opposition. The tabloids are baying for blood.'

'Not a very apposite choice of words, I would think in this situation, eh, Lethbridge-Stewart?'

The Brigadier's voice increased in volume as he let his irritation slip free. 'The papers are linking the horrific actions of the two constables in Wells to the tour. And for once I think they have a point.'

'Do you?' The Doctor stepped nearer, his hand caressing his chin, and scrutinised the Brigadier with a quizzical look in his eyes. 'Do you…?' he repeated more pensively. 'Do you know, Lethbridge-Stewart, you constantly surprise me.'

The Brigadier tilted his head back. 'Meaning?'

'Meaning there's hope for you yet. You just take a little longer getting there than everyone else. Now if you don't mind, I do have rather a lot to do.'

He'd been dismissed – like a blasted schoolboy! The Brigadier opened his mouth to bark a riposte, but the Doctor had already turned his back. Lethbridge-Stewart closed his mouth, his face prickly with humiliation and anger, and strode from the room.

'Bristol,' the voice said in Willis's ear. 'They're heading for Bristol.'

'How extraordinarily convenient. For both of us,' Willis replied, leaning back in his leather armchair and watching the sun plunge bloodily into the woods beyond his picture window. 'I should think this tour – what's it called?… the Unwashed and Unforgiving tour? – would be rather a cause célèbre for your… magazine.' The last word was pronounced with poorly concealed contempt: he might just as well have included the word 'odious', as he had intended to do before surrendering to self-restraint just in time. It wouldn't do to push the grubby little man too far.

'They're nothing to do with us!' the voice bristled. 'They're peddling obscenity and butchery.'

'And what on earth does *Class Hate* propagate? Peace and goodwill to all men?'

'You know what we stand for Willis: don't piss me around. I believe strongly in what I'm doing, which is something you could never say about yourself, so don't get on your soddin' high horse with me. Understand?'

Willis knew he shouldn't, but he couldn't resist rankling the man just a little more. 'I know why the convoy is ruffling your feathers so much, my friend: might it not be to do with the fact that whoever is behind this magical mayhem tour is organising a protest that has gone so much further than anything you and your... *organ*... could ever initiate with regard to shaking up the establishment?'

The line went quiet for a moment. He'd certainly scored with that comment. He smiled as he imagined the man seething with fury and wishing all kinds of working-class violence on Willis's upper-middle-class person. He enjoyed the moment, then gave in to practicalities; he did need this wretch on his side after all.

'Your chance will come, Mr Pole. As I said, the convoy coming to Bristol couldn't be more opportune. What superb camouflage it will provide for you to perpetrate your great act against the monarchy. That's if these hippies – or whatever they are – stay in the city long enough for you to use them as scapegoats... and I believe I can put pressure on certain areas to ensure that. Well, goodbye, Mr Pole. A pleasure, as always.' Willis replaced the receiver and his smirk grew. He reached for his glass of Bollinger on the coffee table, and took a very contented sip.

The convoy entered Bristol.

It had been tailed all the way from Glastonbury by two UNIT trucks and a jeep, the Brigadier occupying the latter. However, the Brigadier, acting on his own innate good sense – nothing at all to do with the Doctor's disapproval – had issued strict orders that his men should not engage with 'the hippies' in any shape or form, and that all provocation was to be ignored. Strangely enough, there hadn't been too much of that, but perhaps that was down to the Brigadier's other directive: that the UNIT force keep a discreet distance from the rear of the shambolic convoy.

The convoy entered Bristol, and brought the city centre to a standstill. Chaos ensued as local constabulary tried to herd the rusting collection of vehicles away from bottleneck situations and the Brigadier barked orders at them over his RT to let the travellers go where they willed, just as long as it wasn't out of Bristol again – another expressed desire of the PM. Where they willed, apparently, was south of the river. Totterdown.

Totterdown was a district of Bristol that had been levelled by a Second World War blitzkrieg and never quite managed to heal its bomb-site scars; it was an eccentric wasteland bounded by brightly coloured houses tilted against the steep hill on which the district was built.

The convoy led UNIT up Bath Road, one of the main routes skirting Totterdown, and then, to the Brigadier's delight, turned right into Arnos Vale cemetery. There was only one way out of this immense Victorian burial ground, he was informed; and that was the gateway through which the travellers had entered. He promptly issued orders to the local constabulary to seal off Bath Road to civilian traffic, and the convoy was successfully contained. The PM, if maybe not the damned Doctor, would be suitably satisfied.

'It's funny,' Nick said as they pulled up beside the imposing crematorium chapel, constructed along the lines of a classical Greek temple, 'but no one seems particularly bothered about Rod. Nobody's really mentioned him since he disappeared.' He shot an accusatory glance at Sin, who was sitting cross-legged on her seat, demurely smoking a joint.

She looked at him and shrugged. I don't *give* a shit.

Thanks, Sin. I used to love you. *Still do, you sap.*

Nick hurriedly turned his back on that thought and glared at Jimmy, who was leaning over the driver seat looking guiltily at him.

'He bummed out,' the driver offered. 'The tour must've freaked him.'

'Nothing freaked Rod. He didn't have the imagination.'

'Well, he's gone.' This piece of far-searching philosophy was from Jo, who had become rather friendly with Sin since Glastonbury. Rather too friendly in Nick's mind; she even seemed to have adopted Sin's unhealthy (in Nick's eyes, if not in the eyes of any other member of the convoy) infatuation with the band and the tour. Nick knew why he was staying with this mission, and it hurt him to admit it. He couldn't leave Sin.

He stared glumly out of the window at the massive overgrown cemetery that climbed the hill above them. It was more of a wood bristling with elaborate tombs that ranged from simple crosses and unadorned headstones to baroque sepulchres and fantastic crypts hidden amongst almost impenetrable undergrowth. The convoy was pulling up in the small car park beside the Garden of Rest. A few headstones tilted with the impact of clumsy manoeuvring, and some vases cracked under desecrating wheels. The cattle truck took out an obelisk with a brittle crunch and rolled to a standstill. Soon the gates were shut behind all the vehicles and the convoy became an encampment once more.

The bums watched the travellers arrive with befuddled amusement. They squatted around a dead fire at the top of the cemetery near where the pedestrian gate led out on to Hawthorne Street. They laughed raucously and spat and pissed themselves and did other things that bums do because they are blasted out of their minds and don't care, because life has left them precious little to care about, even if they could remember how to. Six of them in all: Moggy, fat and bewildered, proclaiming to anyone who'd listen – and that was nobody – that all he'd ever wanted out of life was a laugh; Cliff, wasted and only in his late thirties, the stain of his own piss ripe upon him; Lionel, big-boned and aggressive, his beard festooned with yesterday's beans; Heather and Nose, the couple who drank together and were now growing old and insane together; and lastly filthy old Hedges, mad-eyed and mumbling, still retaining an Elvis quiff and the black suit he'd worn to his wedding.

These merry boys and girls were the Arnos Vale alcoholics, continually grasping for their bottles like purple-faced babies at feeding time. Heather and Nose were engaged in a conversation which neither of them understood, waxing more vehement and violent with each other as they failed to get their respective meaningless points across. Moggy groped for his red wine as if clawing at his last hopes of sanity, and succeeded only in spilling it which made him roar. Lionel cuffed him, hurling obscenities in a voice husky with throat cancer. Cliff scratched at a scab on his balding head, and fresh blood seeped down over his brow. He barely noticed it, staring like a rheumy fortune-teller into the depths of his bottle; it told him nothing he didn't already know. 'I said to her,' he muttered, 'told her I didn't want to come back… never come back, and you know what?… Never did. Never went… back.' His blonde hair stood up here and there on his scalp like weeds. His nose was a blistered bulb. Hedges stared at him with gory eyes but said nothing, his mouth working drool.

'Never missed a day's work,' Moggy was boasting to no one. 'When I was… when things were… better.' He seemed oblivious to the blow the Neanderthal Lionel had dealt him. A foul squirting noise disturbed the relative peace of the upper cemetery as Moggy voided his bowels. Nobody objected. Nobody cared. He could sleep in it, like he always did. The purple haze of meths had long since stolen any sense of propriety. Visitors to the cemetery always avoided this dead-liver colony beneath the blind, stone angel. This was an exclusive club; meths drinkers only need apply.

But now they had something else to occupy their burnt-out minds: the commotion within the lower reaches of the cemetery made even these alcohol zombies react. While Heather rocked beside the ash of the dead fire, crooning to her bottle, the others staggered to their feet and stumbled down the path to claim a better view. Maybe, in the depths of their stewed brains, some curiosity remained. Or maybe they thought they could blag some more booze.

Hippies and punks, skinheads, Rastas and rockers, all together in one organised movement. And they weren't fighting. Something powerful indeed was happening here, Nick reflected as he sat on the wide stairs of the crematorium chapel and watched the roadies prepare yet another gig. This was the largest audience yet – he hadn't been able to visualise the size of the convoy until now, as more and more vehicles had been tagging on as it wound through the Southwest. Many travellers had followed the slow-moving collection of vehicles on foot, which hadn't been a problem considering just *how* slowly they had progressed. Just like they had all the time in the world. And in that moment of early summer, the realisation struck Nick that for once they had.

And now this ragged army surged before the cluster of tombs the band had chosen to be their latest stage. Hippies smoked joints, punks spat and belched and swigged beer, but nobody seemed to give a toss about the cultural or musical differences that normally divided them. They were embracing a single cause – thirty-something bikers with Led Zeppelin on their leather backs to spine-haired Vicious clones with Sham '69 tattoos. And Nick had never seen anything like it.

Dusk was falling. The battered generator, lugged from the cattle truck and positioned on top of a large sarcophagus, glinted in the last of the sunlight. One of the roadies carelessly slung a guitar into the overgrown grass; another denim-clad roadie leant the bass guitar a bit more delicately against a headstone, while the giant emerged from the back of the truck cradling drums. Wires were trailed through the long grass and connected to the amps roosting on tombs. The stage was set. The crowd stirred impatiently. Nick sucked smoke deep into his lungs, his heart pummelling. His forebodings were momentarily gone: this *was* the most exciting band in the world, bar none. He'd seen the Pistols, and they had been scorching; he'd seen the Damned and their cartoon chaos; he'd seen the strutting Clash; he'd seen The Ruts before Malcom Owen bought the farm. Nothing was as powerful as this bunch. *Nothing*.

They were beyond being a mere band, that much was obvious. They were hate incarnate. They were fury, revulsion, wildness, fear: everything that made your blood bump.

And here they were now.

The restlessness of the crowd ceased. Silence.

'This is desecration…' hissed Jo, standing up to get a better view over the crowd.

'Yeah,' agreed Jimmy. 'Great, innit.'

Jo was suddenly pulling at Sin's hand. 'Come on, let's get up the front,' she burbled with youthful glee. Sin clasped her hand and followed willingly. Nick watched as the two girls pushed their way through the unconventional throng. For a moment – and it was just a brief moment – his doubts returned. *Come back, you bitch. Can't you see what they're doing to you?*

What they're doing… to me?

Then he was on his feet too, Jimmy with him, as the four musicians made their way through the gravestones to collect their weapons.

At first the crowd remained silent, then it was as if there was one collective inhalation of breath, held for a fistful of electric seconds, which was released with a titanic roar as the singer took his place behind the microphone stand, gripped it tight in one fist.

Dying sunlight flared from his wraparound shades, sparked on the cymbals behind him. All four musicians were wearing tattered black overcoats like Western-style dusters over their mummer tassels. They looked more bizarre, and more threatening, than ever. The singer had a dark stetson rammed on his green punk hair. Leather gloves with metal spikes adorned his hands. He coughed hoarsely into the mike and the crowd ceased their baying.

The guitarist leant against a headstone to the singer's left, top hat askew on his head, its crown flapping in the breeze. His minstrel trousers were smeared with dark stains. The skinhead drummer lowered himself on to his stool, tombs flanking him. The bassist, taller than anyone Nick had ever seen, struck a few notes from his instrument, grinned evilly at the audience and began a threatening riff.

This was it.

This was why they followed the band.

Adrenaline terror and joyous aggression caught him up like a doll in a cyclone as the band blasted into their first number. Nick was jettisoned into hell, screaming orgasmically, his brain a pounding thing that would burst like a squeezed orange any second, his heart drilling through his chest. He was on fire, he was the coldest he'd ever felt, he had the biggest hard-on imaginable. He was in love.

He was in hate.

And the world would fall apart, and nothing mattered but this inferno of incredible ragesound.

Nothing mattered.

Yes, this was it. This was what made it all worthwhile.

In the prosperous heart of Bristol's financial district, the decorous wine bar the Money Tree was *the* place to parade your pinstripe. Stockbrokers, insurance brokers, commodity brokers and bankers – the cream of the young Turks – honoured the extravagant drinking hole with their presence. The bar was a converted bank, its vaulted walls echoing now with cultured tones and braying laughter instead of the subdued bustle of weekday transactions. The best designer suits, the best haircuts – not too long, not too short, conservatively caught between the battling late Seventies fashions; market dealers not yet in their thirties taking time off from hustling the fiscal streets to pose at marbled tables and pontificate with ruthless peers.

There were also the poor imitations of course: the ambitious shadows, emulating their heroes with sycophantic precision. Junior execs who would most likely not progress much beyond that level; bank clerks and sales reps rubbing shoulders with the big boys, their suits cheaper, but oh so immaculately pressed. These low-ranking wannabes were the ticks in the exquisitely tailored hides of their idols; struggling to conceal Bristol accents as they ordered their Double Diamonds, borrowing catch phrases they'd overheard about the state of the market – and which market it was, perhaps they didn't even know.

The women posing around the plush but incredibly soulless wine bar knew the score; gold-digging secretaries or struggling lower-paid execs in low tops with big smiles. Lured away from preoccupations about blue-collar boyfriends by the flash of cash. Fifty-pound notes were so much more pleasing on the eye than the scrumpled quid Dave or Terry offered over the bar down the local.

Above the gleaming brass bar, crystal chandeliers glowed tastefully. The setting sun played on them, streaming through the great arched windows. More arches, exquisitely marbled, opened on to the recessed lavatories while white, fluted pillars ran the length of the long room. Above the complacent, chattering throng, Renaissance characters frowned down reproachfully on this modern decadence from gilded frames. The fiercely manufactured elegance was neoclassical, and the fact that the building had once been a Lloyds Bank simply added to the irony.

The singer wielded his microphone stand like a spear, prodding it out into the audience for them to roar the chorus into the mouthpiece.

'SCUM!! WE'RE THE SCUM, SCUM OF THE EARTH!!'

Then he snatched it back, belched out more obscenities masquerading as lyrics, his face contorted with ogre rage.

The guitarist hunched over, hacking rhythms from his

instrument. The bassist was spitting blood into the crowd, his mouth growling wide, wider than any mouth should go. And the drummer was joining in the barbaric fun, nutting his cymbals with his scarred club of a head. He finished this display with a stream of shining green vomit that splattered his snare drums.

'How do they *do* that?' Jo shouted into Sin's ear as they stood at the very front of the twisting, leaping crowd, buffeted this way and that. She had to hold on to the Chinese girl for safety. Sin didn't answer – but she remembered the foul stink of the liquid spraying down on to her, and she smiled a secret smile and began dancing, pulling Jo around with her.

A foul odour came off the band like heat. Rotten compost cabbage animal spew smell. Jo's nostrils flinched from it, but she knew she was grinning regardless. The little Chinese girl's enthusiasm was infectious, and Jo felt a violent joy that was all her own rip through her. She was a wild child dancing a discord dance as the Earth churned beneath her careless feet. And why *should* they care? Why should the Doctor dash frantically through the universe putting right things that would probably sort themselves out anyway, if he only left them alone.

Always rushing around, meddling.

When he could be dance-dance-dancing.

Who gave a toss about anything?

All the signposts pointed to the same place didn't they, in the end? All roads led to Home.

Better to sit in your armchair and do nothing. Do nothing or dance the discord dance...

The guitarist charged abruptly to one side, his boot lashing out. He kicked a leaning gravestone flat on its back, then spun, all in one lithe movement, machine gunning horrendous riffs into the loving audience. The singer posed, legs apart, mike detached from its stand and pumping at groin level; threw his head back and then let fly a torrent, a *spew* of white squirming objects from his mouth.

Maggots.

They cascaded into the crowd, festooning spiked hair and hippie beards alike… and several hundred voices screamed with insane fervour.

The bassist was atop a tomb, swinging his bass dangerously. Then he was airborne, came crashing down on a gravestone, falling with it, rising, pummelling his bass continuously, shades still clamped across his eyes.

Jo realised Sin had stopped dancing. She could see the white grubs squirming in the luxuriant blackness of the Chinese girl's gorgeous hair, could feel them in her own *and didn't care*; she watched as Sin was suddenly seized by the singer, and a strange sexual horror swept her as she realised what was going to happen – horror and dark, dark glee.

The singer was pressing that noisome mouth, from which so many maggots had spilled, against Sin's, was snogging her violently, wantonly. Then he shoved her away, and was that something white and squirming falling from the Chinese girl's lips? Sin was smiling, reeling as if drunk, and the music took them all.

The Arnos Vale alkies were in the city centre now. They couldn't remember what had made them come this far. They didn't know why they had collected the sexton's tools from the cemetery shed near the gates. And for once, their oblivion was nothing to do with alcohol, although, of course, they had consumed vast amounts of that.

Nose, Hedges, Moggy, Lionel and Cliff; differing ages, differing backgrounds. United by their dilapidation. They had staggered all the way from Totterdown, over the railway bridge, under the flyover, clutching bottles in one hand and rakes, hoes and shovels in the other. They didn't argue for once; didn't talk at all. They merely swayed and tottered on their meaningful way.

Oh yes, tonight they had method in their madness. But it was not their own.

* * *

Richard Thwaite, a commodity broker in his late twenties, was the first to guess that the stocks were about to plunge disastrously to an all-time low for him and his buddies. What convinced him of this was seeing the two don't-mess-with-me-I'm-hard bouncers, who had supported the doorway outside like two burly, tuxedoed pillars, come tumbling in through the swing doors spraying blood.

Bad shit, he mouthed to himself, not comprehending exactly how bad the shit was going to get this evening. One of the bouncers had the head of a rake embedded in his neck. Then the doors opened further, and Richard saw what was on the other end of the tool.

A bum. Dribbling, filthy suit, purple face: the lot. A *bum*, in this exclusive haven.

That made him get off his seat. He had always loathed bums. They were people who had lost control, who had turned their backs on their own humanity and dignity. Losers and failures. And Richard despised losers most of all. Losers were the creatures you stepped over in subways, carefully avoiding the outstretched grimy claws begging for money. They were the refuse that the council always forgot to sweep off the streets.

The large-breasted young thing beside him was also getting up, almost in slow motion – certainly too slowly to avoid the wino who came lurching across the marbled floor at her like a wound-up toy, waving a shovel and gibbering nonsense. Richard didn't have time to stop the swing of the shovel, even if he had the inclination. Which he certainly hadn't – he was too busy saving his own finely soaped skin.

He watched anyway as the blade of the shovel connected with his companion's lovely face, albeit from the apparent safety of the other side of the large round table. But he didn't count on the bearded derelict who came through the glass doors at a run, his run turning into a leap as he spotted a victim – as he spotted Richard.

What almost offended Richard the most about his predicament

was the smell. His last thoughts were not of his wife waiting patiently at home, watching the clock and wondering at exactly what point in their brief marriage her perfect husband had begun going wrong. They were concentrated on the indignity of being butchered by a crazy wino with a scythe who stank like a sewer thing. And then the prices hit absolute rock bottom for Richard.

Screams echoed around the vaulted wine bar. The Arnos Vale alkies waded into their adversaries, slashing with broken wine bottles, mutilating with hoes, ripping at smooth, well-fed faces with filthy fingers. Moggy pounced on a sleek brunette with a low-cut dress, dropping his meths in his excitement. The girl shrieked with revulsion and the terror inherent in the idea of two social opposites so inelegantly united, then her breasts were bared and Moggy was burying his coarse features in the forbidden fruit.

Some of the suits made a break for the door. But Lionel had retreated there to take up his new occupation as wine-bar bouncer. Only this bastard didn't let anybody *out* he didn't like. And his scythe agreed with his philosophy.

'If your name ain't down...' he croaked, 'You ain't getting out!'

The scythe swung and dug, swung and dug.

Cliff, Hedges and Nose were doing fine too.

The Money Tree at number twenty-nine Corn Street had once been executive heaven. In the space of fifteen minutes it had been transformed into executive hell.

Chapter Ten

Once more a blood message had been left. This time scrawled by the winos all over the decorous walls of the exclusive wine bar.

Charmagne Peters read it along with her journalist peers; the police had finally allowed them access. She turned to study the looks on the faces of the other hacks. A lot of hard-bitten stoicism, some poorly hidden glee, and just a little revulsion – not a lot, but some. To them it was an opportunity for a great story. To her, it was something different.

Although what *that* was, she could never have said.

Personal. Yes, this was in some way personal, and she resented all the other journalists for being there.

She recognised a few of them from Princetown and the Oblong Box, some from the nationals, others from local rags. But none of them had been on the story right from the start – the first reporter on the scene at Princetown had been herself, so maybe that was why she felt so defensive.

It was more than a story.

She remembered her dream. *(Keep running, cos it's nightmare time.)* It was recurring almost twice a week now. And it had been five years since she'd been to Romania as a student and seen the sewer children. They had not advanced on her like in the dream; she had not been on her own in a deserted side alley. Yet nevertheless the children of Sighisoara had haunted her ever since, and the image of them begging from the tourists and more affluent members of their own society at café tables, driven away by angry – *indignant* – proprietors, was what had inspired her to become an investigative journalist in the first place: she wanted to correct these wrongs. And that wasn't just naive self-righteousness, it was something she felt deeply. *(Just like she could feel this tour burrowing deep inside her, like it was part of her.)* But she'd certainly never dreamt of them since her visit – not until the night before the Princetown gig.

And now this.

This blood graffiti.

This, *this* reached a deep secret spot as well. Not for her the superficial satisfaction at the chance for career advancement that was evident in the reactions of the journalists milling like cockroaches around the scene of the crime, cameras blitzing.

This was something else.

REND THE RICH, the blood graffiti told her, dribbles spiralling down from each letter to congeal on the marble floor.

UNWASHED AND UNFORGIVING…

The Brigadier allowed the police access to the encampment reluctantly. While he was at odds with the Doctor on one score, namely that the tour should be given free rein at all – he was all for disbanding it immediately – he agreed with him that harassing the bloody hippies would only cause further trouble. And what would the police be able to discover anyway? The actual perpetrators of the crime at the wine bar had been taken away, blatantly meths- and blood-sozzled. So what were they hoping to prove here? That the band had subliminally brainwashed some local alcoholics to butcher a bunch of stockbrokers? What did the civil boys think they had on their hands here, a punk-age Charlie Manson and his family?

The Brigadier frowned. The analogy was a little too close for comfort. But it seemed to fit: some crazy cult working their evil influence on impressionable minds. Why had it taken him so long to come to that rather obvious conclusion? His perceptions seemed to be a little dimmed lately. The band were a death cult. Maybe he ought to pass that little nugget of inspiration to the Doctor. If the Time Lord ever managed to tear himself away from his tinkering, that was…

Another thought struck the Brigadier, a natural successor to the first one, and he gazed long and hard at the cattle truck and the detectives interviewing the roadies outside it.

If the band were the family, just who the hell was playing Charlie?

The police were walking away from the truck now, and the Brigadier could see the open sneers on the faces of the roadies. The largest one chucked a cigarette stub contemptuously in their direction. The Brigadier noticed something rather unusual as the detective and his sergeant stalked past the rear of the truck and made for the cemetery gates. They had interviewed the roadies about any possible connection between the band and the alcoholics' murderous deeds – *but they hadn't interviewed the band themselves*.

For the second time in the space of mere minutes, the Brigadier felt as if he'd just realised something he should have caught on to a long time ago. And then, unusually for someone with his precise, disciplined mind, he completely forgot it again.

She had been able to slip past the UNIT guards on the gate as they were liaising with their officer over whether to let the police in or not. When she saw the extent of the encampment, just how much it had grown since the Oblong Box, and realised just how vulnerable and incongruous she felt on her own amongst the travellers, she began to wonder if coming to the cemetery had been such a great little idea after all.

But then, did she really have a choice?

Charmagne paused next to a purple camper van as she pondered that. Of course she did. She could walk out again right now.

Of course she could...

The cattle truck caught her eye, parked beneath some overhanging yew trees, a felled stone obelisk beside it. The police were conversing with some military bigwig who had insisted on following them inside the cemetery with some blank-faced soldiers for company, and, judging from the expressions of the respective parties, it wasn't exactly an empathic meeting of minds. Then the police, obviously having been granted access, headed off towards the truck. Charmagne decided to explore other avenues instead.

101

She deliberately chose the most hostile-looking group she could find. That way she was sure of a reaction; she didn't want noncommittal material. The four punks were squatting round the remains of last night's fire, empty tins of beer strewn around the nearby headstones like New Wave grave decorations. They eyed her with a mixture of wariness and derision as she approached. She almost walked on by, but her journalistic instincts forced her to make contact.

'All right, folks?' They ignored her greeting, staring at her blankly. One of them clutched a bag and his eyes were very red, and very empty. Pretty bloody vacant, all right. However, she'd come this far; she wasn't going to stop now.

'My name's Charmagne, I'm from...' She hesitated. The *Plymouth Chronicle* would sound so absurd in this context she would have laughed herself. 'I'm from the *Daily Mail*.'

On second thoughts, she reconsidered, as two of the punks snorted with contemptuous mirth.

'D'ya wanna story, love?' one of them asked. His hair was dyed black and spiked, his leather jacket proclaimed DO IT DOG STYLE down one sleeve.

'Have you got one for me?' She smiled her most encouraging smile, not too winsome, not too cocky.

'Depends what ya want.'

'Can you tell me about the Money Tree?'

'Been lookin' for it all me life,' he shot back immediately.

She gave him a little laugh, just to make him feel good. 'The wine bar?' she prompted after a while. She was very conscious of the fact that the other punks weren't saying anything, just staring at her; two with derision in their eyes, one with nothing. She wasn't sure which was worse, until the one with blank eyes offered the bag to her and she smelt the glue. She smiled carefully at him and declined his kind offer. He continued to hold the bag out for a while, as if he couldn't understand her refusal. She turned back to Dog Style expectantly.

'Alkies kill brokers in cemetery tool massacre? You mean that wine bar?' He tucked his head down, slipped a fag between his lips, tilted his head back up.

Yeah, great Clint impression. You really are *cool, maan*… 'You've read the headlines too? But do you know anything else that's not in the papers?'

'Like?'

'Like why they did it. And was it anything to do with the tour?'

'Now why would it be anything to do with the tour?'

'You read the papers.' She was becoming annoyed by his laid-back attitude. 'You know what was written: you tell me.' This was just a hippie with a different hairstyle; there was nothing new or radical going on with this lot. Glue instead of dope. Anarchy in the UK? The same old shit, more like.

Except she knew it wasn't. She was seeing them in the mundane setting of daylight comedown from the night before. There was no band to stir up the vibe. This was the convoy relaxing. You couldn't maintain that wild energy all the time. She contained her disappointment; she wanted confrontation, controversy, *quotes*, for God's sake.

Was that all she wanted?

'Some rich bastards got chopped – that's all that happened,' Dog Style finally replied. 'You expect us to give a shit about *that*?'

'And the band?' She glanced over at the truck. The roadies had strolled off to fiddle with the amps and speakers which were still roosting amongst the graves.

The punk shrugged. 'What are you suggestin'? That the winos were fans? Got a little carried away by their enthusiasm with the music, decided to take out their pent-up aggressions on a bunch of stuck-up stockbrokers?'

'Something like that, yeah.' She stared him straight in the eye. He smiled.

'Then you ain't as dumb as you look. Now, if you excuse me, I gotta take a piss.' He was unzipping as he rose to his feet. She took the hint and turned away. Well, maybe she had some quotes after all. But she knew she could never settle for just that. The cattle truck was the source of the mystery. The band were still in there presumably, and the only time she ever saw them come out was when they played a gig. She began stepping through the multitude of hippies and punks and misfits of all descriptions who were squatting on the grass or on the bonnets of battered vehicles. The roadies were busy, so she'd take a look for herself.

She got within four yards of the cab of the truck and could see nothing inside. She moved closer. The windows were opaque with dried mud, only a small section of the windscreen clear of the filth, and the cab was pushed too close into the trees for her to be able to walk round and look inside from that angle. She decided to check the back doors.

The huge padlocks securing them were rusty but firm. She fiddled with them distractedly for a moment, and then noticed the hole. She bent to peer through it.

The stink made her recoil. She felt her gorge rise, and coughed fiercely.

Decomposition and cabbages. She forced herself to look through the hole again. Blackness. She waited for her eye to adjust, and then…

Another eye was staring back at her.

An eye beyond the door.

An eye… an eye that could belong to no human… no animal.

No screams, just total paralysis. This eye was grey as snail flesh, without iris or pupil. It blinked, stone-like lid closing then lifting to stare again. Something reached inside Charmagne's chest and molested her heart. She felt raped by that filthy eye but, like someone caught between sleep and wakefulness, could…. not… move.

'See something you like?'

The voice broke the spell. She turned, collapsing against the corrugated steel door. The giant chief roadie was standing there, massive arms folded, dirty grin on his face. He unfolded his arms and, leisurely reaching out one hand, crushed her right breast casually, cruelly.

'Cos I sure see something *I* like…'

His raucous laughter followed her as she stumbled blindly towards the cemetery gates.

'Nice and catchy,' Derek Pole said as he slid the *Daily Mirror* across the crumb-strewn café table towards his companion.

Jeremy Willis glanced down at the headline:

STOP THIS EVIL TOUR!

The subheadings were even more lurid:

DISBAND CONVOY OF DEATH-HIPPIES AND HATE-PUNKS!

SHADOW CABINET DEMAND GOVERNMENT TAKE ACTION AGAINST 'CONVOY OF SEDITION'

'Convoy of sedition, eh?' Pole sneered. 'One of yours I take it?' He picked the paper up and read aloud: 'Jeremy Willis, shadow transport minister, yesterday launched a full attack on what he describes as a complacent, ineffectual Government, prevented from taking firm action against the sinister hippie convoy and its cult band because of indecisive leadership and inefficient policies. Willis blamed underfunding of the police force and an uncommitted cabinet for allowing such obscene "outrages against humanity" to remain unpunished, demanding stricter amendments to criminal bills concerning the unlawful gathering of peace-threatening movements.' He put the paper down again and smirked at the minister.

'Got a way with words haven't ya?'

'Oh, but so have you, Mr Pole,' Willis smirked right back. 'I only have to pick up a copy of your magazine to realise exactly *how* eloquent you are.'

Pole lost his smile. 'I'm glad you're a regular reader.'

Willis smiled graciously. He gazed around the seedy little transport café. A yellow sign read BIG BOY'S BREAKFAST. Below that invitation were similar appeals to lesser waistlines. 'Are you sure you couldn't have chosen somewhere more insalubrious for our meeting?'

Pole ignored this. He tapped the paper again. 'I'm making light of all this shit, Willis. But I don't like it. Not one little bit. Too many people are making too many assumptions about this tour. And they're linking it to my magazine. What with the papers screaming class war and everything, it's no wonder the Old Bill's been sniffing around my place.'

Willis raised an amused eyebrow.

'You think it's funny? Remember I'm working with you on this.'

'Is that a threat, Mr Pole?' Willis waved the waitress away. Pole called her back and ordered a cup of tea.

'It's whatever you want it to be, mate.' Pole lit a cigarette, blew some smoke towards Willis. 'But I think you can relax, my friend. They got nothing on me.'

Willis maintained his smirk to prove that doing anything other than relaxing was far from his thoughts. The waitress returned with Pole's tea, and Willis waited until they were alone again before speaking.

'I've got some news for you that will take your mind off the police, Mr Pole.'

Pole leant back in his chair, tilting his head to one side expectantly. 'Yeah?'

'*Good* news. It seems fate is smiling on your little Gunpowder Plot. The very same day the princess is due to visit Bristol there is going to be a demonstration in the city centre. A pro Country Sports demo, which, if the travellers are still in Bristol – and I am doing my utmost to make sure that is the case – will almost certainly draw the two groups into inevitable conflict of some kind. After all, isn't that what this tour's all about – protesting against the affluent in our society? And who's more affluent than the rural country sports brigade?'

Pole was smiling. He didn't say anything for a moment. Then, tapping his cigarette into the ashtray, he leant forward again. 'You know, I could almost get to like you, Willis. But then I realise what you are, and I regain control.' Willis bowed his head with mock graciousness, an oily smirk on his face. 'Are you absolutely sure the princess won't cancel her visit because of the protest?'

'Why should she? It's her set after all, isn't it? And with enough pressure in the right places, the police can be convinced that the travellers and the royal cavalcade will not stretch their resources too much to warrant a rescheduling. Of course, you've got to make sure that if – and I'm sure it'll be *when* – the travellers arrive at the protest, some of your agents kick off and start a little… excitement, shall we say. And then the police will most definitely find they have a lot on their plates…'

'Leaving the darling princess at my mercy.' Pole's voice was low, but as he and Willis were alone in the café, and the waitress was at the other end of the room, he had no reason to worry about being overheard.

'There will be a skeleton police and security force protecting her of course, but the vast majority of the constabulary will be at the other side of town. Supervising those infamous travellers will be far more of a stringent issue than watching the princess visit her university of choice. How jolly accommodating of her to decide to eschew Oxbridge, and how grateful you should be to those ragamuffins for deciding to bring their odious tour to Bristol.' Willis stroked his moustache thoughtfully. 'You really are a lucky man, Pole; things couldn't have worked out better for you.'

'Or for you: don't forget what you're hoping to gain out of this.'

Willis ignored this remark, preferring to continue his condescending assessment of the situation. 'This is what your whole life's been building up to, Pole, even if your riots *haven't* – as you promised me so vociferously they would. The biggest coup of your activist career, and you'll hardly have to organise a damn thing. The travellers will stage it all for you.'

Pole scratched the thinning hair on his scalp, and leant forward, his small eyes squirrel-like and hard. 'And you get to stamp in the face of your political opponents, don't you, Willis? What better way of discrediting the present Government than by having the bloody *princess* kidnapped? Cos people still revere the monarchy, don't they? They still soddin' *love* the parasites. The whole country will have to stand up and listen to your lot then, eh?

Social unrest caused by joblessness, homelessness, lack of public spending and cuts to every service, resulting in the monarchy itself receiving a body blow in protest.

'Let me tell *you* how it is, for a change, Willis. If the Government falls at the next election because of my coup, you know exactly how well *you'll* stand should your crowd get voted in. Just how popular is your leader? He's a weak puppet figure and you, and all your powermonger cronies, know it. He'll go *before* the election, leaving you with a very good chance of becoming the next leader of the opposition. And then come polling day... well, you never can tell. You'd do anything to achieve that, wouldn't you, Willis? Even dirty your hands dealing with me. And that's far more offensive to your senses than taking out the princess. It's just a crime that I have to work with *you* to get what *I* want.'

'Who else would finance your volatile endeavours? Not to mention your magazine?' If Pole had hoped to get a rise out of the politician he was sadly disappointed. Willis remained cool as the proverbial long green fruit, but many times more unsavoury.

And so the two sat opposite each other in a greasy-spoon transport café, class standing between them like a canyon. Each was repelled by the other as if by a physical odour – and yet they had formed a twisted bond, and their mutual need was greater than they could force themselves to admit. Pole, thinning hair, grubby T-shirt, worn jeans, would sell his soul (and sometimes, working with Willis, he was convinced he had done so) to destroy the monarchy he had detested all his life; Jeremy Willis, immaculate, suited, conservative side-parting, hungry eyes and soft white hands had ambitions that were entirely more self-directed. We'll leave them there for the moment, contemplating each other with distaste, and with more in common than they would *ever* allow.

Bessie took the ford too fast and a clutch of indignant geese were sent squawking off in all directions as twin waves plumed from under the Edwardian roadster's wheels. The Doctor didn't even notice, so intent was he on the pulse emanating from the sensor rigged to the dashboard.

It had taken him days to isolate the second pulse from the first and to triangulate exactly where it was coming from. It was very weak and buried under layers of electromagnetic noise, but he had finally succeeded in excavating it. The first pulse was faint but constant, beating from the cattle truck; for the moment he could ignore that, and had dampened it. More pre-eminent in his mind was what exactly was causing the shadow pulse. It seemed to be reacting to the first emanation, almost as if it were calling to the truck.

The Doctor steered Bessie through a quaint Wiltshire village, oblivious to the thatched roofs and black-and-white cottages. He was preoccupied with one thing only: answering that summons before whatever was in the truck answered it. The road ahead was blocked by a tractor; a fat farmer with his buttocks peeping cheekily out from above his cords bounced along happily on his seat, completely unaware of the impatient Time Lord directly behind him.

The Doctor honked his horn, but the sound was lost over the raucous blatting of the tractor's engine.

'Good heavens, man, will you get out of my way!' he bellowed, edging Bessie right up behind the bouncing buttocks. He suddenly missed a placatory remark from his habitual passenger, and his hearts tightened and his impatience grew.

He blasted the horn again.

Jo leant against a stone angel and watched Sin flirting with a long-haired hippie who, with his torn Stranglers T-shirt, looked like he might be on the cusp of transforming into a punk – she caught herself wondering what she'd look like herself with short spiky hair and fishnets. Maybe quite sexy. Perhaps she could talk to Sin about it; they could work on each other. She noticed Nick sitting a little apart on a tomb, smoking and trying very hard to pretend he didn't care. Nick was nice, good looking, kind, but maybe a little too serious. Sometimes she got the feeling he didn't want to be with the tour, and yet at other times he was caught up with the buzz like all the rest of them.

Yes, that included her, all right. She wanted to see this thing through; she wanted to see a confrontation – and she knew one was coming. The band was bringing change, re-dressing this land of shame. And the Doctor?

He just better not try to stop it. She'd grown tired of his meddling.

She was leaning back in the afternoon sun, her back warm from the base of the stone angel, when she glimpsed someone she knew. She sat bolt upright, her lazy smile snatched away.

Bastards!

They couldn't leave it alone, could they? Couldn't leave *her* alone. This had to be the Doctor's bright idea, sending Mike Yates in. And how bloody 'inconspicuous' he looked! She would have laughed if she wasn't so annoyed. He was sitting away from the main huddle of travellers on the steps of the crematorium, smoking a cigarette of all things! My *God* what was he wearing? A sheepskin tank top! Beads round his neck!! *Huge* flares!!!

She felt herself flush with shame and yes, real anger. He looked a complete prat. A cartoon hippie. Jesus, who'd dressed him – the bloody Brigadier?

He was going to ruin everything. If he spotted her and came over now, her new friends would believe she was spying on them. And while that had been the original intention, it certainly was no longer the case now.

She made her mind up. She'd have to go over to him, tell him to leave, that everything was fine. Send him back to those idiot army boys. From a distance, she could pretend he was just a weird acquaintance if Sin or Jimmy happened to be looking.

He must have already noticed her and simply been waiting for the right time to approach her, because he didn't look surprised when he looked up and saw her heading his way.

She forced herself to smile pleasantly, shutting the anger inside.

'Jo,' he said warmly, holding the cigarette like a schoolboy caught behind the bike sheds.

She didn't waste time. 'Mike, you have to go.'

His sheepish smile vanished, and his usual practical expression slipped into place. 'What's the matter?'

'*You're* the matter: you look too obvious. Anyway, you're not needed here. Doesn't the Doctor think I can look after myself after all I've been through because of him?' She'd let out some of the anger despite herself and he frowned.

'Are you sure you're all right, Jo?'

'I'm feeling better than I have for a long time, Mike. I've got friends, *normal* friends who actually believe in something other than just tampering with other people's lives –' she broke off. She was doing herself no favours if she wanted to get rid of him. She should pretend she was still following the Doctor's instructions.

Instead of the mummer's.

The thought shut her up even more, but it shouldn't make her lose her resolve, no more than the look of concern on Yates' boyishly sensible features should.

'I think you're overreacting, Jo. I don't think you're annoyed at the Doctor's lack of faith in you at all. Could it be more to do with the fact that I've discovered you might be just a little *too* undercover?'

He was such a pompous prig! Always had to be right. God knows why she'd never seen it before. 'These people are pissed off, and I can see why. They have every right to be sick of a conscienceless, consumerist society where all that matters is who has the most money and how best they can spend it on themselves. There's no room left for dreamers.'

'Is that you talking, or your new friends?' Mike himself was looking a little angry now.

'Well it certainly isn't the Doctor, for once. I've got my own mind now, Mike, and I'm using it.'

'I wonder, Jo. I wonder if you are. The Doctor believes this band is exerting some kind of influence over its followers, brainwashing them. I'm beginning to think he was right. I think you've been with this convoy too long.'

That made her shake with rage. If he thought he could just snap his fingers and pull her out of the tour he'd – she clenched her fists and turned her back on him. Then she stopped and turned round again. 'If you try to interfere, I'll blow your cover, Mike. And I can't promise what'll happen to you then.' His look of amazement made her feel good. She walked across the grass between the graves to where Sin was waiting for her, watching with shrewd eyes.

'Give me some of that,' Jo said with a wicked smile, taking a big fat joint out of Sin's hands.

'Trouble?' Sin asked, face expressionless.

'Just a former boyfriend. A right jerk. I told him where to get off.'

Sin looked over at Nick. 'Join the gang,' she said heartlessly, and laughed.

Yeah, go on... laugh.

Laugh like you're a heartless bitch.

Because it doesn't matter. I know you're *not*. Not really. You're a strange girl who's got caught up in something she doesn't understand. You don't know your own mind, Sin. It's like you're mixing with a bad crowd or got involved with heavy drugs. *You don't know your own mind.*

Mixing with a bad crowd? That was funny. And also the understatement of the century. Now he was beginning to sound like his old man, and might just as well have been him for all the desire she'd been showing lately. She didn't give a shit. How many times did he have to be told?

Nick got up off the tomb he was sitting on and strolled stiffly towards his former girlfriend. She was chatting to Jo and another bloke he didn't know. He didn't like the look of him. Nick tried to look mean, and cool, but had the keen impression he was just looking ridiculous. Sin looked up as he approached, a cruel smile on those lovely lips.

'Yeah?'

This was even worse than he'd thought; they were all staring at him mockingly, and the geezer with the Stranglers T-shirt was sucking on his cigarette around a smirk that made Nick want to slam him. But he wouldn't do that. He would play it cool.

'Just wanted a word…'

'Any particular one?'

'Yeah.' His dander was up despite himself: 'How about "childish". How about "selfish".'

Sin grinned more widely, to show how little he could annoy her. 'That's double your allowance. You mean selfish because I don't want to see you any more. You mean childish because I don't appreciate your boring outlook on life. Then baby, I'm guilty as charged.'

Nick flushed. He was on the point of walking away, but knew that if he did he would never come back, and she would be truly lost to him.

'Can we talk in private?'

'You ain't got nothing to say I want to hear, Nick. You've made it clear you don't approve of this tour. Why don't you take off and leave us to enjoy it?'

'Enjoy? Jesus… People are *dying*, Sin. This isn't a game!' She had lost her cruel smirk now; her eyes were hard and emotionless like painted eyes. 'What the hell's happened to you?' Nick asked. 'We used to be so close. I remember you saying how much you needed me, how much –'

'How much I *cared*?' she finished for him with icy sarcasm. 'You're embarrassing me. Go and take your bleeding heart somewhere I don't have to see it. I'll tell you one thing: I only care about this tour now. It's everything I always wanted: excitement, fulfilment, adventure. Go and get a *job*, Nick. Go and get yourself a *nice* girl.' She laughed, and the Stranglers fan joined in. Even Jo sniggered.

Nick looked down at the ground, nodding slowly. He turned and walked towards the camper van.

* * *

The Doctor steered Bessie into the car park near the small school and unclipped the sensor from the dashboard. It was bleating faintly but steadily in his hand, perceptibly stronger than when he'd started out on his journey, yet still quiet enough to be described as dormant. The Doctor walked down the footpath beside the school, sensor tucked into the pocket of his green velvet jacket.

Children were running and screaming and fighting in the adjacent playing fields, and some of them pointed at him and laughed. He ignored them. Crows were also laughing at him, hoarsely and unpleasantly, from hawthorn trees leaning over the path. He ignored them too.

The path ended in a stile that led into a lush field, sparkling with cobwebs and the moistness of a brief late-afternoon rainfall. The Doctor's attention, however, was distracted by what stood in the meadow. He leant against the stile and stroked his prominent chin.

'Of course,' was all he said. He withdrew the sensor and held it out towards the field. The detector bleeped comfortably in recognition of the energy source. A nearby sheep stopped its grazing and looked up at him without curiosity. Vacantly.

Others gazed at him too, all with the same uniform blankness. The Doctor had never had much time for sheep. But they had never filled him with dread before. Of course that was nothing to do with the sheep.

But with what they reminded him of.

Then the church bells began to ring as if all hell really *had* broken loose.

She knew she would have to go back. There really was no choice in the matter. Had there ever been, from the moment she'd woken up in Plymouth on the morning of the Princetown massacre? She'd sensed something as she brushed her teeth and stared at her fine-boned features and slightly lost-looking blue eyes in the mirror. She'd *somehow known* that day would bring about a change in her life. Now all she could do was follow the path she'd chosen; see where it led.

She had to go back to the truck. Had to see what that filthy grey eye belonged to.

Sod that! Go back to your cosy flat and boring job on your local rag, girl. Do it now before you change your mind again. Go now. Please..?

What else could she do but ignore the voice? So back to the cemetery she went.

She approached it from the south side this time, from the narrow residential street at the top of the hill that gave access to the overgrown burial ground via a narrow single gate. Of course it was manned by UNIT soldiers. But there were only two of them, and she knew she'd be able to get past them.

She flounced up to them, all blonde hair and beautiful smiles. She had undone a couple of buttons on her blouse for added effect, and she was not ashamed at all. One of the soldiers looked at her cleavage before looking at her eyes. The other watched her impassively. He might be a problem.

'Sorry, miss: no entry,' the impassive one said. The other smiled at her. She smiled back.

'You have to help me: I left my purse in the cemetery yesterday, and I don't want any of those hippies to find it.'

'What were you doing in there yesterday?'

'Your officer let me in specially,' she lied smoothly. 'It was the anniversary of my husband's death. I wanted to visit his grave.' The impassive one stared at her shrewdly. It was obvious he didn't believe a word of it. His companion came to her rescue, winking at her patronisingly.

'I'll take her in to look for it, Geoff. She'll be all right with me.'

'I'll need to contact the sarge,' Geoff said, not looking as enthusiastic as his leering companion about the situation.

'She'll be all right. Trust me.' The soldier was already swinging the gate open, and ushering her through. 'Just keep right behind me miss; it's so overgrown in there you could easily get lost. And there's lots of weirdos about.'

Losing herself was so much easier than even the dim-witted squaddie could have realised, though of course it was entirely on purpose. She simply slipped behind an obelisk wrapped in ivy and hollyhocks and plunged down a bank into the depths of the wood, hopping over half-buried graves and dodging round headstones squeezed by python-like tree roots. She could hear his indignant shouts from above, but he would never find her in this thicket.

All she had to do was fight her way down to the bottom of the slope through the jungle of tombs, nettles and beeches, then locating the truck would be easy. Five minutes later, after sinking through a thin veil of undergrowth that covered the broken lid of a sunken vault, legs kicking frantically in space while she clung desperately to a network of roots, she realised she should have taken more care.

She managed to haul herself out, cutting her hands on the jagged edges of the sepulchre lid, and staggered to her feet. She could hear the anguished yelps of the soldier further away than ever now. She smiled ruefully as she imagined what the moustachioed officer with the swagger stick would do to him. Serve the perv right. That reminded her to button herself up again; after all, like the man said – there were a lot of weirdos about.

She followed the overgrown footpath through nettles glinting with fine strands of web, then through a glade of garlic lilies and finally emerged from the wood into bright sunlight. The crematorium reared above her with Doric columns and tall, murky windows. The sweeping marble steps, split by weeds, were occupied by punks, hippies, bikers and skinheads. They watched her as she came out of the trees, but let her pass unmolested. There was something about their eyes, all of their eyes. Something… vacant. Nobody said a word.

It was a gauntlet. A crowd sitting on the steps to her right, a crowd squatting round camp fires and vehicles to her left. Nobody said anything to her, or to each other. Silence, except for the eerie wailing of a lone cassette player. 'Silver machine' by Hawkwind.

All eyes upon her.

She knew she'd made the wrong decision. She should turn round, go back in search of the soldiers.

She turned round.

The gauntlet had closed.

Teenage punks of both sexes, rock chicks and bearded hippies on the wrong side of thirty, were closing the gap behind her. All staring impassively, vacantly.

'I *knew* you'd seen something you liked.'

The voice was low, mocking. She didn't need to turn to realise it was the giant roadie. Then his huge arms were closing around her, dragging her towards the cattle truck. The crowd watched as though they hadn't registered what was happening, or simply didn't care. She screamed at them to help her. The roadie laughed, slung her over one shoulder and opened the rear doors of the truck.

Darkness rushed at her as she was bundled inside.

Chapter Eleven

'You're the laziest bastard I've ever known.'

'Good for nothing's what my dear mama used to call me.'

Kane was stretched out on a tomb in Cirbury's churchyard, enjoying the mid-June sun and a bottle of Newcastle Brown Ale. Cassandra was standing over him, carrying a wreath. He was sloppy in black T-shirt, ripped jeans and biker boots; she was elegant in pastel blouse, white slacks and Harmony hairspray. She had ostensibly come to visit her mother's grave; Kane was there because he had nothing better to do.

'If the cats can sit around on graves all day, why the shit can't I?'

'I'm not going to dignify that with an answer.'

'Is that for me?' He waved a boot at the wreath.

She smiled. 'Simon's play starts in a couple of days. Are you going to cause any trouble?'

'Not if you shag me right here, right now.'

She sighed. 'You really go out of your way to prove you're no good, don't you?'

'Didn't your mother ever tell you, don't fall for the bad boys?'

'My mother's dead, Kane.'

He winced, and lunged upright to snag a fag out of the packet on the grass beside the tomb.

'Sorry.'

'What?' She put a hand to one ear. 'Did I hear right? Kane Good For Nothing Sawyer said sorry?' She turned her back and walked through the graves to her mother's memorial. He called after her.

'No kiss, no promise. On your head be it.' He lay on the tomb smoking and drinking for a while, watching her from across the churchyard.

They had started kissing in the classroom. He must have seen her dawdling in there after the rest of her year had filed out followed by the teacher, Caston, who he'd always hated. She'd known he would come; she'd seen him through the glass in the door as she sat listening to her boring biology lesson. Of course she'd known he would come. She was one of the cutest girls in the school, even if she did say so herself.

That was the first kiss. She was thirteen and well developed for her age, he was fourteen and wise beyond his years – at least she'd thought so at the time. A dark sort of wisdom, maybe a confused sort of wisdom. But that was just part of the attraction. He'd picked up on her signals and now at last he was going to act on them.

Of course he was the bad boy, the one her mother would have turned white over if she'd known. He was weird, and scruffy, had an attitude, and his hair was unfashionably longer than that of any other boy in the school. He wasn't clean. He didn't care. His eyes were a little frightening in their intensity, and his face a little wolfish, but she liked him.

She'd snog him.

So she did.

Of course his hands started to go everywhere, and she had to sort that out, but it was only what she'd expected after all. His predictability in that respect disappointed her a little, but what the hell, he was a wild kisser.

Then he suggested they go out in the playing fields. Nobody would see them out there. They left the classroom flushed and excited, and she didn't think they'd been spotted. It was home time and there was no reason to suspect big brother had guessed what was going to happen and would be looking for them.

He waited until she and Kane were under the old oak tree and lying on the grass, kissing as if their lives depended on it. Then he had come out of nowhere. And he'd brought his friends.

That was it. The end of her and Kane's little… 'thing' – the only word she could think of to describe it. It had been so long ago. Her brother had made her go home… alone. The next day she'd tried to speak to Kane, to find out what her brother had said, but he wasn't having any of it, wasn't having any of her.

Seventeen years ago.

And now?

She reread her mother's memorial, and time seemed so insubstantial. It felt like she could just walk around the corner, down the lane, into the playing field and under the oak, and he'd be lying there waiting for her – fourteen again, and almost innocent. She pictured him now, considered the lifestyle he had chosen for himself. There was no way back, even if she had never been quite able to forget that kiss. Her first. Her best.

She was nearly thirty, and had no one. Not for want of offers – she knew she was beautiful. There was just something inside her forcing her to wait for the right one to come along.

And that right one would *never* be Kane.

He watched her lithe figure as she stood over her mother's grave, and scratched his chin ruefully. *I know you want me, Cassandra Girl, and let's face it, there's nothin' wrong with that. You're only female, after all. But well, a bloke's got to play it cool. Don't want folk thinking old Kane's an easy lay, now do we? Don't want to spoil his good rep.* He grinned, slid off his perch and wandered over towards the church itself, drawn by idle whim. Or maybe not. He felt drawn to the building in a way he certainly never had before. He'd only been in there twice in the past: once at his christening; the second time pissed at midnight mass when he'd drunk the blood of Christ in one gulp, emptying the cup, and thanked the vicar for the free tipple.

What brought him here now? A desire to get out of the hot sun? Maybe. He pushed open the wooden door and entered the church, still clutching his Newky Brown.

He hated it immediately. The sanctimonious gloom, the ascetic pews that gave you back- and arse ache. The hassocks – how he wanted to lob those around. The stained-glass windows. Hadn't he tried to smash one the other day? Perhaps he'd make up for that now. Who was there to stop him? No soddin' vicar in sight. He strode up the nave, heading for the pompous pulpit, the Bible lying closed upon it. He scooped the book up and flung it across the church.

What had God ever done for him? He toasted the pulpit with his Newcastle Brown. 'Here's my God, arsehole.' He finished the ale and propped the bottle on the lectern. On impulse he crossed to the altar and hawked a lump of phlegm into the holy water. Then minced back down the nave to the curtain that hid the bell rope. Pulling aside the curtain, he grinned wolfishly at the dangling rope.

'Let's rock…' he rasped, and leapt on to it.

The bell clanged sullenly far above him. He kicked and swung madly like an overgrown kid, eliciting discordant peals from above.

Tiring of his childish sport, he released the rope and wondered what to do next. He didn't wonder long: there was a closed door next to the open one that led up the stairs to the belfry. What pushed him towards this door? Was it the same impulse that had brought him inside the church in the first place? Kane didn't know, didn't care. He had to explore.

Maybe because he had nothing better to do.

Maybe because he was bored.

The door was unlocked and he opened it and followed a short flight of stone steps down into a crypt. His boots kicked up grating echoes. It stank of earth and it was dark, but light from a small window showed him the dirt floor and another curtain, this one crimson velvet, drawn across an alcove at the far end of the crypt.

He wasted no time pulling back the curtain. The latticed window was at the far corner of the crypt and only threw a little pale light over what lay within the alcove. Kane reached for another cigarette.

A girl of stone, lying in state and clutching a baby, sculpted into the lid of a solitary tomb. Her eyes were blank marble and yet conveyed such an aura of sadness that Kane froze, cigarette lifted to his lips.

So, so sad. (Can you feel the sadness, Kane?)

There was a name etched into the base of the tomb, beneath the maiden's stone feet.

Kane lit his cigarette and in the flare of the match he read the name.

His mouth formed a rictus. Sweat sprang out upon his brow. He was cold, so horribly cold at that moment.

The marble etching said simply EMILY SAWYER.

'Your name, I presume?'

A stranger had followed him into the crypt. He wore a velvet smoking jacket, frilly cuffs and had a bizarre, white, bouffant hairstyle.

Charmagne lay on the floor of the truck in the most absolute darkness she had ever experienced in her life.

There should have been sunlight showing through the cracks around the doors and certainly through the rusted hole: there wasn't. It was as if deepest night had fallen outside as well as inside the truck. She lay for a moment, too scared to move, traumatised by the darkness. She had heard the roadie slam the doors and the click and rattle of the padlock. She would have to try to escape anyway. But not... just... yet. She felt like a child again – if she moved, something dreadful would snatch her. *Something with a gruesome grey eye.*

Waves of horror rippled through her, making her sure she would vomit. Then she was moving. Leaping to her feet and hurling herself against the doors – against where the doors should be.

There were no doors.

She fell headlong, banging her knees and elbows against the corrugated metal floor. She sat up, stunned for a moment, trying to think logically. The giant had tossed her in through the doors, just inside them in fact. They had to be right behind her. She stumbled up and groped carefully behind her, in the direction her common sense dictated *behind* had to be.

Nothing.

No doors.

She was breathing heavily now, and the first tears had spilled down her cheeks. *You got what you wanted, you got to look inside the truck. Now just please let me get out again.* She groped sideways, reaching for the metal wall.

There was no wall.

Feeling panic uncorking itself within her, she lurched to the other side of the truck, reaching blindly for the wall she knew had to be there.

And wasn't.

Her scream echoed madly within the metal vehicle.

'LET ME OUT. LET ME OUTTTT!!!!!'

My God please let me out.

'It's his name, all right.'

A new voice, a new visitor to the crypt. And that made three. The new arrival was the old cleaning woman Kane had glimpsed at the church doorway when he'd contemplated bottling one of the stained-glass windows a week or so before.

He was waiting for an explanation. Cleaning lady and frilly man didn't seem in a hurry to give one, gazing at the marble tomb in silence. Kane decided he'd better force one out of them.

'Is someone having a laugh at my expense?' He stood before the velvet-jacketed stranger in a threatening posture. The man was taller than him by about three inches, and he stroked his chin thoughtfully as he turned his wise eyes upon Kane. That was no answer, though.

'Well?!'

'I assumed it must be your family name from your extreme reaction, my dear chap,' the stranger said in elegant tones.

'Don't you pissin' "dear chap" me.' Kane was furious. He didn't like this situation – oh no, not at all: it was freaking him. 'What were you doing following me down here – are you some sort of pervert?' The man certainly looked a bit dodgy in his frills and velvets.

The stranger straightened to his full height. 'I am nothing of the kind, young man. I heard the erratic ringing of the church bell, and wondered if someone might be in trouble. I found the crypt door open and discovered you here, staring in obvious shock at this monument.'

'I heard you, too, love,' the cleaning lady piped up. 'That certainly ain't the way the regler bell-ringers does it, and that's fer sure.' Her face was a bowl of wrinkles bound by wisps of grey hair. Grape-green eyes peeped cheerfully at Kane. 'Bit of a shock to yer, was it, love? Findin' that there memorial? Don't s'pose you'd have had cause to hear of it from anybody else, seein' as not many folks gets to come down here.'

Kane stared at her like she was a witch. Were these jokers playing mind games with him? Shit, he needed another drink. 'So who is it?' he said, and his voice was more of a whisper. He turned to stare at the marble form again, with its lost, vacant eyes and pitiful baby clutched tightly to its chest.

'Why, lordy, but it's yer ancestor, love. Emly Sawyer. She who was cruelly neglected, specially when she was with child. 'Tis a sad story, and no mistake, and not one I expect yer family would keep in memory. Some things is best left buried.' However, now that she was warming to her theme, the old lady was obviously not of this opinion. 'Her father abandoned her, see, when she fell pregnant. She was.. now what was the words?... Disowned, reviled and so fell into moral decline, my love – at least that's how the story was passed down to me by the Reverend Tieburn hisself.'

'I know exactly how she felt.' Kane was recovering his composure now, and beginning to wonder why seeing the form should have freaked him so. Perhaps it was the aura of tragedy hanging over the marble tomb – and then seeing his name connected with it.

'This here memorial is a father tryin' to put right what he done wrong. She died, see, in poverty and want.'

'And the baby?' Kane asked, poking a boot at the tiny form cradled in its stone mother's arms.

'Oh, the Church looked after it when its mother passed away, of course. The girl's father made sure of that. A father's shame paid for the child's upbringing in a godly house.' The old lady gave what was supposed to be a sanctimonious smile, but in the dim light of the crypt it looked lewd and creepy. Her eyes had lost their cheerful aspect too. Kane's head was buzzing with questions, yet at the same time he wanted to get out of here.

'So when did all this happen?' he managed, trying not to imagine the old lady's face transforming into something nightmarish in the gloom.

'Maybe you should go to the village library, love. You can read all about it there, I'll be bound. Not that you'll want to.' And now it was too late – her face had turned into a vampire crone's, feeding on his curiosity with unholy relish. Kane found himself thinking of a horrible black-and-white German film he'd seen once: *Vampyr*. There'd been just such a ghostly harridan in that. He reined in his fantasies, because the crone was continuing her rambling.

'It's one local legend they likes to forget round 'ere, my love. You see fer yerself: go find the book.'

All this time the stranger in the velvet jacket had stood quietly by, with a sort of thoughtful impatience. Now he roused himself from his contemplation of the tomb and stopped the old lady in her tracks.

'Legend? Surely this is actual history?'

The woman grinned at him. 'Depends how yer read it, sir. Most folks like ter think 'tis just a story. But the book holds the entire sordid tale. It were s'posed to be burnt, but I know it never were. Some things is just too hard to get rid of; they has a habit of hanging around – like a bad smell, if you like. Strong stuff it were, and should never have been on the children's shelves.'

The stranger looked even more thoughtful. Kane decided that now that his own family history had been divulged, it was the frilly man's turn to give. But the stranger was already turning to leave the crypt. Kane put a hand on his arm.

'And what's your story, mate?'

The dandy smiled, and casually removed Kane's fingers from his jacket. 'Oh, I'm just a passing stranger. But I imagine you get rather a lot of those here.' With that he minced grandly up the steps, leaving Kane with the old cleaning woman, who was still watching him with those bright green eyes, as if longing to tell him more tales.

Her shoes rang on the metal floor of the truck as she stumbled blindly around. Then suddenly the hollow clanging stopped. The floor was soft beneath her feet; springy… like…

Impossible!

The roadie had slipped her some kind of drug, some hallucinogen – that was the only answer. That, or she was losing her mind.

Losing her mind, tripping, or whatever – she was walking on grass. The darkness was receding, as if dawn were breaking inside the nightmare truck. She could feel a wind sighing like a ghost through the grass, and the cold light of morning showed her the endless heath all around.

Sheep were grazing near and far, and for a moment she was convinced that, impossibly, she was back on Dartmoor. When she saw the hut in the distance however, she realised that, just as impossibly, she was somewhere entirely different. And much further away.

This is a dream. You're going to wake up back in your flat in Plymouth, and you'll drive to the office and there'll be a neighbour dispute to report on or… or…

Or a gig on the moor at Princetown to visit.

She knew that hut, and as she walked towards it, drawn like she'd been drawn ever since that fateful morning in her flat, she knew she was walking back into her childhood.

And she really didn't want to go there! Not to that hut, not to that lonely crofter's hut in the absolute middle of nowhere on the east coast of Scotland. Don't make me go back.

Please.

The hut was close enough for her to see the cobwebbed windows now, the element-bullied wooden boards that held it up, the rope bridge crossing the brook winding beside it.

The bridge was as she remembered it, too: the missing slats were still there, just as they'd been when she'd skipped across in search of her father, heart swelling with the thrillfear of finding this fairy-tale cottage and of being lost and alone on the moor.

He'd left her – and she had never understood why. Nobody had ever been able to tell her. They'd tried: but she'd never listened, because it hadn't been right. He'd left her, and that was it.

She'd been playing hide-and-seek with him as they trekked through the glen. She'd hidden in some trees and giggled as he called for her. She'd waited until he'd gone over the rise and then she'd slipped out of her hiding place, still giggling. She'd picked some daisies beside the stream and sat in the sun making a daisy chain, and the cries of her father had grown first more anxious, and then more distant. Just like the mother of Flip the penguin in the storybook she'd read the year before. And that was when she stopped making the daisy chain and leapt to her feet, feeling suddenly scared. Flip had hidden from his mother because he wanted to carry on sliding through the ice, even after it started to get dark. His mother had called for him, waddling over the ice floes, and Flip had hidden. Then his mother had stopped calling and Flip could play all he wanted. Then it got very dark and Flip was alone. And scared.

Just like little Charmagne was now. Except Flip's mother had come back for one last search for her son and the little penguin was no longer alone. And little Charmagne…

Little Charmagne had already lost her mother to a traffic accident. She didn't want to lose her father too.

So she skipped over the bridge, scanning the moor for any sign of the old man, and of course there was nothing but the crofter's hut with its impenetrable windows smeared with cobwebs.

Daddy was inside. *That's* where he was hiding. She swayed over the bridge while the brook sang sweetly beneath her feet, and then she was across and traipsing up to the buckled wooden door.

Little Charmagne reached for the handle. She pulled it down and pushed the door open.

She saw her father sitting inside. The room was bare apart from the plain wooden table and the plain wooden chair, and cobwebs: so many cobwebs, like a witch's lair. It *was* a fairy-tale cottage after all. Nothing there to tempt him inside. So why had he left her?

Why hadn't he come back for one last look for her, like Flip the penguin's mother in the storybook?

He was sitting with his old grey head slumped on his chest, one hand dangling down beside the chair, the other resting on the table.

It looked like he was asleep.

'Why did you leave me, Daddy?'

Why did you leave me?

Little Charmagne stood in the crofter's cottage and screamed at her dead father.

A world of time away, a clutch of years away, a handful of seconds away, twenty-five year-old Charmagne stood in the crofter's hut in the middle of nowhere in the nightmare truck and screamed at her dead father.

'WHY DID YOU LEAVE ME?'

The dead old man in the chair lifted his head up to face his daughter. A length of cobweb stretched from his mouth to an empty plate on the table.

'Heart attack, love. Didn't they ever tell you?' His voice was whispery and dry as if his throat were crammed like the hut with cobwebs. 'I looked, but I couldn't find you, and I was so tired, I had to play a game of hide-and-seek of my own.'

His old face was stiff with rigor mortis, the words squeezed out of a locked mouth. The eyes were cold and frozen and…

Grey. Grey as snail flesh. Grey as the flesh of his face. Grey, like stone.

The figure in the chair stirred and Charmagne saw the rags that hung from its twisted frame. She saw the things that squirmed upon the hairless head; she heard the rasp of air coming from the mouth and realised the Ragman was laughing. Thick-legged spiders, living knots of darkness, trickled out of the mouth and down the bridge of web towards the plate.

'It took me so *looooooong* to find you...'

Chapter Twelve

Kane's hand was on the library door. The hand was shaking. He'd been back to the church since childhood – admittedly only once when he was pissed, and once more today. The library he hadn't visited since...

His throat felt gripped and his breathing was thin, because –

Because this was a bad place.

Bad things had happened to him here.

Didn't bad things happen in everyone's childhood?

The crofter's hut was gone. Snatched out of existence like it never was. *Oh yes it was it was I know it was...*

She was in the cattle truck. She could feel the metal beneath her shoes. Dark.

But she wasn't alone. The Ragman was with her.

It still possessed her father's features – she could see them in a faint glow as if dawn were struggling to arrive in the impossible truck, just like it had before she walked the moor. The creature was four yards away, close enough for her to smell him, and the smell was farmdeath shambles: blood, hay and garbage.

Her father's nose, hooked; her father's chin, protruding like a bony nub. Her father's eyes, but not her father's eyes. Stone-grey, dead pebbles, snail things without iris or pupil.

The Ragman.

Hunchbacked, thin as a ghoul, cloaked in vile tatters. Unspeakable hair – it wriggled, it writhed. *Hair?*

Worms.

Slow-worms nailed to the rock head, stirring limply, blindly.

Charmagne knew she was screaming, but there was no sound in the horror truck. No echo.

Nothing.

Her hands were over her mouth, but she knew she was screaming.

And then the Ragman showed her things.

Kane pushed the door open and the first thing he saw was the check-out counter. The receptionist.

The library shook, but the quake was in his head. He was sweating.

Remember me? I'm back. You forgot me all these years, but now I'm back to haunt you.

Remember, remember.

DON'T WANT TO REMEMBER! DON'T WANT TO LOOK AT THAT AGAIN!

No choice, no choice. Walk over here, there's a nice window seat near the Dr Seuss books. Remember? The Sneetches, The Sleep Book, Yurtle the Turtle, *they're all here…*

Oh, and one other book. That's it, over here. On THAT shelf. Warm, warmer… But of course it's hidden away, isn't it, just where you shoved it all those years ago. Put your hand behind those books, that's it, that's a good sodding little boy. That's it…

REMEMBER??????

And there it was in his hands again after twenty-two years, impossibly hidden, as if waiting for him, and him alone, to find it.

Now she was standing beside some ancient stones in a field, and the moon was high and full. Again she was not alone. A young couple were embracing nearby, oblivious to her presence. They wore old-fashioned clothing: she was in a gorgeous scarlet dress, he was in jerkin and hose, buckles on his shoes, his hair lustrous and black. Their features, like their clothes, were fine. Haughty, carefree. They leant against a gnarled standing-stone and kissed in the moonlight.

The midnight breeze brought with it a trickle of music. If Charmagne stepped around the stone nearest to her she might be able to see where the sound was coming from. She did so, and there they were: five travelling mummers sitting around a camp fire across the meadow, separated from Charmagne and the embracing couple by a grassy trench running the length of the field and rimmed by more standing stones, all of them twice the height of a man. Daisies glowed in the moonlight, scattered across the meadow and in the gulley like drops of spilt milk.

The mummers were dressed in striped jerkins and trousers thickly adorned with brightly coloured paper streamers. They were playing lutes and singing softly along to old songs. When they moved, bells jingled from their boots and sleeves.

Charmagne watched them, and knew they were scorned. Lights from the village winked in the near distance. They weren't welcome there; they weren't welcome here. She was about to see that first-hand, for one of them was rising from the fire and approaching her now. No, not *her*, because of course she wasn't there at all. The mummer was approaching the couple; he had spotted their solitary lovemaking and was about to crash the party. He disappeared from view for a moment as he descended into the trench, then he was up again on the other side. Jingling.

Charmagne watched.

He was begging. He had taken off his cap, and its bell jingled as he held it out to the kissing couple. Had they still not heard the bells?

Or were they ignoring this miscreant from across the divide?

The mummer obviously thought so, and decided to cross all barriers in one fell swoop: he touched the young man.

Charmagne watched.

The young man released his love. His face, *her* face, were masks of outraged arrogance. He snatched his arm free and struck. The mummer fell, awkwardly, dropping his begging cap, his feet slipping on the dewy grass, his head pounding against a standing stone as he went down.

Charmagne heard the crunch. She saw the red smear where his skull had cracked.

The young aristocrat stood over the corpse for a moment, gazing, his face ablaze with revulsion and excitement. The woman clung to him, lips shivering, and then… smiling. She tugged at him and he turned to see the smile, then kissed it hungrily.

The body lay where it had fallen. The blood trickled down the uneven surface of the rock, and Charmagne saw that it formed a face, a ghastly, grinning blood-face.

The face was moving….

Pushing outwards, stretching from the rock. Made of the rock, with a mask of blood covering features that were grinning, obscene.

A grey head now protruded from the stone: mouth, nose, eyes, drip, drip, dripping blood on to the grass.

A neck followed, rock-coloured too. Then the body, squeezing forth like a calf from its mother, spindly shoulders squirming as it struggled to free itself.

It was out of its stone womb, this grey figure, naked in the moonlight, sniffing the air like a beast, licking at the blood that dripped down its face, trembling all over as if wallowing in the spurt of violence, drinking in the pertinence of what had caused it.

It smiled.

This newborn creature with a head full of hate – *smiled*. A child appreciating its first vestigial emotion.

And the smile was horrible.

Snail eyes watched the oblivious lovers. It stalked them, a spidery thing of malice. Hands long and thin like stone knives, and the worms were stirring on the scalp.

It stalked them, and Charmagne heard it hiss.

The lovers turned.

It was gone.

The grey thing from the stone was nowhere to be seen.

As soon as the dead mummer began to move Charmagne knew *where* it had gone.

The corpse's head twitched and for a moment the dead eyes were grey as stone. The head lifted, and the lips smiled.

The lovers backed away and found themselves trapped by a standing stone that leant towards them, almost as if to embrace them, and the mummer was jerking like a marionette and stiffly on its feet now, yes, stalking the lovers frozen there in fear against the stone and Charmagne saw it all she saw –

Oh, she saw.

The aristocrat was unravelled. Bits of him scattered by hands that were dead but no longer human. The woman's lovely face was cradled by those bloody hands, and then kissed. She screamed, and the screams would wake the –

They must surely wake the village, at least, Charmagne thought, but the mummer was too busy with the woman to care, and her lovely dress was a tattered thing now as he took what he wanted, grinning a dead grin all the time, as he took her against the embracing stone.

Then the groping thing, the *dead* thing, the mummer from hell, let her go.

And boy, did she run.

The memories returned with each page he turned. His horror was a trapped thing inside him, and it would never be free, never be exorcised. It had lain dormant all these years, just waiting to be awoken. And maybe *he* was the trapped one, and the horror would not let *him* go now that it was stretching and yawning inside him.

The book was old, and it was full of dust. Just like it always had been. A dust thing. A horror thing. He stared at the pictures – grotesque artwork pencilled from the edge of madness. No sane mind could have conjured such four-colour atrocities. Faces were contorted, either by fear or by malice; limbs were too long, postures unnatural, the whole book stained by barbarous intent. An obscenity then, nestling behind *The Cat in the Hat*.

The text was scrawled below the midden artwork, and it was rife with glee in all things horrible. The story unfolded beneath his trembling fingertips: the couple – the mayor's daughter and the magistrate's son; the mummer; the thing squeezed from the standing stone. The artist had really tripped out in his depiction of the grey creature and its subsequent vile acts when it appropriated the body of the mummer.

Kane could smell the binding, the paper of the book. It smelt of tombs, of slinking rats, of bones. It smelt of eye gouge and tongue rip, and dirty hands rudely imposing inside eviscerated bellies.

But the pictures were worse.

Kane read on.

The villagers approached the field of stones. The mayor led them, and they carried blunderbusses and a rope. The undead mummer was waiting beside the pieces of the magistrate's son, its hands gloves of blood. It still grinned, a grin too wide to belong to living tissue. Blunderbuss shot buffeted it, slapped it back against a standing stone. Dust puffed from its body as the pellets struck home. It came on, took one of the villagers, uncorked his head from his body. Grin. Blunderbusses. Blood.

One page was just a full frame of blood. Kane could almost feel it staining through the paper into his fingers.

The rope was flung around the corpse thing's neck; four stouthearted villagers dragged it to a nearby larch, hoisted it into the air. The mummer was not kicking, not struggling at all, only grinning.

A page devoted entirely to that rictus.

The mummer freeing itself with a slash of its wicked fingers, rolling to the grass, unwrapping the ribs of the blacksmith, splattering another page with more gruesomeness.

Then…

The retreat.

Back into stone, blunderbusses bellowing after it. The creature sank into the standing stone from which it had emerged as if slipping into a portal of quicksand. The 'busses kicked up splinters of rock and the thing was gone.

In the truck.

In the dark.

The Ragman and Charmagne, and the things he shows her.

She can see them in the dark: all the children. Boiling out of the sewers like an endless spring of rats. Advancing on her, hands outstretched, a litany on their lips.

Nu mama nu papa nu mama nu papa nu mama nu papa nu mama nu papa nu mama nu papa.

NU MAMA, NU PAPA!!!

And Charmagne, forced to scream. Scream the single important truth of her life and the reality that has marked her more than anything:

'I'M AN ORPHAN TOO!!!!'

She was kneeling on the metal floor of the truck, and the Ragman was gone. She could hear her own sobbing echoing in the confined space – and it *was* a confined space, and, of course, always had been. A crack of light coming from under the back doors allowed her eyes to adjust to the darkness. Her hair was soaked with sweat, her clothes stuck to her body. The smell of the truck was overbearing. Butchery and filth.

Her eyes were adjusting, but what they were beginning to see was no less alarming than what she had just witnessed.

She could see the vague outlines of a jumble of musical equipment: amps, speakers, guitars, a drum kit, generators. And lying sprawled amongst this mess like discarded life-size dolls she could see the vague outlines of four men.

As she watched, they began to move.

The mummers were still sitting around their camp fire, still playing their tunes. Either they were oblivious to all the carnage that had ensued across the meadow, or they simply did not care. The magistrate found them guilty on the spot regardless, and the mayor heartily concurred. A justice of the peace was not required on this wild night. They were bound to the very rock that housed the beast. Four villagers lined up before them and zestfully unloosed their blunderbusses until the rock was splattered with more blood and brains.

Then, with much straining and grunting, and the aid of five

ropes and ten villagers, the large rock was unearthed from its mooring. The mayor supervised the process, and conceived its purpose: the rock, still wrapped with four bleeding bodies, was levered aboard a large and very stout cart.

'Take them far,' the mayor roared into the night, charging three villagers with the arduous task. 'Take them to the furthest corner of the land, from where the stink of their evil can no longer pollute our village. Dispose of them like the midden heap they are, where there be no goodness, where nature ends. Let this rock of horrors be their memorial.' The three villagers boarded the cart and began their journey. That journey took them beyond the edge of the frame, beyond the edge…

Off the page, and into Kane's mind.

Chapter Thirteen

'Found something interesting, old chap?'

The Doctor leant against a shelf and gave Kane a reassuring smile as the young man looked up. The smile vanished as he took in the evil illustrations inside the book Kane was holding. Kane's eyes did nothing to alleviate the Doctor's uneasiness: they were haunted, *branded* by terror.

'It's all right, there's nothing here to scare you,' the Doctor tried to reassure him. He leant forward to take the book and Kane reacted violently. Leaping to his feet, he snatched it away from the Doctor's grasp and scuttled over to a far corner of the library, where he sat on a window seat clutching the book and glaring at the Time Lord like a dog jealous of a juicy bone. The Doctor considered approaching him again, and then thought better of it. The long-haired young man looked capable of anything right now; the mania in his eyes could explode into physical violence at the slightest excuse.

Better let him lie.

Besides, the Doctor had seen those gruesome pages, and Kane's resultant transformation upon reading them, and that rather confirmed his theory.

The cleaning lady at the church had fired his curiosity. It wasn't much of a mental leap to suspect some link between the woman's hints of a dark history to this village and the source of the energy pulse. Maybe Kane, or more precisely the book, held the key. Acting on impulse, the Doctor crossed over to the ageing librarian positioned behind her counter which smelt of old hardback books and gave her his warmest smile. She eyed his velvet smoking jacket and frilly shirt dubiously, but returned his smile after a moment. She was every inch the librarian: horn-rimmed spectacles, severe white bun pulling the skin of her rosacea-flushed face back into a red mask.

'Can I help you, sir?' She held a book stamp in mid-air rather than putting it down, as if by wielding the tool of her trade she could justify her existence to this elegant if flashy stranger.

The Doctor inclined his head towards the corner where Kane sat alone, once more engrossed in the book. He could see the cover from here and it depicted shadowy men with blunderbusses and a gaunt grey creature stalking them. He could see no title.

'I was wondering about the book that young man is reading...' He beamed at her with full-throttle charm. 'I was interested in exactly how long it has been on the shelves here.'

The librarian, despite her formidable glasses, obviously couldn't see as well as the Doctor could, because she came from behind the counter and took a few steps towards Kane before halting. The Doctor noticed her back tense, as if she'd been touched by someone she really didn't like. She returned to the counter, deliberately not looking at the Doctor. Her face had lost its redness completely.

She picked up another book and flipped open the cover to stamp it. The Doctor waited patiently.

'Well?'

'I'm sorry sir,' she said without looking up.

'And what are you sorry for exactly?'

'I've never seen that book before in my life,' she stammered, furiously stamping the book.

The Doctor inclined his head and pursed his lips ruminatively. 'I think we both know that's not entirely the truth, don't we?' he said gently.

The librarian looked up, her eyes wide. Her chin wobbled a moment, and then she blurted out:

'I was *sure* it had been burnt. Long ago, when I was a child.' She paused, and the stamp was shaking in her hand. She looked at it as if it were an alien artefact and put it down before continuing. 'It gave me the worst nightmares you can imagine,' she said in a hushed, conspiratorial tone. 'The *worst*.'

The Doctor leant across the counter and put one hand tenderly on top of hers. She looked up at him quickly, then down again. She made a move to pick the stamp up again, as if by resuming her normal duties she could efface any unpleasant memories that were lurking like sharks beneath the waters of her mind. Instead she merely touched it, as if for reassurance.

'The librarian of that day ordered it to be destroyed shortly afterwards – after my mother complained.' She frowned at the Doctor. 'I dare say there must have been *two* copies…?' She didn't look convinced herself. 'Either that or… or they couldn't bring themselves to burn a book of such local interest.' She shivered noticeably, and the Doctor saw behind the crusty spectacles – saw the scared little girl hiding in her eyes.

'Yes,' the Doctor said thoughtfully. 'Tell me, would you happen to know where the book came from, and who was the author?'

The librarian frowned at him. Then shot a glance in Kane's direction. The Doctor followed her gaze. Kane's unshaven face was milk-white behind the large cover of the book.

'Why, the author was the same as the illustrator. And should have been imprisoned for it, if you ask me. Or at the very least certified. Because he was mad, or so they said when I was little. So very mad. Mad, and very, very *bad*.'

The Doctor raised his eyebrows encouragingly. 'Really? And what exactly did he do?'

'Besides create that obscenity, you mean? I only heard rumours… rumours that could never be proved. It might not be professional of me to wag my tongue so many years after the events.'

'No…' the Doctor said with mock complicity, 'I suppose not.'

'Dark things. That's all I know. Rites amongst the stones. Bloody deeds… I… I really couldn't elaborate. But suffice to say a local publisher decided to take a gamble and publish the unwholesome thing, and the library decided to stock it. As to the author…' She leant towards the Doctor, lowering her voice.

'Do go on,' he prompted.

'Why, the author was no more than one of *his* lot.' And once more she glanced furtively in Kane's direction. 'One of those lazy Sawyers. His grandfather, if you really want to know. Always were a bad lot, those Sawyers. A *bad* lot.'

The Doctor glanced at Kane.

He was staring right back at them, the book in his lap.

They had climbed to their feet, and now they were shuffling towards her in the dark.

Four musicians – four mummers – in the dark…. in the truck.

She could not see their faces, she could not hear them breathe.

But she could see the silhouettes of their tatters, could hear the scrape of their boots on the metal floor. And, as if the Ragman had popped another vision inside her head, she understood what they were.

As they came for her.

'But Sarge, wouldn't it be far better to disperse the travellers, rather than allowing them to go where they want?'

The young corporal's eyes were hard and angry, and Benton knew she was speaking for the majority of the squaddies. But there was also something else in her wide blue eyes. Something a little like hate, and Benton didn't like that at all. He shrugged at her.

'Not for us to worry about now is it, Robinson? Besides, they're out of harm's way while they're in there. We've got them contained rather nicely.'

'Are you sure we've got them contained, Sarge? Or is it that they're just not ready to move on yet? I get the feeling they're taking the piss because we're not doing anything about them.'

Benton had no reply to that. 'The Brigadier's just following orders from above,' he finally snapped.

The blonde corporal wasn't satisfied by the answer. She glowered through the spiked gate at the cemetery which was now succumbing to twilight. Camp fires were blossoming amongst the tombs. 'Doesn't make it right, does it Sarge?'

Benton grimaced helplessly. 'Like I said, nothing for you to worry about.'

'Until someone else gets killed,' she shot back. She was only small, but she managed to knock a few inches off Benton just by her attitude. He felt his cheeks burn.

'Now look, your job is to obey orders, not voice opinions.'

'Everything all right here, Benton?'

The familiar crisp tones of the Brigadier made the sergeant whip around guiltily. Although *he* hadn't been the one questioning orders, it was still someone directly under his command, and he felt responsible. He crashed to attention, as did Corporal Robinson.

'Everything's in order, sir,' he said smartly.

The Brigadier eyed him shrewdly, and then turned to the corporal. He nodded his head at her as if weighing up the insubordination he had so obviously heard while they had missed him in the gathering dusk, and Benton couldn't resist rolling his eyes in frustration. He was always being caught on the slack. He really *should* tighten up on his men. *And* women. Captain Yates wouldn't have stood for it for a moment. Benton was too soft, and he could tell the Brigadier was thinking the same.

Lethbridge-Stewart stared through the gate. Some of the travellers raised double digits at him from a nearby camp fire. He eyed them impassively, completely unfazed.

'I'm glad everything's under control, Benton.' He shot a glance at the sergeant, one eye ominously narrowed. 'Very glad indeed.'

The moon watched him drive, an old, fat moon keeping pace with the silver-haired Time Lord as he motored through the country lanes, watching out for him on his urgent errand or maybe gloating over his anxieties. Yet it was just the same old familiar moon when all was said and done, and this was just the planet Earth.

Just the planet Earth, yet once again the Doctor had managed to find himself involved in one big and very *unearthly* mess.

He knew exactly where the cattle truck was, and therefore the location of the original pulse, so there was no need to use the sensor any more. He had left midnight behind somewhere in the Wiltshire lanes, and now he was chasing towards dawn, the night wind combing his hair back from his brow. His face was grim, and his black gloves were tight on the wheel.

He curved round a bend, the moon flirting with him through the branches of some voluptuous oaks, and there was a figure in the centre of the lane.

The Doctor didn't see him at first. As the oaks slipped away to his left, a barebacked range of hills had been revealed under the moonlight and, glowing bone-white on a hillside as if sketched there with luminous paint, was the huge figure of a chalk horse.

The Doctor took his eyes off the amazing sight and concentrated on the road ahead. And there was the man in the lane.

Except it was no man. It was a scarecrow thing of rags and stone-coloured flesh, head bald but for a Medusa writhing of blind, oversized worms. Eyes reflected the moonlight malefically and, throwing up one arm to protect his face, the Doctor swung down hard right on the steering wheel with the other.

The Edwardian roadster ploughed into the hedge on the side of the lane, hurling the Doctor forward across the top of the windscreen. The car lurched to a halt embedded in the thicket, and the Doctor slumped over the steering wheel, stunned.

The moon stared down at him as if in rebuke over his clumsiness, bathing the car, the hedge and the empty lane in its impassive light.

Dawn caught up with the Doctor as he finally succeeded in heaving the car out of the hedge and back on to the road. Pale first light, and birds shaken out of their slumbers and indignant for it, shattering the silence with their vociferous chorus. They reminded him of his lack of sleep, and that he would doubtless also lack the opportunity to get any in the future, but this was something he was becoming used to.

And to think he'd believed exile on Earth was the equivalent of the Time Lords shoving him away in a retirement home!

He sat behind the wheel again, removing half a nettle from around the steering column, and looked ruefully at the car's muddy bonnet. He thought of the figure that had been in the road and then vanished, and he forgot his ruefulness, even his tiredness; he remembered that Jo was with the truck, and that perhaps he had procrastinated long enough if that was truly what he had been doing. Could checking up on all possible data instead of acting on the information he already had be called procrastination? Or was it simply following the natural curious instincts of a scientific mind? He knew what the Brigadier would have said, but then the Brigadier had always relied on instant action without weighing up all the possibilities first – looking for cause and effect rather than blowing things up had never been first on his list of natural responses. Bless him.

Damn him.

Maybe this time he would have been wise to let the Brigadier have his way. Maybe this time he had let things go on too long before making a direct move, and maybe he had endangered Jo in the process.

He swept over the brow of a hill and the Avon valley lay spread before him in the exuberance of dawn. Bristol waited for him near the horizon, gateway city to the Southwest, and beyond was the lazy twist of the River Severn, all but lost in morning haze. The Doctor rammed the roadster into top gear and sped down the hill towards whatever might await him.

He hadn't contacted the Brigadier with the information he had regarding the origin of the second pulse, or indeed to find out the latest news on the convoy. But of course he had the daily papers to tell him everything he needed to know on that score; and of course they were still picking over the bones of the tour and anything insidious they could connect to it. And then there were the politicians, both incumbent and hopeful, growling at each other and biting each other's flanks in their desire to come out on top and smelling of roses.

The Ragman.

The Doctor slammed on the brakes and Bessie jerked to a stop beside a black-and-white timbered tavern. He had been looking at the pub sign, and his shock at seeing it depict a gaunt figure dressed in tatters with slow-worms rearing from its scalp had caused him to stamp his heel down automatically.

The name of the pub was the Ragged Fellow, and it crested the top of a hill on one of the last stretches of countryside before the cancerous suburbs of the city began eating into the greenery.

The Doctor climbed out of the car, black cloak swirling behind him. The figure on the pub sign was without a doubt the same as the one he had seen in the lane, and also the same as the one he'd seen on the cover of the book Kane had been reading in the library at Cirbury. The name Ragman had spun into his mind on the instant of seeing the pub, a prompt from nowhere.

It was probably too early in the morning for the pub to be open, but he tried the door anyway.

It was unlocked. The Doctor stepped inside and found himself in a bar with flagstones on the floor, barrels against the wall and wooden tables. Pictures of country scenes on the walls, red-jacketed riders hunting foxes on the hand pulls (oddly, it appeared to him that the hunters' faces looked drawn and terrified while the foxes were smiling), fruit machine in the corner. Absolutely nothing out of the ordinary (except those hand pulls...) Had he expected anything otherwise, really?

He leant against the bar counter and shouted.

'Hello, landlord!'

He repeated the call before someone eventually appeared: a stout woman with red hair, and enormous breasts barely covered by the red dress she was wearing. It was an evening dress and absolutely unsuited to the time of day, but that didn't deter the Doctor in the slightest. What did was the fact that she was glowering at him with obvious irritation at having been summoned from whatever early morning duties she had been performing.

'I think you mean *landlady*,' she corrected him acidly, her overly rouged cheeks burning still brighter with resentment.

'Er, quite,' conceded the Doctor rather sheepishly. 'I was, ahh… actually wondering if –'

'Of course we're not serving,' interrupted the fierce landlady. 'What kind of place do you think this is? I only opened the door to collect the milk.'

'Naturally. Actually it wasn't alcohol I was interested in.'

'And if you're expecting breakfast you can carry on doing just that: expecting. You won't get it, that's for damn sure. This surely ain't no transport café. Does it look like one?'

The Doctor was becoming a little irritated himself now. 'No, madam, and I wasn't suggesting for a moment that it was one. Now, would you be kind enough to allow me to make a simple inquiry?'

'You want to ask me directions!' the harridan thundered. 'Now you're thinking this is a tourist information bureau!'

'No, madam, I was thinking nothing of the sort!' He glowered right back at her, bullying her into silence with his imposing stature and indomitable gaze. When he was sure she was not going to open her mouth again, he allowed her a charming beam. 'Now, if you've quite finished making assumptions, what I *was* going to ask you was simply if you knew the origin of the name of your establishment.'

She gaped at him blankly.

'Where did you get the unusual name of your pub?' he elaborated patiently.

'What, the Ragged Staff?' the landlady said, obviously perplexed. 'What on earth's so unusual about that? Why there's at least three of 'em in Bristol alone, never mind Bath.'

The Doctor blinked at her, momentarily lost for words. The hand pulls caught his eye, and of course the foxes were not grinning at all. He spun on his heel and left the pub.

Outside, the full blaze of a midsummer's day was engulfing the countryside and gilding the black-and-white exterior of the inn, including the wooden sign which, quite unequivocally, bore the name the Ragged Staff as well as a prosaic depiction of a bearded but blatantly benign shepherd clutching a gnarled old stick and nothing more.

He sat in the driver's seat and turned the ignition angrily.

Now it was no longer just himself that was causing him to procrastinate. Someone, or something, else was playing little mind games with him.

One hour later he pulled up in front of the police cordon that blocked all traffic from entering the road leading to Arnos Vale cemetery.

He patiently explained exactly who he was to the officer in charge, and waited with a little less patience while the policeman ducked inside his car to contact UNIT and check the credentials of what he obviously believed to be a flaky eccentric wanting to spy on the hippies from hell.

The officer came back a moment later with a rather politer attitude and waved him through. The Doctor drove past more police cars and then UNIT trucks and jeeps, all parked alongside the high cemetery walls. He stopped directly outside the imposing spiked gates and leapt out of the roadster. He spotted Benton immediately and strode over to him.

'Doctor!' the sergeant greeted him with the unconstrained relief he always displayed whenever UNIT's scientific adviser popped up in the middle of a crisis.

'Good morning, Sergeant. How is everything? Any news from Jo?'

'The convoy situation's entirely under control, Doctor, but we've heard no reports from Jo. But then we don't need to.'

'Oh, and why is that?'

Benton jerked his head towards the encampment beyond the gates. 'Because we can see her most of the time, that's why.' Then his broad face cracked into a cheeky grin. 'And we can see Captain Yates rather more often than I'm sure he'd like, as well.'

The Doctor let that pass. 'Right, well you'd better let me in.'

Benton looked unhappy at the idea. 'You want to go in there? Is that wise?'

'Whether it's wise or not is no longer the issue. It's become a necessity, and one I've put off for far too long already.' The Doctor ignored Benton's misgivings and appeals for him to alert the Brigadier first, and waited for one of the soldiers to unlock the padlocks strung round the metal bars.

The huge gate swung open, complaining all the way, and he was in the hippie encampment.

Jeers greeted him. Punks spat near his feet. Someone tossed a joint in front of him inviting him to 'Toke on that, ya old queer,' but he ignored all of this. He was looking for Jo, but not in an obvious way. It was becoming increasingly apparent that if she was still with the convoy she must be deeply undercover by now, and it could be very compromising for her – let alone dangerous – should he approach her too openly. Mike Yates was obviously unconcerned about any danger to himself: after the Doctor had made his way through several groups of travellers sitting round burnt-out fires and enjoying the first beers and joints of the day, his attention was drawn to a gesticulating figure dressed in a ridiculous attempt at hipness standing beneath some trees quite apart from anyone else.

The Doctor still hadn't spotted Jo, but no doubt the undercover captain would be able to give him the lowdown on her wellbeing. And then, of course, there was the main reason for his return to the convoy: the cattle truck and whatever awaited him inside it.

He looked over his shoulder, not wishing to blow the captain's cover. None of the travellers seemed to be paying them any overt attention, so he strolled beneath the trees and around some headstones to where Yates was lurking beside a weather-gnawed obelisk.

The Doctor looked the captain up and down quizzically. 'Yee-es,' he said after a pause, with a smirk most unbecoming to a Time Lord. 'Well, I must say you don't look out of place at all, Mike.

Peace and love, man, is I believe the appropriate greeting.'

'Anarchy and chaos seems to be more the order of the day, Doctor. And you can spare me the witticisms.' Yates looked strained and uncomfortable. The Doctor lost his smile immediately.

'Jo?'

Yates glanced away momentarily, then his usual earnestness forced him to meet the Doctor's gaze. 'She's been acting strangely.'

The Doctor frowned. 'What do you mean, strangely?'

Yates sighed. 'I'm convinced she's under some influence. She's displaying a rather disturbing herd mentality.'

'Are you sure she's not just acting in case someone should overhear you talking to her?'

Yates paused, then his jaw tightened. 'No, it's more serious than that, I'm afraid. She's definitely not herself. She seems to have swallowed the whole convoy idea hook, line and sinker.'

'Then you're going to have to watch over her very carefully indeed, Mike,' the Doctor said gravely. 'And make sure you keep her away from the cattle truck.' He turned away as rain began to patter on the leaves.

'So where are you going?'

'To the cattle truck of course. And this time I'm not going to let anyone stop me.'

He left the captain lurking under the trees in his 'disguise' and made his way along the paved lane past the crematorium to the collection of vehicles that surrounded the truck like a bunch of disciples hovering round their guru. Some hippies glanced curiously at him as he slipped around a double-decker bus with the roof torn off, but nobody challenged him.

If possible the truck was even filthier than it had been at the start of the tour, but this time there was no sign of the giant roadie, or any of his pals. Rain tapped on the metal roof and tickled the Doctor's face as he stood with his back against the metal flank, making a last check that the coast was clear. Then he swung round to the double doors and, whipping out his sonic screwdriver, positioned its nozzle directly over the padlock. There was a whine of power and the lock fell away sweetly, clumping to the ground.

The left-hand door eased open with a guttural croak, and the smell and the darkness rolled out at him. The Doctor didn't hesitate, vaulting nimbly up to the step and easing the door softly shut behind him.

'Pig.'

The word was spoken not as a shouted insult but as a quiet confirmation of suspicion. Yates turned and the Chinese girl was emerging from the shrubbery in front of him. She was followed by several punks and hippies, and Jo. Yates determined not to look at his friend, but faced the cold-eyed Chinese instead. As suddenly as it had started, the rain ceased to fall. The glade was quiet.

'Why pig?' he asked carefully, reaching for the packet of cigarettes he only smoked when he was being observed.

The Chinese girl knocked them out of his hand. She turned to a tall punk next to her who wore dark eyeliner and an earring in the form of an upside-down crucifix bearing a snake.

'You saw him; he was talking to a member of the Establishment, thinking we couldn't see him. Conspiring to betray us. He's a police spy.' She turned towards Jo who was staring at Mike without any expression. 'And he's *your* friend.'

The punks and hippies standing in the little clearing swivelled towards Jo.

Sin's face was a thing of hate as she pointed at Jo. 'Pigs!' she spat. The tall punk beside her took up the chant and soon the others were joining in, vicious glee making them ugly.

'Pigs! Pigs! PIGS!'

The first thing the Doctor noticed in the darkness of the truck was just exactly *how* dark it was. His questing hand found the slim pencil torch inside his cloak pocket and he directed it ahead of him, thumbing the button.

He expected to see a confined corrugated iron space, jumbled with musical equipment.

What the torch beam revealed, however, was entirely different.

There were no walls or floor, but an endless dreary tract of black weeds. The beam faltered a good fifty yards away, only hinting at the twisted landscape of despair. Trees were black bones that teetered into dust as he watched; hillocks bore sculptures that might have been the mutated remains of buildings fused and tormented by horrible forces. Nature had been raped. He could taste the death of the world: a slight breeze left its sick flavour on his tongue like the kiss of a decomposing lover. No more cities, no cathedrals, no palaces, no temples. All the petty vanities and sophistications swept away like dust. Someone, or something, had unleashed the beasts of anarchy.

The beasts of anarchy? The phrase had slithered unbidden into his mind like something alien and intangible and very nasty. It meant nothing to him, but it conjured more unease. Reeling with the shock of it all, he took a tentative step forward and his shoe slipped into a viscous steaming pool. He could smell the contents, and he moved his foot hurriedly, stepping around the wide tarn of blood.

The Doctor realised his hearts were racing against each other, and that primal fear was rearing up inside him. 'Reality-wound,' he said aloud, as if the application of logic would shy away the horror. It didn't. A shivering wail kicked up out of nowhere – the hopeless moan of terror of a child locked in an eternal nightmare nursery where rocking horses cackled, dolls jerked mad fingers and teddy bears danced obscene dances, disembowelling themselves to the evil chimes of a musical box. And, imagining the images, the Doctor saw them.

Saw the images, heard the sounds.

And then, like ghosts, they were gone, to haunt the bedrooms of millions of crying children throughout the civilised world.

The Doctor was walking across a landscape generated by what could only be the festering thought processes of a madman.

A madman or a monster.

He walked on through the crickleweeds, past more red tarns, and streams of gore along which human heads bobbed, skin seared like melted toffee. Once he passed a crumbling stairway that led to a torso balanced on the top step as if it were a waiting prize. Severed, burned hands were scattered on each stair. Arms thrust out of the ashy soil like gruesome plants. The Doctor walked on determinedly, ignoring the bone obelisks that were erected amongst the weeds as if hikers had trekked this way, losing their minds as they went and constructing hellish cairns to mark their passing.

His torch beam eventually found the rock on the horizon, raised on a dais of rotting human bodies and surrounded by a moat of blood. It was obviously a centrepiece to this whole horrendous tract of unreality. He approached it carefully, torch sweeping the barren surroundings for any movement and finding none.

A young woman with long blonde hair lay on the rock, arms and legs outstretched. The Doctor paused at the moat, then leapt across to the island within. He almost lost his balance as his shoes slipped on a jackstraw heap of arms and legs. He steadied himself against the rock and stared at the woman. He was sure he had seen her somewhere before: pretty, maybe in her mid-twenties. He touched her pulse and was surprised to find it beating gently. Surprised to find life in so much engineered death. He became aware that the energy-detector wand he'd detached from Bessie's dashboard was throbbing manically inside his cloak, and he withdrew it and held it over the rock.

He had found the source of the original pulse.

The pulse was an echo identical to the emanations he had detected at Cirbury. The rock was identical to the standing stones he'd found there too, ancient and implacable in their field of ages.

The wand kicked in his hand, twisting like a water diviner's, and the Doctor turned. He knew what he would see before he directed the torch beam behind him.

He froze at the sight, but his voice was icily controlled as he spoke the name that came to him as if on a telepathic breeze.

'Ragman…'

Jo stepped away from Mike. 'He's no friend of mine,' she said emphatically.

'Pigs! Pigs! Pigs!'

The chant was becoming louder, and attracting more travellers to the clearing.

Sin's eyes were boiling with unmitigated loathing. Nick put a hand on her arm, in an attempt to defuse the madness. She put the nails of her other hand to his, scratching troughs of flesh away.

'He's part of the Establishment,' Jo continued slowly, hatefully. Mike looked at her carefully. Her face was a mask of fervour. 'He's a pig!'

Jimmy leapt on Yates from behind, his arms thrown around the captain's neck in a python hold. Yates flung him aside with practised ease. Nick stood back, taking no part in the lynch mentality. A punk spat on Yates, another picked up a stone and flung it at him. He dodged it, and someone leapt at him wielding a broken branch like a club. Yates threw him over his shoulder, cracking the punk's head against the obelisk.

Sin stepped forward and there was something in her hand. A silver cigarette-lighter. She pressed a knob on the end and a four-inch blade sprang eagerly out. At the same time another stone spun off Yates's temple, diverting his attention long enough for Sin to dive in with the flick knife. The captain's eyes actually met Jo's as the blade slashed across his right cheek, and in the burn of pain he saw her flinch and then resume her determined coldness.

Nick grabbed for the knife, but the tall punk pulled him away. Jimmy slammed an exclamation mark on the proceedings by smashing a bottle of Newcastle Brown across the back of the captain's head. Yates dropped face first into a bed of nettles. Sin stepped astride his body, held the lighter knife aloft in both hands, poised it above the back of his neck. Even Nick stood transfixed in the moment of frenetic violence.

A shot rang sharp and clear and a chunk of masonry spun away from the obelisk next to Sin. A female soldier stood in the gap in the clearing, blonde hair tucked up beneath her cap, one eye shut, the other, pottery blue, focused down the length of her rifle barrel. Her finger flexed on the trigger as she swung the barrel to centre on the Chinese girl.

'Corporal Robinson!'

The order cracked out as loud and sharp as the rifle shot a second or two earlier.

A flash of extreme frustration twisted across the soldier's face, but she held the rifle in position until the Brigadier pushed his way into the dripping clearing. Sin melted into the foliage. The other punks followed suit, hightailing it into the woods that pressed all around them.

The Brigadier squatted to check on Yates, then stood up to confront the corporal.

'Shoulder your weapon, Corporal.' His voice was clipped and angry. Robinson did as she was ordered, resentment all too clear on her face. The Brigadier stepped closer to her, eyeballing his subordinate but saying nothing. She dropped her gaze and stood to attention. Satisfied, he turned to the other soldiers who had followed him into the clearing, including a concerned-looking Sergeant Benton.

'Look after Captain Yates, Sergeant,' Lethbridge-Stewart ordered, gesturing at the unconscious captain's body. He followed them as they carried the limp form out into the open space beside the crematorium, surveying the watching encampment for trouble. *Daring* the travellers to make some move, almost willing them to do so.

All this inactivity and restraint was killing him.

And where the bloody hell was the Doctor now?

Kane was back in his favourite place: sitting on a tomb in Cirbury's graveyard. The book he had stolen from the library was in his hands. The librarian had ushered him out at closing time the day before, but she had not noticed him shove the large book inside his leather jacket. Or perhaps she had, and was glad of it. Glad to see the blasphemous volume leave the library for good.

He hadn't been able to finish it that evening in his bedsit above the fish and chip shop. Damp on the walls had assumed elongated faces and there had been a tapping at the windows that he was sure was more than rain. He had hidden the book beneath the wardrobe, determined to let it rot there.

Of course, the next morning he had lugged it out with all the relief and assurance that a bright new day will bring. The churchyard seemed a fitting place to finish the story.

The three villagers are making their illustrated return from their errand, their sanity long gone. Their eyes are empty things, and they walk like lost souls. Of their journey to dispose of the mummers' corpses and the monster rock they have only wild and garbled tales to tell, the ranting of the insane. They promise the mayor and the magistrate that the village has not seen the last of the Ragman. He will return one day.

And of course, as is always the way with these sort of tales, return he does. Spectacularly.

Here the artist really freaked out. The last few pages were soaked in blood, with brief glimpses into hell in the midst of the red tide. Kane dropped the book, numbed to his soul. He staggered away from the tomb leaving the volume where it had fallen, face down in the buttercups.

A snail made its idle way past the book of horrors, antennae questing curiously, and then hove slowly away in search of pleasanter pastures.

Chapter Fourteen

PROTECT COUNTRY SPORTS cried one banner. Another proclaimed: HALT THIS ATTACK ON THE RURAL WAY OF LIFE.

Nick had never seen so many tweeds and Barbour jackets. He felt an insane urge to spray them with red paint; indeed the urge to kill was hot within him. The infection, he called it: the Unwashed and Unforgiving infection. He glanced nervously at his companions. There was going to be trouble, that was obvious.

Castle Green was an expansive stretch of parkland covering the site of the old eleventh-century castle, long since gone. Some pieces of old wall were all that was left, and the moat ran underground, a hidden medieval world beneath their feet. The north side of the park was taken up by the elitist Country Life supporters. The south was full of travellers on a special day out from the cemetery, with beer and drugs instead of picnics. UNIT had let them go unmolested, and Nick could only guess it was because the authorities believed more of a riot would start if they tried to contain them. If that was the case, UNIT were fools. Instead of having a riot on their hands, they were going to have a bloodthirsty massacre if recent class-related events were anything to go by.

Could they really be that stupid or were their motives ulterior, transmitted from above? The shadowy Above. That caused *all* the trouble. All the shit.

Whatever, the admittedly substantial police and UNIT forces sandwiched between the two groups were certainly going to have their hands full today. So far, nothing serious had broken out apart from a few hurled beer bottles and insults. Give it time, and there would be blood. *(And it would be oh so good.)* He felt a cold breeze pass through him as he remembered the eager desire for violence he had experienced at the Oblong Box. He glanced at Sin who was wearing a thin leather jacket and high-heeled boots, her face expressionless apart from her eyes, which, like they always seemed to be these days, were full of hate.

Hate. Why so much hate? She had always been passionate, and yet frivolous. Times they were a changin' and the beautiful, innocent Chinese girl he had fallen in love with had transformed in the space of a few weeks into a twisted soul.

And Jo with her.

Jimmy was mad, but then he'd always been an angry young man, desperately seeking somewhere to vent his rage. This summer he'd certainly found it.

This bright, bright summer of hate.

Bristol University Hall. A cavalcade of cars. Paparazzi. Police, of course, but merely a token skeleton force. Bodyguards.

The royal visit is going ahead as scheduled. And here comes the princess now, stepping from her limousine, flanked by musclemen, caught in a fusillade of clicking cameras. Up the stairs of the magnificent old university administration building she comes, nineteen years of age, not particularly striking, in fact rather ordinary – but some have said (*Hello!* magazine among others) that she has a pleasant, homely face. The bodyguards press around her like flies, and there at the top of the steps is the honoured dean, looking very honoured indeed as the cameras blaze away.

And here is Derek Pole, just behind the surging ranks of photographers, who are in turn behind the red ribbon barriers gauntleting the steps and the pavement. Of course he has lied to Jeremy Willis all along: the revolver inside his bomber-jacket pocket is snug and hard. He holds his camera against the bulge and takes a few amateurish snaps of the princess as she moves towards a spot where she will be directly in front of him.

Of course there will be no kidnapping. That was *never* the plan.

Pole's entire life has been leading up to this hot, prickly, pounding moment. He can taste blood in his mouth, his excitement is so extreme.

Here she comes…

* * *

The cattle truck had left the cemetery too; the skeleton force of UNIT men remaining there had even opened the gates for its largely unwitnessed exit. Now it was passing through the streets of Bristol, a filthy, growling thing.

'What are you?'

The question was simple, yet the answer came in a complex series of images that kaleidoscoped inside the reality-wound of the truck without the being so much as speaking a word.

The Doctor stood in the darkness, and the being's history was all around him, glowing with alien starlight.

It started with a journey. This journey began on the far shores of infinity – so inconceivably distant it would stretch the sanity of a human, then snap it like a spider thread. So, *so* far, at the other end of the vast black desert of space that was the universe, littered with the bones of stars and the dust of forgotten worlds. Here the creature was conceived within a womb of rock spinning through the radiation-bathed flue of a black hole, passing on, cosmic spawn without rhyme or reason, simply *being*; cast adrift through barred spirals and asteroid belts, surfing meteor wakes and moving ever on…

On, on.

Galaxies bloomed and died around its passing. Species ended screaming in the silent void of space, and the creature cared not at all, knew nothing of his stargate floating. Merely was, and thought not.

The rock tumbled on, through tides of time, through eddies of the infinite, guided by an indefinable call that echoed only within the core of the cradle rock.

The call grew louder, more tangible, and now the Doctor can recognise galaxies, systems, planets. The rock was locked into an interstellar flight path of inconceivable, perhaps mystical, programming, and it had passed through its incredible voyage practically unscathed. The rock was moving towards planetfall now, answering the ley summons of primal energies locked within the earth of one particular field in one particular country of one particular world.

The parent rock recognised those signal energies: they pulsed within its own core. Perhaps it had sensed a kindred force from across the infinite, and felt like it was coming home.

And now the Doctor could see primitive man, awed by this cosmic fall and subconsciously surrendering to alien urges that seethed within his brain. These ancient savages worked on the field of stones already erected on the mystical site they had long sensed as unearthly, as *special*: they incorporated the still-warm rock into the group of stones, and they worshipped it. Maybe it *had* come home, for it was identical to the other standing stones in every way. Maybe it was ejected into the depths of space at some primal point of Earth's spawning, and only now had begun to find its way back, impregnated with alien detritus.

The Doctor found himself pondering these imponderables, and the Ragman either refused to provide enlightenment, or could not.

The Ragman remained silent throughout the spectacular screening, the sick grin on its grey face the only sign that it was enjoying the process, as if boasting of its unique journey into existence.

Ley-line nexus beneath the stones, nurturing the dormant creature, and then the Time Lord witnessed the entity's brutal birthing into society through the midwife catalyst of blood and hate one summer midnight.

The mayor's daughter and the mummer. Conflict and intolerance. Inequality and oppression. These were the first emotions and concepts experienced by the alien life-form, experiences that shaped an emerging ego and appetites; that drew him from his chrysalis of stone.

The Doctor sensed the creature's frustration: the environment was not right for this predator from the beyond. His full emergence would have to be postponed. Social strife was limited, the spirit of levelling far too undeveloped – there were no wayward children to lead on a merry dance of dissolution. The being sensed his own weakness and lack of growth, and retreated until times were a changin' enough for him to revel.

Until a time when anarchy was bursting the land at the seams and violence and division incited the monster once more to step from stone.

The Doctor spoke, and his words dissipated the images like soap bubbles popping in a sudden breeze.

'Stop!'

He held out a gloved hand for emphasis. 'I've seen enough, and still I don't understand.' His voice was husky with fear he could not control in the presence of this entity. It was a fear he felt only seldom, but which was all the more piquant for it. Yes, he feared this grey man from the fringes of nowhere, he feared what he might do with this world; that he might unravel it like a ball of wool, and think nothing of it. 'Stop these pictures, and talk to me. Why are you stirring such hatred among the people of this world? What can you possibly hope to gain?'

The creature shimmered and receded to become a distant tiny figure lost on the bleak horizon of the reality-wound, then just as suddenly sprang into close-up mere yards from the Doctor, slow-worms twining, eyes baleful. The transporting disorientated the Doctor so much he backed away, a weakness he realised the alien assumed to be obeisance before a more supreme presence. He let this vanity pass, and pressed forward with his questions. Knowledge was the key, understanding would prove to be the solution. It always had been in the past. And the vanity of his opponents had always helped in supplying understanding, and in their subsequent downfall.

Even as the Doctor entertained these reassuring thoughts, he suddenly knew they would not apply this time.

He spoke out, regardless – just as he always had done in the face of alien terror.

'Like I said: what can you hope to gain by this madness? Already your tour is being manipulated by humans for their own

Machiavellian political ends. Is that what you want? The forces of repression have many subtle avenues and expressions, and all the newspapers are full of their successes. Successes created by your fiddling. You think you are creating disorder, whereas you are merely strengthening the hands of those who would crush your wayward children for ever.'

The Ragman smiled. He smiled, and then he spoke.

The voice was a bizarre mismatch of British accents and periods, sliding from Tudor grandiloquence to twentieth-century gutter slang. Hushed, then strident, whispered then guttural. A changing journey through mores of expression and enunciation that were hypnotic to the ear.

'Everything must be levelled.'

These were the first words to pass the grey slug lips. Then came more: and as they came, four shapes shuffled out of the darkness to guard their mentor. The reanimated amalgamation of four seventeenth-century mummers, executed and then buried on Dartmoor, and the doomed punks who arrived at the same spot three hundred years later. The Doctor understood their existence and their creation in a flash of telepathic intuition and, while his skin crawled at their unnaturalness, his mind reeled at the morphic powers inherent in the Ragman that were used to fuse eight separate essences into one Frankensteinian supergroup of resurrected flesh, bone and irony.

'Hate 'n' insurrection, channelled by my mummers and their strife music, will prise wide the fissure 'tween rich and poor. Society will slide into the hole for ever. This hole will be where greenery turns to black; sophistication transforms into nihilism; architecture to ruin. I mean it *maaan*!' And here the being gurgled unpleasantly with what the Doctor could only assume was laughter. 'Everyone will be equal.'

'Everyone will be dead,' the Doctor stated simply, aghast at the extent of the Ragman's vision.

The being nodded its boulder-like head, and the worms twisted idly like seaweed in a current.

'Death be the only true state of equality.' A set of panpipes was suddenly at the monster's lips, and he was playing notes of such haunting horror the Doctor felt compelled to fall to his knees. He saw a vision in his mind of this murderous Pied Piper leading his children screaming into a cataclysm – the only solution the alien could accept as the logical answer to his twisted and abnormal philosophy.

The Ragman replaced the pipes inside his tatters and gestured at the gruesome landscape of body parts and black weeds around them. 'This is but a foretaste of my whims. This is but one land I will level. There are plenty more in need o' my attentions.' The worms writhed ecstatically as the being's excitement rose. The Doctor backed away, terror rising within him like a great wave, and then he was running blindly, desperately, as impossible rain began to fall inside the nightmare truck, turning ash into mud beneath his feet. The Ragman's words echoed around him as he ran, a mad monster's litany:

'Pretension shall putrify. Elitism smoke like a gutted corpse's entrails in the rain. Sophistication will become defecation. Grandiloquence shall be *gored* by degradation.'

The Doctor was running nowhere and still the Ragman was in front of him, grinning obscenely, tatters lifting in unison with the slow-worms. The Time Lord stopped, though horror was fisting his soul.

'You're not championing equality,' he panted, 'you're celebrating nullity.'

'They are the same, frilly one,' came the croaking response. *They are the same.*

On the steps of the Bristol University Hall…

Princess Mary hesitates. She is level with Pole. She is also flanked by two bodyguards. She hesitates, and our hero seizes his moment. He drops the camera with a SMASH to the pavement, and he sweeps out the revolver in one fluid movement. He…

* * *

The Ragman approached the Doctor, seemingly gliding through the darkness without taking steps. One grey arm shot out, the hand snapping closed around the Doctor's neck. The Time Lord froze in the being's grip, all will to struggle sucked away. Tilting the Doctor's head back, the Ragman examined him thoughtfully.

'You too are an Everyman, like me, Doctor; a wanderer with no distinction, no shackles – a Man of the People. Like me you enjoy fiddling while societies burn. It feeds you, this constant interfering, this toppling of tyrannies, this trampling of egocentricities.'

The slow-worms wound around each other as if in orgasmic appreciation of the Ragman's words. The eyes blazed with intelligence unfathomable. The voice was a voice from midnight cemeteries, vocal cords eaten away by maggots. A death whisper, and then, continuing, it became a moist gurgle as if the alien were swallowing the blood of his enemies as he ranted his hypnotic litanies:

'I see into your past, your present and your future... *Time Lord*... I see into your eyes and your soul is there. How many have read your secrets? We are both orphans of space... both condemned to wander in search of meaning and both ultimately trapped here. Yet I have found *my* destiny here – in correcting sociological wrongs, even if I do confront them in an extreme way. Have you found yours?' He released the Doctor who crumpled to the ground, eyes haunted.

The Doctor was alone again. His tormentor had abruptly vanished.

Princess Mary turns towards the man with the gun and the whole world sucks in its breath. Photographers are too shocked to snap, bodyguards pose like players of a children's game where to move is to be caught out. Princess Mary turns towards the man with the gun and she smiles. Her eyes are suddenly grey pebbles and she is reaching for the gun, smiling her crooked smile, and she takes it from the man as if it's a present being offered. Now the world breathes out and the cameras fire away like crazy and the bodyguards reel like drunks and the gun is blazing, the Princess is pumping the trigger like Dirty Harry and explosions are ripping little holes in the man's body as he stands there taking it. Then he's falling, blood squirting from those holes and he's hitting the dirt of the pavement and the princess has shot him five times and now she's leaping forward, *on top* of the body and look: she's dancing.

Dancing on death.

She's giggling as she performs her macabre jig, trampling on the leaking corpse, and the cameras lavish her with their praise and even the BBC have got in on the act with their big OB camera which moves in like a greedy beast to devour the action.

The bodyguards have stopped their confused reeling; now they stand, completely lost. They're watching the show too.

The princess finishes her dance, and she turns towards her audience as the bodyguards finally move forward to lead her gently away. She laughs brightly, like a delighted child at Christmas.

'This is Our Birthright,' she says proudly, stepping off the corpse of her would-be assassin. 'To dance on the grave of the filthy poor.'

A few streets away, in the car park of a department store, the cattle truck growls into life and pulls away from the kerbside where it has been waiting, seemingly abandoned, all morning.

And the day goes mad.

Chapter Fifteen

CLASS WAR, the headline of the *Daily Mail* bawled, AND THE ROYAL SOLUTION. The *Guardian* was more poetic: THE PRINCESS AND THE PAUPER. The *Communist Worker* positively roared its own take: MURDERING MONARCHY. The *Sun* had the best laugh with: ONE SHOT HIM FIVE TIMES M'LUD.

Jo was reading all of them, as Nick tossed the newspapers to her one after the other. Now she glanced at the *Mirror* which had trotted out some headlines from Derek Pole's own magazine *Class Hate* to accompany its article: DON'T WORK, WON'T WORK: A REDUNDANT MONARCHY. SMASH THE RICH. Jimmy was chuckling obscenely as he drove the camper, repeating some of the choicer extracts like punch lines as Jo read them aloud.

'Could the royals have gone too far?' he echoed, turning The Clash's 'I Fought the Law' up on the dash player. 'I fought the parasites, and the parasites won. Well maybe not this time, eh, Nick? Maybe this time they *have* gone too far, and all those stupid sheep they call soddin' subjects will finally realise the bastards have gotta *go*!' He cackled with wild enthusiasm, tailgating the Beetle crammed with travellers in front of them, his energy levels kicked into top gear and impatient with the crawl of the convoy.

They were on the move again. Nobody knew why; nobody knew where to. But hell, they were on the move again, and that was good enough for Jimmy.

Nick didn't answer his friend. He was staring out of the window as the last of Bristol's suburbs dragged by. 'She can't remember,' he said finally, as if to himself.

'You what?' shouted Jimmy over the riot of guitar.

'The papers say she can't remember what happened,' Nick continued dreamily.

'Conveniently lost her memory for five minutes, yeah right,' scoffed Jimmy, sparking up a cigarette, his face a mass of bristles and sneers. He had always struck Nick as looking like someone who had once had a violent past but had since become a reformed character. Lately, the reformation had been kicked out of him. Now he wanted blood. *Just like all of them*, Nick pondered bleakly, and then amended the thought: just like all of *us*.

Jo spoke up: 'It says in the *Communist Worker* that the 'possessed for five minutes' statement is just an excuse, and that the princess was most definitely *consciously* acting out the royal family's blatant disgust and hatred of the lower classes. Basically, that she let herself get a bit carried away with it all.'

'And now she *will* be carried away for good,' Jimmy bleated. 'Lock the bitch up in Broadmoor, that's what they should do.'

Nick said nothing. He was thinking about the Country Life demonstration and the almost complete lack of trouble on that day; and the subsequent events that had so massively eclipsed the protest. It troubled him. It was almost as if the spirit of mayhem had drifted away from the travellers for a fleeting moment and settled elsewhere. He caught Sin glaring at him and returned her cold stare with a growing disgust he could no longer hide. He was becoming as infected as all of them. He wanted blood too; but somehow he'd kept his conscience, even if he could do nothing about it. Every time he tried to speak out he quailed inside, as if something were reining him in. He could express himself only in passive loathing for what he had become and for those he had once loved.

He stared out of the window as the countryside opened up around them. He wondered if UNIT were still tailing them, and knew without needing to check that they were, and that they would be making no moves to interfere with the convoy's progress; still following the same non-engagement rules they had been adhering to all along.

He knew that was the case, but what he didn't understand was...

Why?

Kane bought his ticket and took his place in the village-hall stalls.

In the first row of course. He was very drunk now. Had been pursuing the art all day. No one had attempted to prevent his entry into the hall, but that was understandable. He'd kill any sod who tried, and that readiness for violence showed in his wild and sleep-deprived appearance. His eyes were bloodshot, his long hair was a tangled mess. He hadn't spoken a word to anybody in days. He gazed up at the curtain as the villagers settled themselves in their seats around him and waited to enjoy the show.

Kane shifted his bleary attention to the programme in his hands, as if it would make some sense out of his life. *The Epic of Gilgamesh*, the oldest recorded work of fiction, it said. The tale was originally carved on clay tablets in ancient Mesopotamia thousands of years ago. The programme gave a brief summation of the plot: the egocentric King Gilgamesh ruled his people with an arrogant will, dominating their lives and allowing none their individual liberties or freedom of expression. He was a lonely tyrant, however, and longed for a companion in arms.

Kane lit a cigarette.

'Excuse me, it's a no-smoking venue, I'm afraid.'

Kane turned slowly to face the speaker. It was a young man in a shirt and tie, balding prematurely, who was showing people to their seats. Kane stared at him, cigarette poised at his lips.

'Sir?' the man prompted again nervously.

Kane dragged slowly on the cigarette, not taking his eyes off him.

'Please, we have to think of the fire regulations.' The man was beginning to sweat.

Kane turned back to face the stage and took another drag. 'Let the show begin,' he said in a strange voice. As if on cue, the lights dimmed.

'Grandfather?'

'Grandfather?'

Someone was calling for him. Someone he hadn't seen for such a long time.

'Grandfather, is that you?'

No. Not *her*. It wasn't time for him to meet *her* again. He'd left her. Abandoned her, hadn't he? Running away from his responsibilities, just like he'd always done.

Run, rabbit, run.

Across the universe, along the yellow asteroid road. Always chasing the rainbow. And finding a pot of blood at the end of it.

'Grandfather? Are you coming out to play?'

He could see her now. She was walking across the insane tract of the reality-wound *(because that was all it was that was all it was that –)* and she was dragging behind her something like a big stuffed doll. No, not a stuffed doll. A stuffed man. Her husband. Of course. He died, didn't he? Old and diseased in a hospital bed, while she was still young. Nice fate: to watch the person you love grow older and older, to see the sorrow and yearning in their eyes as they stare back realising that it was the truth after all – that you will stay young for ever. Or so it must have seemed to him. And maybe there would be bitterness too. Resentment, at the trick of fate.

Never marry an alien.

Didn't I tell you that one, Susan. Didn't I?

She was still dragging the corpse after her, and yes, it *was* old and white-haired and wearing hospital pyjamas.

Go away. It wasn't my fault. Love kills, didn't you know?

Even if you don't actually die.

The curtains swished apart. *The Epic of Gilgamesh* was commencing. Simon was the first on the stage, and Kane stared at him. He hadn't seen him for years, but the young man, slightly portly with chubby cheeks and weak chin, was still the boy who had tortured him on the school playing field. Just across the road in fact. Kane thought abstractly about the distance in yards and the distance in time, and it didn't make much sense, but then perhaps it wasn't supposed to. Life was all a matter of absurdities: he found himself thinking about his grandfather's corpse.

He'd broken into the morgue the night before the funeral to see if they'd tampered with the old bastard's body. He'd only been ten, but he'd heard tales and he wanted to see if they put make-up and shit on him. Didn't give a toss about him being dead of course. He'd found the coffin, unopened, against one wall. His grandfather was inside it, miserable-looking as he'd always been in life. Kane had thought they might have tried to pinch his cheeks into a macabre smile, but what he'd found had been funnier still: to lift the pillow on which his grandfather's rotten old head was lying and give him a more dignified air, the funeral assistants had stuffed magazines behind it. Pornographic magazines.

Now that was bloody funny. The young Kane had thought so. So did the old Kane. He began barking with loud laughter and his distracted, drunken, crazy thoughts meandered away from his childhood visions to the bastard who had evoked them, who was standing a mere ten yards away, tall and proud in flowing robes. And suddenly they locked eyes.

Simon froze in midsentence. His eyes widened, his fey poise wilted. Then he recovered his composure and snapped back into his role. 'I am the strongest here!' he bellowed, deliberately staring at Kane, lifting up his pudgy arms and vaingloriously blind to any irony. The chorus kicked in with:

'Is there none to challenge Gilgamesh?'

Kane lit another cigarette and noticed from the corner of his eye that someone was moving into one of the empty seats two down from him. He didn't need to look round to know it was Cassandra, Simon's sister, and that she was watching him worriedly.

'*I* am the strongest here!' bawled Simon again, surveying the audience with petulant bravado.

And again, Kane barked with raucous laughter.

The chorus twittered on with their story, ignoring the dishevelled drunk in the front row. As wind instruments accompanied their melodramatic posturing, they spoke of a meteor falling from the heavens and bursting open to reveal an

171

antidote to the megalomaniac king: a leveller, the wild man Enkidu, who will supposedly oppose Gilgamesh but in fact will inevitably accompany the king on his journey through ego. This much Kane knew from the programme, even though he had only dimly assimilated it in his drunken stupor. The actor playing Enkidu, the challenger, was in the wings about to make his grand entrance – Kane could see him fidgeting in the darkness.

'Is there none to challenge Gilgamesh?' wailed the chorus again.

Kane stood up, ground his cigarette out, and vaulted on to the stage. He staggered slightly as he moved forward. He could see the amazement on the face of Enkidu as the actor waddled on stage. He could see the horror on Simon's as his old enemy bore down on him.

Simon opened his mouth to speak, but his lips merely flapped pitifully. His callow cheeks whitened. The village hall was silent, silent as a funeral home. Kane seized 'the king' by his toga and spun him round so that his back was to the audience. Blank-faced, he gave Simon a massive shove that sent him flailing off the stage and into the audience, just missing his stunned sister who let out a little shriek of alarm.

Kane stood there for a moment in the spotlight, unshaven, shabby, drunk. His eyes were locked and strange.

'He's coming,' was all he said. Then he jumped down from the stage and strode out of the auditorium as the villagers erupted into excited chatter.

'Stonehenge, Prime Minister,' the Brigadier said into his RT as the jeep crawled several hundred yards behind the last vehicle in the convoy. 'It's the only logical destination for them, considering we're now travelling through Wiltshire. Mystical home for travellers, and all that.'

A chalk white horse was visible on the hillside to their right. The Brigadier glared at it disapprovingly. 'Yes, sir. We can throw a cordon around the monument, but wouldn't it be better to contain them within the circle? I see...' He frowned at his staff sergeant who was steering the jeep. 'Public outrage about the possibility of the stones being defaced? But sir, what about public outrage at what has already taken place? Surely –' The Brigadier sighed. 'We'll keep them out of the stone circle. Yes, sir.' He broke the connection and stared ahead thoughtfully.

'Trouble, sir?' asked the staff, braving the Brigadier's obvious bad mood.

'Hmm?' The Brigadier gazed blankly at his sergeant for a moment. One of the hippies in the back of a filthy Renault was making lewd hand gestures at him. He watched the offender with a weary expression. 'Trouble, Staff,' he confirmed. 'We've been ordered to protect a bunch of stones. It seems the powers that be cannot take *any* more assaults on the public domain. Elections are in the air, I'm afraid, and our English Heritage being damaged really *would* be the final straw.'

He sighed again and pressed a button on his RT. 'Sergeant Benton,' he barked as soon as a connection was made. 'Deploy every UNIT vehicle towards Salisbury Plain. Stonehenge, to be precise, Sergeant; and we've got to get there before the convoy.' He signed off, and turned to the staff. 'Right, let's find a short cut, and fast.' He cocked an eye at the white horse. Its wide mouth seemed to be braying with laughter.

At the head of the convoy, the chief roadie led the way on a battered Vincent. Directly behind him, the cattle truck growled through the country lanes like a grimy dinosaur searching for prey. The windscreen was practically opaque with dried mud. The roadie pulled up at a crossroads where a signpost pointed schizophrenically in three directions. Without hesitation, the roadie steered his motorcycle along the road leading towards Salisbury, then pulled into a lay-by. The cattle truck swung slowly in another direction, exhaust blatting out clouds of black fumes.

Then something very odd and very precise occurred: the first half of the convoy followed the cattle truck; the latter half peeled off after the roadie, who veered his bike on to the road again and

173

roared off into the gathering dusk as his obedient portion of vehicles crossed the junction.

Not a word had been spoken to any of the convoy drivers. They just *knew* which route to take. It was that simple.

Jimmy was at the wheel, his dash player hissing on a dead tape.

'Why are we going this way?'

Jimmy didn't answer Nick's question. He was staring through the windscreen at the cattle truck directly in front of them, driving on autopilot.

'Jimmy! Half the convoy went after that roadie. So what made you decide to go *this* way?'

'Huh?'

Nick could see Jimmy's face in the rear-view mirror. It was blank. His eyes were dead.

'Jimmy!' Nick got out of his seat and made his way up to the driver's seat. 'What's happened to you, mate?'

'What?' Jimmy turned to face him, and suddenly the cheeky grin was back on his face, his eyes were lit with their old mischief. He cocked his Confederate cap back on his brow and scratched his spiky hair. 'It's only rock 'n' roll…' he said in a bad Jagger impersonation as he fumbled for a new tape. It was one of his favourite catch phrases.

'Shit, Jimmy, get a grip. You must have some idea where we're going and why?'

Jimmy blew Nick a mock kiss and slammed the tape in. '…But I like it, like it, yes I do.'

Nick gave up, and took his seat again. Confusion and not a little fear seized him. But he was damned if he could do anything about it. Quailing again. He glanced at Jo and Sin. They were staring at him like two evil but hardly identical sisters. He pulled a cigarette as UK Decay blared out from the tinny speaker.

The Six O'Clock News was just starting. Derek Pole's face was splashed across the television screen.

'Will the monarchy recover?' the studio newsreader was asking a royal correspondent on an OB screen live from outside Buckingham Palace.

Jeremy Willis wasn't listening. He didn't care about the correspondent's answer. In one hand he held a newspaper. Pole's face was on it, next to a black-and-white shot of Willis himself. The link between them had been revealed by police once Pole's identity had been ascertained. The offices of *Class Hate* held papers and other things Pole should have destroyed which tied the two irrevocably together. Cheques paid into Pole's bank account, issued by a certain member of the shadow cabinet, were also offered up for public scrutiny in a police statement to the press that bordered almost on the smug. Money to finance *Class Hate*. It was a glorious revelation for the Government.

Glorious.

Ashes. Willis's career had been poured into a cremation urn.

The telephone had been ringing all day, since the very early hours. Now it was silent. But that was only because Willis had yanked the lead from the wall. He had drawn the curtains too, but he could still hear the impatient rapping on the glass. His doorbell trilled intermittently.

It was enough to drive a sane man mad.

The newspaper with the glorious revelation on the front page was in his left hand. In his right hand, a gun. Willis couldn't remember the make or model. It didn't matter.

What the hell did, any more?

He lifted the gun to his head.

He saw his own face fill the TV screen just as he pressed the trigger.

Side Two

'… Now we're gonna dance to a different song…'

Chapter Sixteen

"'Rat!' he found breath to whisper, shaking. "Are you afraid?"' Jo
was sitting next to Sin by the camp fire and staring coldly at Nick
as she spoke the words long-remembered from childhood. Her
mouth curved into a cruel but sexy smile as she continued:

*"'Afraid?" murmured the Rat, his eyes shining with
unutterable love. "Afraid! Of HIM. O, Never, never! And yet – and
yet – O, Mole, I AM afraid!"'*

Nick pulled a cigarette from his pack, keeping his gaze level as
he returned the blonde girl's stare.

The Doctor was sitting in the stern of a rowing boat travelling
slowly upstream. He held an oar in each hand, but he was not
using them; they trailed little wakes through the dimpled water as
the craft slipped along. Ahead of the boat a great stone bridge
with three arches loomed out of the purple twilight – or was it
the darkness before the dawn, he wondered idly. The banks on
either side were largely invisible in the shadows, but he could
smell the intoxicating odour of the meadowsweet. The river
gurgled on by as his companion pulled gently at the sculls. The
Doctor was thinking of Jo, wondering what she was doing right
now, and so he wasn't paying much attention to the rower until
that person spoke aloud, just as a solitary predawn bird chimed
sleepily.

'Now it passes on and I begin to lose it,' his companion said,
and the Doctor glanced over at his friend, at the large water rat
dressed in human clothing. He smiled a bewildered smile as the
Rat continued.

*'O, Mole! the beauty of it! The merry bubble and joy, the thin,
clear, happy call of the distant piping! Such music I never
dreamed of, and the call in it is stronger even than the music is
sweet! Row on, Mole, row! For the music and the call must be
for us.'*

And the Doctor, entranced by his friend's words, set to with the oars. And soon they were passing under the central arch of the great mossy bridge and a deeper darkness closed them in, and the dripping and truckling of the river echoed eerily around them and the Doctor was afraid. But just as quickly they were out again, and a purple horizon skirted the meadow bank to their right, and from ahead there came a soft and distant rushing of water. The river divided and they were now following a long backwater, and the first flush of dawn was expanding enough for the Doctor to be able to see the banks on either side, drooping with osiers and silver bushes.

The gentle rushing sound grew clearer as the two rowers propelled their craft through the dawn. Suddenly the Rat dropped his oars and sat up stiffly, head cocked in a listening posture. And now, at last, the Doctor could hear what his friend had already heard: a distant, eerie piping, haunting and beautiful, floating over the reeds and willow herbs from some point ahead.

A semicircular weir awaited them, curving its foaming arms around a small island mysterious with dense willow and silver birch and alder. The piping was clearer still, calling them on, filling their hearts with fearful joy. The Doctor said nothing at all as his companion steered the craft into the island's osier-decked bank and moored it carefully. He followed the Rat ashore and the panpipes ceased playing and silence fell around them. No birds sang as yet, and even the sound of the weir seemed hushed.

Together they passed through the foliage towards the centre of the small island, and there they found a lawn glowing bright green in the dawn light and on the green, sitting under a crab apple tree, He awaited them.

The Doctor saw his great furred limbs first of all, and the cloven hooves resting on the grass. Above the goat legs, the naked chest was broad and pale, the silent panpipes clenched against one nipple. The Time Lord's awed gaze travelled upwards, taking in the grey boulder of a head, crowned with twisting life, and the cruel slash of a grinning mouth. The eyes blazed ferally while curved horns swept back from the play of the writhing worms.

'*Rat,*' the Doctor found breath to whisper, shaking. '*Are you afraid?*'

'Afraid?' murmured the Brigadier, standing stiffly in the water rat's clothes, and arching an eyebrow at his companion. 'Why on Earth should I be afraid, Doctor? And look, we've found Miss Grant, at last.'

The Doctor peered in the direction the Brigadier was indicating with his swagger stick and, sure enough, in the shade of the crab apple tree, nestling in between the hooves, Jo's pretty head lay on the grass, severed messily at the neck. Her eyes fixed accusingly on the Doctor's as if to say –

But the Doctor was falling to his knees, hands clasped around his white head, and he could hear as he closed his eyes in torment that the monster was piping once more at the gates of dawn.

Jo, Sin, Nick and Jimmy sat around the fire beneath one of the great stones and watched as the mummer moved from group to group, playing his lute. They had not seen him for some time, and Jo struggled to remember when exactly that last time *had* been – things were getting so hard to recall, she thought with some confusion. She remembered Mike, and a little pang of something like remorse touched her heart – and that confused her even more, because he was a traitor to the cause; he was the enemy, the Establishment. He was everything they had to destroy, stood for everything she no longer believed in. The sight of the mummer in his gaily coloured tatters, mincing across the meadow in cracked old leather boots and minstrel cap, chased away such disconcerting thoughts and lifted her spirits once more. He was nearing their camp fire now, and she shifted her gaze to Nick as he sat slumped beside Jimmy, miserable and afraid.

What, exactly, was his problem? Couldn't he see what was going on around them? They were all caught up in the most monumental moment of change this land would ever know – and he was running scared. They had the chance to put all wrongs right, to level the playing field so that this country, and then maybe the world (and why not?), could be free of bigotry, prejudice, inequality, brutality, selfishness, greed. The mummer was going to show them how. Couldn't Nick see that? Or was his reluctance and antipathy purely down to the fact that he no longer had Sin? Selfish bastard. He deserved everything he had coming to him, then.

And what was that, exactly?

She ignored the quiet, rebellious question, and touched Sin's hand. The Chinese girl smiled carefully at her, and continued rolling a spliff. Jimmy was singing tunelessly to himself, patting his knees arhythmically as if to confirm his complete lack of talent. But then that was all right – in the world that was coming his previous social unacceptability and status as number one pariah would be completely assuaged.

The mummer was coming. He was stepping between the stones, through the daisies, eyes shining darkly as he strummed his lute. The merry air played across the meadow as stars spun through the dark skies above and a slight breeze ruffled the grass. A few hundred yards behind him, in Cirbury's public car park, Jo could see the silhouette of the cattle truck surrounded by its entourage of dilapidated vehicles. The village nestling beside the car park and the field of stones seemed not unduly perturbed by this mass arrival of dubious characters – aside from sending a deputation of local policemen backed up by curious villagers to investigate the rare phenomenon. They now stood watching from the fringe of the encampment, as if all this were some bizarre Midsummer Eve fête they were looking forward to.

Jo gazed up at the moon riding towards fullness. It was half-past midnight on the day of the twentieth of June. Tomorrow would see the summer solstice, and anything could happen really, couldn't it? She felt like saying so to Sin, but just then the mummer finally reached them and instead she fell silent and listened to his words. Even Jimmy stopped drumming impatiently on his knees and lay back on the grass to take it all in. Nick stayed slumped, head drooping, eyes clouded.

The mummer's eyes were upon Jo, or so she thought; but they seemed so all-encapsulating she was sure the others were just as certain that they were the sole object of his attention. She could see herself small and waif-like in his dark shark eyes, and she was smiling into the depths.

Shark eyes? Yes, maybe; but they promised so much. They promised an end to that old tyrant, the Doctor – and it had been so long since she'd even bothered to think of him that she hardly needed to wish for an end to him now. The mummer would take care of it for her anyway. He was the tidier of loose ends, the leveller. Now she could live her life the way she wanted to, instead of being dragged from one horrendous conflict to another by a man who purported to be on the side of freedom, yet needed the narrow-minded might of the military and all its conservative, stifling authoritarianism to back him up.

Sod him!

Let him be blown away in the wind like… like the spore of a seeding daffodil. Oh yes, the mummer would tidy *that* loose end all right.

His long fingers played softly with the strings of his lute as he stood in the centre of the little group, looking at one, looking at all. The tune was sad and stirring, gently medieval and brutally modern all at once. The spikes of his straw-coloured hair peeking from beneath his cap seemed to stir slightly in the breeze and Jo gazed, fascinated. His prominent nose quivered as he breathed in the night air and his large, voluptuous mouth widened to an astonishing degree as he smiled and spoke of the world that would soon be theirs.

And as he spoke in rich, melodious tones, quaint and rustic, eloquent and sharp, Jo was a pupil again and, for the first time ever, she was actually *listening*.

Sin was a child too, and his words transported her to some innocent place she had long since forgotten existed. Although most of his words had little direct pertinence for her, she interpreted them in her own way, and found peace and contentment in them, and that was enough. She remembered the time he had entered the Devil's Elbow, she remembered the child beside the stream reaching for him; most of all she remembered what it was like to be... happy?

And Jimmy the Wild, he was thinking of violence, and clashes, and rage, and yet it was all so *good*, because for once he was revelling in strife that was righteous strife; he was the hero in a modern morality tale where the coppers really did deserve to take a dive in the final reel. He felt vindicated for all his past misdeeds and, yes, he was the rebel with the bloody greatest cause.

And Nick... Nick listened quietly, chin on his knees, hands clasped around his legs.

And the mummer talked.

And talked...

And the camp fire crackled and popped, and the moon grinned as it rode through the night, and all around the field of stones the travellers were at peace.

'Our journey has reached its end,' the mummer announced, and his fingers slid over the strings of his lute and notes trickled sharp and cold into the fire-lit night. Some distance away at the edge of the field the police officers and local villagers watched from behind the (safety?) of the wire fence, like cardboard characters that did not move.

'This journey began in violence, and now it must end the same way. But freedom was always bought with violence, were it not?' With that, the mummer tossed the lute into the fire and spread his hands wide, grubby fingers poking through leather mittens like straw through the gloves of a scarecrow. The strings popped with discordant squeals and the wood warped to black.

'This here journey began for I in the Bogside; soldiers firing at will – as soldiers are wont – and the common people falling. But falling for truth even as they bled. This journey continued as I watched police clash with thugs and believers in racial freedom

184

at the burgh of Lewisham; names and places change, but the noble riots go on, and I am with them. This is your age, my children. The age of riot. See, I have roamed at the site you call Notting Hill and seen the good blood in the streets, though I have wandered there before the first bricks were laid; I 'ave been to all the troubled areas, seen it all: the fury, the hope, the belief. Most recently, I strolled beside your princess (whose princess? not *mine*, will *you* have her either?) as the gun flared in One's blue-blooded hand, severing the last link between rich and poor, and with five bullets destroyed the future of this detestable monarchy. Now there is a royal public hanging... rejoice.'

The mummer bared his teeth in a wolfish grin. The eyes held all these histories inside them, and revelled in their violence.

'But the march is over and the work almost done....'

Yet there came a challenger to the storyteller: a lone voice from the group of friends huddled around the fire. A quiet, shaking voice, and one which made Sin stare with hate, Jo with contempt, and Jimmy with bafflement.

'And you've done a good job, Mr Mummer.'

Nick was looking up now, arms still folded round his knees. His eyes were scared, but resolute. The clouds had gone from them, though his face was bone-white.

'All these places...' he continued, '...you were really there?' It was a sceptical accusation, his voice laden with tired cynicism.

The mummer took a step towards him before answering, and Nick's face became even whiter in the firelight. The final catgut string of the lute burnt away with a lonely wail. Silence for a sweaty fistful of seconds as the mummer turned the full gaze of his implacable shark eyes on the spike-haired young man.

'In spirit, if not in flesh,' he replied at last, his voice a menacing drawl, the menace of which was lost to all but Nick.

Nick nodded, then furnished his own slant on the mummer's words: 'In thought, if not in deed.' And suddenly, he saw the truth of the whole shambles: Rod's face floated up from the darkness of his mind: there he was, walking up to Glastonbury tor in the dead stretch of night, alone, having said goodbye to his friends for the last time. Nick saw what was waiting for him at the top and tears were in his eyes, and a great righteous fury flared up from his heart.

'I've been to those places too,' he said slowly, and his voice was no longer shaking but iron hard, as the tears trickled down his cheeks, not dissipating his strength but rather intensifying it. He looked at Sin.

And she saw the tears and the inner strength and her eyes widened momentarily, and horror and loss filled them, for one blissful moment only. Then she was the cold, hateful Sin again, and Nick made his speech.

'Yes, I've been to all those places too – in my head. Along with hundreds of other places like them, and I saw a different story. Not glory. Not glamour. Not a celebration of violence and discord. I saw only fear and desperation. A need to change, not destroy. What do you offer, Mr Mummer? A solution? Hope?...' He laughed. '*Freedom?* No. What you offer is a walk into the heart of hate, purely for the wild joy of it. And hate is all you've got.'

The mummer's eyes were no longer lustrous and dark. They were grey, grey as hard stone. And Nick stopped talking, and his head drooped on to his knees once more, and Sin looked at him, once, then looked away.

The fire burned. A knot of wood burst, then hissed. The mummer left them and walked across the field of stones towards the cattle truck.

Chapter Seventeen

It was like a hellish version of the TARDIS's dimensional transcendence, but knowing that did not save the Doctor from his own private horrors. He was bound to a stake as fire kissed the tinder wood and a crowd of bellowing ragged people celebrated. And, under the hoods and tatters, he recognised every one of them. There was Susan, there Vicki. And bearing the flickering torches that had kindled the faggots, Ian and Barbara grinning with bloodlust.

'Not you, Jamie,' he moaned, as another figure hurled a stone that gouged his cheek. 'Oh, not *you*.'

And although he knew he was simply caught like a leaf in a perceptual whirlpool inside the filthy cattle truck, it did not make the flames burn any less. He was a wicker man offered up to the hungry gods of his own delusions and fears and, inside his head, he'd found the one place where there really was no haven.

Zoe was mincing up to him and her rags were dropping away, freeing her to dance naked and wild before him. She threw her arms and head back and moved sinuous as a snake to the sound of his screams. He saw his skin blackening, and the agony was unendurable.

The stones came thick and fast then, all of them hurled by people he had loved and lost.

But now he was back in the control room of the TARDIS, holding on to the console while the craft shook wildly as if grabbed in the jaws of a monstrous cat. Lights flicked on, off, on, off. The floor bucked and threatened to hurl him against the indented roundels of the far wall. He held on, braving the psychic storm. The observation screen glowed into life and simultaneously the thrashing of the ship ceased, leaving the Doctor still clutching the console, sweating and panting.

He looked over his shoulder at the screen. It showed only an unfamiliar star system, shifting, beautifully coloured coronas embracing alien worlds; an asteroid-gemmed canvas of virgin territory. He longed to explore it, the chaos of the preceding moment all but forgotten. That is, until the scratching sound reached his ears.

Something was tearing at the outer hull of the timeship, scratching to get in. The sound echoed around the length and breadth of the TARDIS, mighty strips of environmental force-field gouged away with each clawful – and it had to be claws, judging by the noise. Claws that would strip away the onion layers of the ship and grope for him if he stayed put.

He hammered at stiff buttons on the mushroom-shaped console, prodded switches that came away in his fingers and, horribly, the TARDIS was screaming as it was clawed to death. The Doctor heard those screams as he finally succeeded in grappling with the dematerialisation lever, the location of which he had incredibly, albeit momentarily, forgotten. The TARDIS shook as if a big boot had stomped on its transdimensional spine, and the system spanning the screen blurred into nothingness to be replaced by the purple orgasmic thrusting of the space-time vortex. The Doctor collapsed against the console.

And then the scratching recommenced.

Impossibly, there was something out there, clinging piggyback to the TARDIS, riding with it through space and time and ripping its way slowly inside.

Irrational terror caught the Doctor and had him up and running for the door. He passed through, staggering blindly into the corridor beyond as lights pulsated greenly and sickly and the symphonic death rattle of the TARDIS crashed in his ears.

His fear chased him through corridor after metallic corridor, each the same, each seemingly endless – all apart from one which, inexplicably, was overgrown with nettles and weeds. In the centre of this passage a simple stone tomb nestled. The Doctor kicked his way through the undergrowth, slow-worms easing away from his shoes to slither under the memorial.

There was a name etched on the eroded lid, and the Doctor

gazed at it in fascination. So the TARDIS was dead, *he* was dead, and the craft had become a floating tomb adrift for ever in the vortex. The thought had him running again, as if he'd forgotten the essential truth that there was nowhere to run *to*. Through the nettles and hogweed, then through the far door, down endless corridors and up to a final door which led back inside the control room, to stare at the screen and what it showed him.

The scanner revealed a portion of the outer shell of the TARDIS and the spindly spider thing that clutched it with black, irradiated limbs. The teeth of the beast, as well as its claws, were ripping at the exterior, leaving long scorings. The repulsive hitchhiker turned towards the screen and the Doctor saw the face: his *own* face, mutated by the unknowable forces of the vortex, eyes locked with madness, mouth grinning and losing teeth that spun away into the void. The white hair was alive like a sea anemone, coiling and thrusting even as the flesh charred away to drift into the time stream, but yes it was his own face. And yet not. Evil as much as the cosmic erosion of the vortex had eaten away at it; perversion pulled at the corners of the leering grin. Bare id incarnate lusting after a whole universe, playing the beast with four backs with the craft that would take it where it willed. Insanity urging it to destroy what it needed. The Doctor's own ego, loose and satanic, scratching away the layers of his goodness.

The Doctor fell to his knees, eyes tight shut, hands over his ears as the TARDIS cried with everlasting sorrow.

The Cirbury villagers watched the roadies unload the cattle truck the next morning, hefting amps, speakers, instruments and cables over the stone wall and into the field of stones. There was plenty of discussion of course; this was the 'convoy of evil' after all – or half of it, anyway. But, strangely enough, there was no undue consternation. The newspapers told them the main batch had headed off for Stonehenge, and that made much more sense. Stonehenge was a symbol of old and arcane things; it was a natural magnet to social outcasts and hippie types. Cirbury, while just as old and equally as mystic, had for some reason never entered into the public consciousness to the same degree as the Salisbury Plain monument. If anything bad were to happen, it would happen there; and the soldiers also believed this – television newscasts showed the UNIT forces protecting the stone circle in an impressive display of armed doggedness.

If a few of the villagers were troubled by passing thoughts about the apparent short-sightedness of not deploying at least a token force to supervise the Cirbury part of the convoy, their thoughts were just that – passing – and immediately left those who had entertained them with a dull feeling of curious tolerance towards the colourful invaders of their historic community.

The general consensus was that nothing bad could happen here. UNIT would protect them if there was anything to worry about and, besides, they had a handful of local bobbies keeping a pragmatic eye on things.

Yes, a curious complacency was the order of the day amongst the villagers of Cirbury. Except in the case of one young man.

Becoming more dishevelled and wild-eyed with each passing day, Kane was also in a permanent state of drunkenness. The villagers referred to him as an alcoholic now, adding to his long list of socially undesirable epithets, and he was roundly shunned. The sunny morning of 20 June found him waking beside one of the standing stones out in the field, his body stiff with cold, his hair wet with dew.

He rolled over in the grass and sat up, his bones aching, his head competing with them. A bottle of Jack Daniel's lay three-quarters empty beside him. He pounced on it like a bird spotting a worm and, twisting off the cap, thrust the neck to his lips.

He took a long pull, and only then took time to look around him.

Travellers everywhere, camping in the field of stones. Some in tattered tents, others rolled in sleeping bags out in the open. A few tottered around the ashy ruins of fires provoking them into some semblance of life. Kane belched. Not far from where he sat a figure was slumped against another stone, the remains of a fire next to him. Kane remembered that the night before, when he'd staggered drunkenly among the hippies and punks, accosting any who'd listen with urgent and oft-repeated warnings that were met universally with derision and insults, the young man had been in exactly the same position. He remembered that he'd tried to wake the bastard, but with no response. And here the young man was still, head slumped on his knees.

Kane walked over to him and nudged him with his boot. 'He's coming,' he croaked. The young man remained unmoving, so Kane left him and shuffled over the field towards the village, and specifically the pub.

Cassandra intercepted him on the way. She was sitting on the stile that led from the field. She was dressed in a soft leather jacket and a green dress patterned with black shapes. Her dark, softly spiked hair framed her ascetic cheekbones and her sea-green eyes were clear with bright intelligence. Kane stood before her, stained T-shirt hanging out over filthy, urine-soaked jeans, face haggard and scurfed by stubble, hair lank with grease and littered with grass. He smiled vacantly at her and belched.

'He's coming, Cass,' he said by way of greeting, and held the bottle out to her. She refused it with a gesture, soft eyes watching him closely.

'Who's coming, Kane?' she asked in the manner of a nurse addressing a mental patient.

Kane laughed and lugged the bottle to his lips again, draining it with one gulp. 'Raggers, of course.' He spun and hurled the empty bottle against the nearest of the crusty stones.

'Raggers?'

'The Ragman to you. He's come back to Cirbury, and he's mightily pissed off. Heads are gonna roll, Cass.'

Cassandra shook her head confusedly, warding off his ramblings. 'You're in a bad way, Kane.'

Kane giggled, and searched the pockets of his leather jacket for cigarettes. Cassandra put him out of his misery and leant forward to offer him one. He leant against the stile smoking it, swaying slightly.

'You stink like a pig, Kane.'

'Still wanna shag me, eh, Cass? Well, it's too late for shit like that. Things have gone to bad.'

She ignored him. Her face was hard, though her eyes could never be anything other than soft. Her jawline tensed as she spoke. 'You couldn't leave it, could you? You had to come and spoil it for him. His big night, that meant so much to him. You just couldn't stop yourself.'

Kane didn't know what she was talking about. He frowned over at the roadies who were unrolling cables and connecting them to amps and speakers arranged amongst the stones. 'Bad times coming, Cass,' was all he said. 'The band's gonna play us all into hell.'

'Tell me, Kane: what's it like to be you?'

He looked up then, and she saw for the first time the extent of his madness. His eyes were haunted and barren. She flinched, and almost fell backwards off the stile.

'You don't wanna know that, Cass. You *wouldn't* like to go there. Scary places inside *my* head. No one playing games, no children, no… Raggers – *he's* been there, left his shadow behind. See, he's been playing with my family for years and years. Didn't know that, did ya, Cass? Didn't know I come from good stock, once upon a time. I didn't know either, but there it is: Kane Sawyer's ancestor was a rich bastard. Mayor of Cirbury.' And here he broke off laughing, a wild raucous laugh that was like a cold hand on Cassandra's spine.

'And Raggers, well, Raggers messed with my ancestor's daughter. *Messed* with 'er. You know what I mean, Cass? She was dancin' with the devil, and bore his brat. Ha ha. A Raggers brat. And her pop, guess what he did? Yeah, you just won the sale of the century, Cass, cos I know you're keeping up. He disowned her, cos she was tainted by scum and filth. She died cos of his neglect, in poverty and distress. Are you moved to tears yet, Cass?'

'I don't know what you're talking about, Kane.'

'Course you soddin' don't. What did you ever know about poverty and distress?'

'Kane,' she said after a while, her bitterness dissipating fast as she realised how far he was slipping away. 'Who's the Ragman?'

Kane swayed and dropped his cigarette. It lay burning amongst the buttercups. 'Is the pub open yet?' he said quietly.

The pub was packed. Just about every member of the small community was in there, and quite a few of them had drunk more than their usual allocation. But the mood was strangely jovial and benevolent; even when some of the travellers entered.

Jo, Sin and Jimmy were among them. They received a few amused and curious stares but no hostility. 'The mummer said we'd be welcome here,' Sin said as Jimmy ordered the round.

'Did 'e?' Jimmy turned round with a puzzled expression. 'Can't remember that.'

'Yeah,' Sin said, but her face was crinkled with puzzlement. 'I'm sure he did.' Jo was silent, watching the locals swilling and murmuring. She spotted one shabby young man leaning against the jukebox, swaying drunkenly. He was staring at her with unfocused eyes.

'Well, he was right anyway, wasn't he?' Sin continued, gesturing around the pub. 'Despite all the bad publicity the tour's been given, they don't give a shit about us being here.' The tall punk who had helped her sort out the traitor at Arnos Vale cemetery entered the pub with a few other spiky-haired rebels. He spotted Sin and strolled over, casually kissing her neck and putting his hand on her backside. She grinned emptily at him.

Jo was still watching the scruffy, drunken young man. He detached himself from the jukebox and advanced waveringly on her. She stood her ground, thinking he might be one of the convoy 'tribe' although she had never seen him before.

He wobbled to a halt in front of her and his large, hollow eyes fixed on hers.

'He's coming,' was all he said. And suddenly Jo was treated to a mental image of the Doctor kneeling with his hands over his ears, screaming in the back of the cattle truck, and she felt cold, colder than ever before, and then the image was fading, and another face swam before her eyes. She turned towards Sin and Jimmy.

'Where's Nick?' she said, as if she had only just remembered he existed.

Sin shrugged coldly while the punk continued to nuzzle her neck. Jo turned back to the drunk.

'Get lost, loser,' she said and pushed him back towards the jukebox. Then she smiled at Jimmy and accepted her pint. The coldness had gone. And so had Nick's face.

By mid-afternoon the equipment was all set up, drum kit shining amongst the buttercups and daisies, amps positioned in front of grim standing stones, the generator hunched over the lip of the grassy trench that curved around the field. The roadies tuned the instruments and barked repetitively into the microphone. Birds spiced the air with summer song and sheep wandered curiously amongst the stones, watching the bizarre undertakings. The travellers – those who weren't still in the pub – watched too, as curious as the sheep. This was it: this was the big one. The final gig. They all knew it, and there was a little sadness tinged in with the excitement. Villagers looked on too, and felt the excitement creeping into their own complacent souls, stirring wonder and other things.

Corporal Robinson was beginning to feel the strain. She listened to the taunts and jeers from the travellers camped before the UNIT cordon on Salisbury Plain. As yet they had made no concerted effort to force the point, but it was evident they wanted access to the stone circle in time for the solstice. But that they would not get. Even if she had to shoot every soddin' one of them herself. And she could feel the kill-lust hot within her, like the need for sex. And whenever she got *that* particular itch, she always had to scratch it. Same with this.

She glanced at the Brigadier who was standing next to his jeep, talking to Captain Yates. The young captain had recovered from his ordeal at the cemetery, a large lump on his head the sole souvenir of his treatment at the hands of the 'scum' he'd been trying to infiltrate. She looked around for Sergeant Benton, and there he was, inspecting the tight cordon that completely encircled the monument, checking weapons and morale. A good man, Benton. One of the boys – if that didn't seem a strange salute coming from the petite corporal. But while she respected the Brigadier for his iron resolve, equanimity and bravery, the Brig would never be a man of the people; and nor would the slightly fey Yates, come to that. Benton was a solid trooper, a man's man, and yes, a woman's man too. She could even fancy him, if she put her mind to it. But right now she was putting her mind to the scum a few hundred yards away, who were congregating messily on the grass in front of their filthy vehicles. The ringleader seemed to be the large biker roadie who was leaning beside his Vincent, smoking and apparently watching her as she inspected her segment of the cordon. She felt like flipping her rifle down from her shoulder and shooting the bastard there and then.

Maybe later, if things hotted up; oh yes, maybe we can save you for later, you scruffy, dirty, long-haired *bastard*.

It was around six in the evening when the roadies brought the final item out of the back of the cattle truck. A flat-bedded Bedford was positioned beneath the rear doors and, with much grunting and heaving, two roadies succeeded in levering the large rock down into the smaller vehicle. The gate leading into the field of stones was thrown open and the roadies drove into the meadow, heading for the standing stones.

The Bedford bounced and careened over tussocks and through beds of buttercups before coming to a rest at a specified location between two stones, a few yards from the band's equipment. The roadies climbed out of the truck and secured ropes to the large stone, then signalled to some nearby punks to help them.

It took ten of them to pull the hefty rock down from the

Bedford and drag it to the desired spot. When it was finally erected the entire field of hippies and punks grew silent. The awed hush reached even as far as the village. Some members of the community, including five policemen, were at their habitual observation point leaning against the fence overlooking the field, and they too felt the power of the moment. There was no need to put it into words.

The rock had come home. After centuries it was once more in its rightful position.

The field crackled with the primal significance of the occasion.

And falling through the door of the pub, Kane felt it too, almost insensible with drink as he was.

He straightened up, leaning against the wall of the pub, and his eyes were huge and very afraid. Then he slid down the wall, his head nodding forward on his chest as the drink kicked in.

Just across the road Simon was on the point of climbing into his Jaguar, anxious to leave the setting of his grand humiliation a couple of evenings earlier. He would have gone sooner, but for his sister's pleas for him to spend some time with her. Well, that particular (hollow) duty was fulfilled, and he could quit this shit at last. This village of no prospects, this Loserville. No wonder he was the only one to ever succeed – it was such a no-through-road of a place. Along with maths and English they taught you how to underachieve at the village school. Most of his wretched peers all had O levels in mediocrity and the odd A in 'making the best of your lot'. Well, sod that. Making do had never been enough for him.

It was then he spotted Kane.

The symbol of everything this shitty village stood for: here he was, the personification of stagnation.

He closed the car door slowly, and crossed the street.

His smile grew as he walked up to his old enemy. It was a cruel smile, vicious and triumphant. It was the smile of a schoolyard bully who was into spite in a big way. As he stood over Kane he could feel the warmth of the midsummer sun on the back of his finely tailored jacket, and it could just as well have been burning on the back of a school blazer worn by a vindictive boy who squatted astride his victim and reached for the crawling jar.

The crawling jar. God, he hadn't thought of that in such a long time.

Years and years. And they could have been bloody *days*, because he felt exactly the same as he had back then; the same urge to humiliate *totally*, the same impulse to torture. He remembered Kane's fourteen-year-old mouth bulging with squirming horrors, slime running from his soiled lips, mucus from his nose, tears from his eyes. He smirked. *That* was how to be a bully. Perhaps Simon should have given lessons in it at Cirbury Road To Nowhere Comprehensive School: at least the dropouts would have learned *something*.

Seventeen years on from that memorable victory, Simon kicked Kane as he sat slumped against the pub wall.

'Scum!' he spat. 'Always knew you'd be nothing. You just had to go and prove me right, didn't you? You dirty little drunk. You touched my sister, Kane. You *fondled* her, you disgusting creep. You were never good enough for her, and I just wanted you to admit that. Remember the slugs, Kane? Remember the *worms*? Dirt to dirt.' He stepped back and swung his shoe into Kane's kidneys. The drunk grunted and his head flopped to one side.

'And the funny thing is, you never knew why I hated you, did you? Too thick to work it out. Just another local yokel, eh, Kane? Just another bum, from a long line of bums... Except you weren't, were you?' And now the smile was gone from Simon's face, and true paranoia leapt in his blue eyes. He staggered back a step as the extremity of his passions burned through him, leaving him flushed and sweaty and short of breath. Helplessly, he stared at his old enemy and felt, at last, that there was a reckoning between them. Kane was brought down to the ultimate state for which he had been destined, while Simon had scaled the peaks of achievement. Yet his mother's words were as clear as the sobs of his victim on that summer's day in the playing field seventeen years before.

'He comes from a good family, not that you'd know it now. A very old family. The Sawyers used to practically own the village, my boy, in olden days. And we should respect them for that, no matter what their circumstances are today. Be kind to him, Simon. According to local legend this village owes them a lot.'

This village owes them a lot!

Simon was laughing. God, he still remembered that stupid line, even though he could scarcely remember his mother's face without looking at a photograph.

The Village of Nobodys owes you a lot, does it, Sawyer? Why, what did your inbred family do that was so special? Anybody care to tell me?

He hadn't realised he was speaking aloud until Kane suddenly looked blearily up at him, grinned, and said:

'We drove away the monster. That's what we did. But monsters always come back, don't they? *They always come back!*'

Kane was grinning, and confronted by that grin Simon could do nothing but back away across the street, in the path of a Mini that swerved wildly to avoid him, honking furiously. Without another word Simon threw himself into the driver's seat of his Jag, slamming the car door behind him. He turned the key in the ignition, not needing to look round to know that Kane was still grinning at him from across the road. Still grinning.

Simon swung the Jag in a curve, aiming the bonnet at the pub. At Kane.

He completed the tight semicircular manoeuvre, missing the drunk by a couple of feet, then steered up the high street with a growl of acceleration.

He was getting the hell out of town.

But the hell *in* the town wouldn't let him.

He was pulling up to the junction just beyond the last house. Away in the hazy summer distance he could see the white horse galloping across the blue hills he remembered so well from his childhood, the woods fringing the chalk cutting a cluster of gold in the glorious evening light. He paused and changed down as a lorry bustled past on the main road to Marlborough. The sight of the horse calmed him, or maybe it was the realisation he'd left that hated trap of a village hopefully for the last time. Why in God's name had he ever decided to go back?

Well, he knew the answer to that well enough. He wanted to show them, didn't he? Wanted to show all the useless, retarded good-for-nothings that he'd done something with his life. That he'd made it.

Well, he'd done that.

Hadn't he?

He swung the Jag across the junction and picked up speed, heading east towards London. The needle kicked towards fifty, sixty... sixty-five. The last of the standing stones reared up directly beside the road as if to bid him a sarcastic farewell, and suddenly there was a figure beneath it. A gaunt, hunchbacked figure in grey tatters, with grey flesh too, and a horrible head crowned with writhing things and the car was no longer under his control and my God he could see the creature's gruesome features and *they were a twisted likeness of Kane's*!

The Jag, doing a happy sixty-eight miles an hour, ploughed into the standing stone with a horrendously dull impact-sound of crumpling metal and shattering glass.

Nobody in the village even noticed.

Dusk over Cirbury. The community mingled with the travellers amongst the stones as the band took up its position.

Silence fell over the ancient meadow. A few rooks circled the elm trees, rowing with each other in their own particular eldritch fashion. The sheep hurried away to a far corner of the field. The first stars poked through the skies, and the moon swung out from behind a cloud as if to say: entertain me.

The singer stood behind his microphone. His shades were on, of course. His leather jacket looked like it had been dragged through a farmyard; the colourful paper tatters covering his hose trousers fluttered in the evening breeze. His grass-green hair stood up wildly, imparting, along with his saturnine looks, an overall impression of a punk Pan standing before his beasts.

The beasts: guitarist hunched behind and to the left of the singer, top hat with hinge crown, mummer rags, big leather boots, stubble, shades; skinhead drummer snarling behind his snare drum; Sid Vicious bassist in worn leather and ragamuffin tatters.

The singer shrieked once, like a night-hidden fox. Then he leant closer to the mike.

'Welcome to the village of the damned,' he snarled, and the band began to play.

One last time.

Chapter Eighteen

'I say we rush them, Sarge.'

Yates glanced up from his RT as he heard the corporal's words. She was standing next to Sergeant Benton, and her eyes were hard and determined.

Benton shrugged in response, unaware he was being watched by his superior. Yates waited for some more definitive reply from the sergeant. None came. He closed the connection on his RT unit, dismissing the irritation the scene had left him with, and strolled over to where the Brigadier was studying a brief that had just been couriered to him from Whitehall.

'Trouble, sir?'

The Brigadier looked up. 'Hmm?'

'New orders?'

'No. Same orders, unfortunately. In duplicate. For me to sign and return ASAP. Seems the RT isn't good enough. They want me to be in possession of hard evidence in case of recriminations.'

'I don't understand, sir.'

'No, Yates,' the Brigadier said, folding the brief away inside his jacket pocket. 'Neither do I.'

He glanced over at the restless ranks of travellers who were now actively beginning to taunt the soldiers protecting the stones. A few bottles were hurled and though no injuries had been sustained so far it was only a matter of time. The soldiers were becoming restless too, increasingly nervous and angry.

'Whitehall wants me to maintain our defensive position,' the Brigadier said gloomily, his fist clenching on his swagger stick.

'Surely that's wise, sir?' said Yates with a puzzled expression.

The Brigadier turned to him and his eyes were small and hard, emphasising the sharpness of his tone. 'Wise, Yates? How the devil can doing nothing in the face of such hostility possibly be deemed "wise"?'

Yates looked at his feet, taken aback. Then he remembered the reason he had approached his superior officer. 'We really should try to get Jo out of Cirbury, sir.'

'Yes, Yates,' snapped the Brigadier, obviously irritated at the note of reproach, however accidental, in the captain's voice. 'I'm fully aware of my responsibilities towards Miss Grant.'

Then why don't you act on them? Yates felt like answering, but contained himself. It really wasn't like the Brigadier to procrastinate over something as important as this. Perhaps he just had too much on his plate. After all, he seemed to need all his resources here. Still, if Yates volunteered to head for Cirbury by himself, or maybe with just a few soldiers as back-up, he might be able to free Jo from the obviously malign influence under which she had fallen.

'Sir?'

Yates and the Brigadier turned to face Corporal Robinson, who was obviously agitated.

'Yes, what is it, Corporal?' the Brigadier inquired before Yates could say anything.

'The boys want to take them on, sir. There's a bad feeling brewing.'

Yates was speechless. What the deuce was a corporal doing voicing such concerns to UNIT's commanding officer, for God's sake? Was discipline slipping to such a disastrous degree? He waited for the Brigadier's reprisal. Again, as with Benton, it was not forthcoming.

'They're a bad lot, sir, these hippies,' continued the corporal, brushing a lock of sweaty blonde hair away from her forehead. Her eyes were stark with prejudice. 'The boys want to wade in, good and proper. There's a lot of hatred.'

'Indeed,' was all the Brigadier said, hands clasped behind his back as he stared past the bitter-eyed corporal to the cordon of UNIT soldiers ringing the monument. The sun was going down fast.

'I know what they mean, sir.' Robinson hadn't finished yet; she was just beginning to warm to her theme of hate. 'My parents died in a car crash caused by their sort.' She gestured towards the group of travellers taunting the picket. 'Stoned to their eyeballs, they were. Bloody, *filthy* hippies… They shouldn't be free to do this, sir. They shouldn't be *free*…'

Yates waited, dumbstruck by this extraordinary display of emotion and insubordination, for the Brigadier to shout her down, and still… nothing. He glanced at his superior, and was astonished to see a bitterness mirroring Robinson's in his eyes. The Brigadier's mouth was set in a stern line. It was Benton who intervened, but even *his* voice carried no conviction. 'That'll do, Robinson.'

From beyond the monument the chanting intensified as the falling sun threw golden spears of light across the impartial sarsons.

Jo could feel it; she knew Sin and Jimmy must be able to feel it too. The whole village could surely sense the vibrations. The *vibe*. The vibe that had been trembling through them all ever since that first incredible gig back in Princetown, which seemed like years ago now – a lifetime ago. But now it was stronger, thrumming towards some peak, orchestrated by the wild playing of the band.

'It's the ley lines,' Jimmy shouted next to her.

She turned to him, startled. 'What do you mean?' she shouted back.

He shrugged, still watching the cavorting band.'Dunno. But it is.'

Ley lines. Jo tried to concentrate on the idea, thrown rather off guard by guttersnipe Jimmy's sudden flash of erudition. She knew Cirbury and Stonehenge were reputed to be ley-line nexuses, but what did that have to do with Dartmoor, and the band? She had very little understanding of what a ley line was. She imagined the Doctor lecturing her, and the need to know suddenly vanished and hate returned. Memories of all the patronisation, all the condescension, returned in force, stoked by the vicious riffs of the guitarist. Her heart beat in time with the drums and her fists clenched.

You're a reasonably intelligent young woman, Jo.
Did you fail Latin as well as science?
Stir your stumps, Jo.
BASTARD!!

If he were here now she would reduce *him* to soddin' stumps. The constant humiliation and put-downs. She should have been carefree and happy, finding a nice exciting bloke to spend her days with, not chaperoned through time and space by a supercilious old fop in a box.

Sin closed her eyes and the music took her. She felt hornier than she'd ever felt in her life, and it had nothing to do with mere *sex*. This urge went beyond the body. She pictured herself dancing with the great god Pan in some secret glade deep, deep in the darkest wood. A stream chuckled magically in the background and wood pigeons cooed and badgers nodded at her as she danced with the cloven-hoofed one. And now He took her in his arms and smiled a wicked smile and the horns curved back into the tangled bramble-hair and the eyes, oh my God, the eyes… Such fierce beauty she had never beheld. And then she opened her eyes as the music lulled, and the first thing she saw was Nick's body, still slumped against a stone behind the band, picked out by a spot of moonlight. She quickly closed her eyes again and waited for the music to come for her.

Jimmy was dreaming of school. Only this time, when the teacher belittled him for his poor understanding of percentages and fractions and ordered him to stand outside the classroom for catapulting paper balls at the rest of the class, instead of sheepishly doing as he was told, instead of *taking* it – he stood up and climbed on the desk so that all the kids could see him, and faced down the teacher with a snarl that he was only beginning to learn how to use at fifteen years of age. 'Hey, Mr Fryer: kiss this,' he called, swivelling his backside towards the man. Then, as the teacher's face flamed with red rage and he bore down on this rebel of rebels, the classroom door burst open and in came Jimmy's gang. All paper tatters and worn leather, dyed punk hair and ferocious boots; and the girls he'd always fancied and who never spoke to him normally could see that he had the coolest, *meanest* mates as the gang ripped the clothes from old Fryer and displayed his minuscule member for them all to laugh at before pounding him senseless, trashing the class and burning the school. Jimmy was striding through the smoking corridors with his new gang, and the girls were the only ones allowed out of the inferno through the main doors. The rest could burn. Jimmy considered letting his schoolmates out too, but nah, they thought he was crazy so let them burn too. Then Jimmy was pulling away from the flaming pyre of education gone wrong, *roaring* away with the band on big, shining Hogs, and the girls were running after him, and the soundtrack to all this dreamy cool stuff was Generation X's 'Wild Youth', or maybe, yeah, maybe 'New Rose' by The Damned, cos that was probably the best soddin' song ever written and – and…

The band stopped playing.

Along with the rest of the crowd Jo, Sin and Jimmy turned to face the car park a few hundred yards away to their right. A growl of diesel-fuelled engines. The cattle truck was on the move. It grumbled towards the half-open gate leading into the field and then forged straight through it in an explosion of splintering wood. The filthy vehicle came on, lumbering over the tussocks towards them. The band struck up another number, and the playing was faster, the grizzled vocals more urgent as the vibration, the *vibe*, built within Jo, within them all.

The guitarist and bassist weaved between the tall standing-stones, trailing flexes through the daisies. The singer threw his head back and howled, and the drums beat an evil tattoo that pounded inside Jo's skull like something very nasty was trapped in there and trying desperately to get out. The cattle truck swung in a slow trouncing curve until the back doors were facing towards the band and its enrapt audience; then its engine cut out and the singer's shriek ended. The rest of the band carried on playing, fast, faster.

The doors were opening.

Kane came to and wondered blearily what had roused him. His head felt like someone had been having a right royal go at it with a pike. But that wasn't what had stirred him. For a moment he struggled to work out where he was. Sitting outside the pub of course, stupid. Where else *would* he be? The street was quiet and he wondered if it was a Sunday. Sundays in Cirbury were a special kind of hell. Then he remembered.

Everything.

And he knew what had woken him.

The music – he could hear it. The hell band was playing, but he knew instinctively it was not their racket that had jolted him from welcome oblivion. No, it was the low, evil vibration that was moving through his guts. *That was coming up through his feet from beneath the ground.*

He heaved himself up, and his stomach revolted against the action. He turned to the pub and threw up in the doorway, somehow sensing it was the last gesture he would ever make towards his old haunt, and feeling it was a damn suitable one. But the music was calling…

Time to go.

One of the roadies had erected a ramp below the open backdoors of the truck, and now, walking grandly down it from inside like a princess revealing herself to her subjects for the first time, came a pretty young blonde woman. Jo recognised her; she'd seen her before, and wondered where… the Devil's Elbow. And again at Arnos Vale cemetery. Journalist. Jo felt a pang of envy at this special treatment the woman was receiving. Like she was some May queen or something. Yet the journalist didn't seem to be exactly savouring the attention; she moved like she was in a dream, eyes wide and empty. Her white blouse and slacks were covered in dust and cobwebs but she made no move to brush them away as she descended the ramp and stepped trancelike towards the band.

The moon watched her approach, granting her an even more ghost-like appearance, brushing the eerie stones, too, with luminous paintwork. The band continued to play, the music thrusting towards orgasmic peaks of frenzy. The singer's vocals had become one long guttural scream, and Jo also felt like screaming – to release all her pent-up frustrations, and embrace this music of the damned as if it would satisfy her every desire. She was free now, at last. Tears streaked her cheeks and she groped for Sin's hand, and found it. Sin's face was lit with cruel relish, flushed with extreme passion. Jimmy was grinning like a lunatic and the band played fast, faster…

Charmagne moved wraith-like behind the band and took up her position in front of the restored stone, arms at her side, beautiful and calm in the moonlight.

And now someone else was descending from the truck. The back doors swung closed behind him.

The mummer. Colourful paper streamers stirring in the night breeze, leather-mittened hands outstretched as if he were some all-healing Messiah spreading benedictions amongst the chosen, eyes fixed ahead – on Charmagne Peters, on the stone behind her. Cracked leather boots carried him slowly through the dandelions.

Ley lines. The mummer could feel their power ripping through the earth, the primal violence of them, pouring into the willing crowd around the stones and amplified beautifully by the band's psyche-moulding music. The violence was escalating, and upon hitting orgasm the forces at his control would be staggering; morphic forces forged beyond the other side of the cosmos, married to the convulsive energies beneath the stones of Cirbury. The result: a widespread tidal wave of volatile negativity. Pure antipathy.

The summer of hate was just beginning.

Enjoy, my children…

On his way to join Charmagne, the mummer passed Jimmy. Jimmy found himself staring into those depthless eyes – *I can see for miles and miles* he was thinking helplessly, so terrified he almost pissed his jeans and so excited he wanted to laugh and shout and…

Without a word, Jimmy peeled away from the crowd congregating around the band and headed off towards the car park. Neither Sin nor Jo noticed him leave.

'Riot shields?' the Brigadier repeated in outraged disbelief upon hearing Yates' suggestion. 'Good heavens, man! We're an intelligence task force – we're the *army*, dammit, not a bunch of rural bobbies.' He enunciated the last word with heartfelt contempt. Yates flinched as if he'd been slapped. Such an outburst was incredible. The UNIT troops were virtually defenceless against the stones and bottles that were beginning to fly thick and fast now; protective gear was essential. The rage in the Brigadier's eyes was completely uncharacteristic – his lack of reason too. But he was Yates's commanding officer and, like all good soldiers, the captain was trained never to directly challenge a superior. He glanced over at the ring of UNIT men guarding the sarsons. He could tell they were itching to unsling their rifles and blast away at the shouting, screaming mob of hippies and punks surrounding them.

He decided to drop the subject of riot shields for now, vital as he was convinced they were. Something else was worrying him almost as much.

'Sir… I was wondering if we shouldn't deploy a squad to Cirbury,' he announced in the most diplomatic tone he could manage. The Brigadier glared at him, but said nothing. Encouraged, Yates forged ahead: 'It's just that the band is at Cirbury, and they've always been the figurehead for the convoy. Every time the band plays there's hell to pay. Can I suggest we send a squad there just to keep an eye on things?' He waited nervously for a reply. Nervously? This was the officer he'd followed blindly and devotedly through all sorts of bizarre and horrific conflicts and eventualities; this was the man whose judgement and command he had never before even thought to question. He would have trusted him with his life, so strong was his confidence in him. But now? What the hell was happening to him, to... everyone?

He thought of Jo: the blind, manic fervour that had been in her eyes at Arnos Vale. And now he looked at the Brigadier and saw –

'How *dare* you question my authority, Yates? Are you trying to suggest I'm not in control of events? The bloody *police* can deal with the few troublemakers at Cirbury. The real situation is here! The bloody *hippies* are here – can't you see them? The enemy's *here*, man!'

Yates backed away, stupefied by the violence in his superior officer's voice. A bottle exploded against the jeep parked beside them. The Brigadier turned, whipping out his pistol, eyes sparking with fury. Yates could feel the latent violence crackling in the air between the soldiers and hippies. And it made him feel cold and afraid.

On impulse he left the Brigadier standing like an angel of vengeance beside his violated jeep, and headed for a Land Rover parked further away from the stones. A group of reserve soldiers sat inside the vehicle, awaiting their turn to be sent out to relieve some of the Stonehenge cordon. He barked an order at the driver as he eased himself into the passenger seat.

'Sir?' the trooper asked in bewilderment.

'That's an order, private. Do it!'

The Brigadier didn't even see them leave as the Land Rover lurched over the field towards the main road.

Yates was thinking hard. Why wasn't he as caught up in all this mania as everyone else seemed to be? He had been in both camps – hippie and UNIT – over the last few days, so he had been exposed to two fields of influence. Yet he remained calm and unaffected by the – what could he call it? – *mesmeric* bloodlust that seemed to have blanketed his colleagues and friends. What made him so special? He'd hardly excelled himself over the last few days, had he? Got sussed at the cemetery and smashed over the head as a consequence –

He frowned. He'd been unconscious for the better part of a day as a result of that blow, and ever since he'd been subdued and sheepish. In a low mental state. And of course that could be the answer: he hadn't been in a very receptive condition. So how did that help him?

It meant, as Kipling once mentioned (although Yates was sure the writer could never have imagined his wit being linked to such a wild occasion), that he could keep his head while everyone else around him was losing theirs…

But could he sort out this mess alone? And where the hell *was* the Doctor when he was needed most? Yates hadn't seen him since the incident at Arnos Vale. He could have slipped away to Cirbury ahead of the convoy, of course, but nobody had even thought to ask. Maybe Yates *was* affected by this malign influence to some degree. Maybe it was making him forget important things.

Well, he'd just have to concentrate a bit harder, that was all. And right now he had to concentrate on getting to Cirbury.

The Doctor was trudging dazedly through the reality-wound of the cattle truck. The tidal wave of delusions that had ripped through his mind seemed to be receding at last, but this didn't seem to be helping him find an exit. He had to focus his mind deliberately on one goal – locating the back doors of the truck. If he visualised them perfectly, if he concentrated on every rusting fleck, every rib of corrugated metal – even the hole through which he'd peeped when the truck was on Dartmoor – then surely it would help him to break through this perceptual warp.

He had no idea how long he'd been trudging through the black cricklegrass. It could have been merely a handful of hours, and yet it could have been whole days, whole days while Jo remained at risk, while the *planet* remained at risk.

And what could he do if – *when* – he found an exit? It wasn't like him to succumb to self-doubt, but in this case he really did feel helpless. It wasn't a question of rigging up some last-minute contraption to defeat the aliens – he couldn't simply reverse the polarity on the Ragman. The entity would simply laugh at such arrant nonsense. And yet…

The ley lines obviously held the secret to the monster's power. After all, the rock inside which the entity had travelled through space had been imbued with ancient forces analogous to ley energies – along with other, more cosmic potencies – that much the boastful being had already revealed. But the Doctor could only guess at what those forces were, so how could he hope to find an antidote to them? The morphic power to transmute organic materials – to resurrect them from death and infuse them with life-simulating energies – that was truly awe-inspiring; and that, coupled with the ability to create mass mesmeric effects, made the Ragman a daunting adversary to say the least.

And the Doctor couldn't even *begin* to think about defeating him while he was still trapped in this tangible distortion of viewpoint.

He paused beside a black tarn and studied his reflection in the troubled waters. There was light of a kind in this dismal place; a diffused, bloody glow on the horizon that did not tempt him to seek out its cause. He realised that walking indefinitely was pointless. The doors, the walls of the truck were still there – of course they were. He was probably walking around in a circle within the back of the truck like a clockwork toy that refused to wind down. Well, perhaps it was time to stop his aimless wanderings and refuse to play the Ragman's game. He was about to sit down beside the tarn when he saw the blue box.

The TARDIS. Waiting for him behind the black bone of a tree. And yet, of course, just another illusion. Should he waste his time checking? He would still be playing to the Ragman's sadistic rules. Then again, the TARDIS might have responded to some summons

– maybe the Time Lords were coming to his aid again. It wasn't an impossibility. Surely even their short-sighted apathy could not ignore the universal peril the Ragman presented. In fact, what society offered more of a challenge to the levelling hunger of the Ragman than the officious, hierarchical sophistry of Gallifrey?

He walked around the darkly rippling tarn, heading for the TARDIS.

Perhaps there would even be something he could lash up in the control room to help him against the Ragman. Last-minute contraptions *sometimes* had their place, after all.

Yates saw the purple camper van hammering along the moonlit country lane towards them, and turned to the UNIT driver.

'Pull over, that's the vehicle Jo was travelling in!'

The soldier obediently swung the Land Rover into the verge. The camper came on, and it must have been doing at least sixty-five on the dangerously curving roads.

Yates could see the driver of the van, and recognised him as Jo's companion Jimmy. He could see the grey Confederate cap pulled low over the crazy eyes. Jimmy had always had crazy eyes, but now they were more bugged-out manic than ever. At the same time that Yates realised there was nobody else in the camper van, Jimmy noticed them and swung the wheel down hard right, flinging his long vehicle into a direct collision course with the UNIT Land Rover.

Yates acted instinctively. The driver was already flooring the accelerator pedal in a knee-jerk shock reaction but his hands were not working in conjunction with his feet, so the captain seized control of the Land Rover himself, frantically leaning over to grab the steering wheel.

The UNIT vehicle bounded forward in first gear as the camper van rocketed through the space they'd occupied seconds before. Yates saw it veer manically as it slammed over the grass verge, threatening to flip over sideways into the hedge that divided the road from Salisbury Plain on the other side. Then it righted itself and, without pausing, continued its hurtling journey onwards. Soon it was around a bend in the road and gone from their sight.

'You want us to follow it, sir?' the driver asked, white-faced.

Yates gazed anxiously in the direction from which the camper had come. 'No. That's just convinced me more than ever that we need to get to Cirbury now.'

The mummer stood next to Charmagne, in front of the stone from space. He was careful to leave a distance of at least a few yards between himself and the rock, but there was nobody around with sufficient presence of mind to notice his caution. In this comfortable position he could bathe in the escalating power-flow streaming from the rock, the rock that was the focus for all the ley lines beneath the stones. The flames of rage from near and far were being stoked to a crescendo. Near was Cirbury, and far, although it was not so distant as to lose its almost tangible volatility, was Stonehenge. The hatred, the violence was rising, rising...

And the band played fast, faster...

Chapter Nineteen

The Doctor fitted his keys into the lock and the doors of the TARDIS swung open. He entered the craft, and shut them on the wilderness of psyche outside.

He stood within the blue box and for a moment he didn't react. It was barely larger than a cupboard, equipped with telephone and police-instruction notice. It was a box, and nothing more. Perhaps it never had been anything more. Perhaps his past, Gallifrey, his travels – *everything* had been but a dream within a dream. Perhaps there had never been anything more than this box, and his delusions to fill it.

He slumped into a corner and put his head on his knees.

We're gonna smash it up till there's NOTHING left! roared Dave Vanian, as Captain Sensible's guitar wailed joyously, Algy Ward's bass bounced and leapt and Rat Scabies' drums galloped like a herd of rhinos determined to break free from the tinny speakers Jimmy had set up in the camper van.

Jimmy was grinning madly. Mad? He wasn't mad. He was livin' it: for the first time in his life he had a purpose and was pulling out all the stops to achieve it. This was his finest hour, this was Jimmy's exclamation against the world that had always tried to hold him back, to throw him in the slammer, to tell him no.

Well, now he was shouting back. *Yes, yes, YES!! You can't stop me now!* He sang along to The Damned's tribal anthem, and it was everything he'd ever believed in. Of course it was. He'd never been a creator, had Jimmy. Destroying was much more fun. Destroying pomposity, vanity, pretension. Bring it all down! Bring it *all* down!!! There was a devil in him, always had been.

Today it was having its day, that was all.

Mad dog, comin' down the way.

The camper van tore along the road at more than seventy miles an hour. Jimmy could see the sacred circle of Stonehenge on the horizon, lit by moon and stars and surrounded by the green-garbed protectors of the Establishment. Encroaching against that barrier, there were the rebels. The outcasts. The outsiders who never belonged.

Time to change all that, Jimmy thought, and put his foot down even further.

'It's only rock 'n' roll,' he sang crazily as the tape ended and the monument loomed larger in his windscreen.

But I like it.

Soldiers. Pigs in different uniforms, that's all they were. With rifles 'stead of truncheons. Oh well, no problem: here comes the pig farmer. Run for your lives, boys, it's porky-arse-kickin' time.

The camper van took out a gate leading on to the plain without slowing. Splintered wood confettied around the windscreen and Jimmy hollered with glee. The van pounded over the grass, bouncing and lurching as the speedo flickered around fifty-five, sixty. Jimmy tore The Damned tape out of the player, tossed it over his shoulder, rammed The Ruts in. 'H-Eyes'. Turned it up full blast.

He was lurching past the parked convoy vehicles now; could see the crowd of hippies and punks and losers and outlaws all turning to stare as he howled, accelerator glued to the floor, and the music took him away...

AND THE BAND PLAYED FAST, PLAYED FASTER...

And now he was past the travellers and hurtling towards the ancient stone circle, towards the cordon of soldiers ringed around it, some of whom were unshouldering their rifles, taking tentative aim at Jimmy as he sat in the driver's seat and screamed his rebel yell and his soul took flight and this was the most glorious moment of his life and Malcolm Owen was screaming back at him: *'You're so young, you take smack for fun; it's gonna screw your head, you're gonna wind up dead!'* and he aimed the purple camper van at a trilithon directly in front of him, the soldiers in his way forgetting about shooting and throwing themselves aside as Jimmy howled 'How's this for anarchy and chaos you bastards!' and Jimmy…

Jimmy…

Jimmy drove the camper van at sixty miles an hour into a huge sarsen and the world went red, white and…

Black.

The camper van erupted into a mushroom of flame as it steamrollered into the ancient standing stone, slamming it over on to its back. The UNIT troopers hugged the grass and a great roar went up from the crowd of travellers as they saw what Jimmy had done, and that now there was a gap into the ancient stone circle. As one they surged forward, bottles, tyre irons, knives, anything they could get their hands on that would serve as weapons, clenched in fists that were ready to use them.

At Cirbury the gaily coloured mummer smiled a shark smile as a new wave of energy coruscated through him. He waved his hands to capture the attention of the surging crowd of villagers and travellers as the band threw themselves around in a whipped-up frenzy, the music a white noise of hatred and spite. The crowd parted before his gestures, leaving a clear passage leading to the edge of the field where the handful of local bobbies waited for precise instructions from their absent superiors… and waited in vain.

The mummer didn't need to say anything. Travellers and villagers alike turned together and began running silently towards the edge of the field, their faces contorted with bloodlust, maniacal, horrible. The police realised belatedly what was going to happen and made a pathetic break for it, pelting towards the stile leading to the village.

Of course they never made it.

As the guitarist pumped high-voltage sonic fury into the night air, as the singer roared like a gutted grizzly and the rhythm section anchored the sound into a pummelling vibe, the mob caught up with the five policemen.

The mob didn't need weapons. For the most part they used

their hands quite effectively. They used their teeth too. They used everything. The head of a pudgy sergeant was pounded repeatedly against a standing stone until the back of his skull was smattered all over the rock like pieces of bloody eggshell. The eyes of a screeching constable were gouged out by the Cirbury milkman, and his ribs were then kicked into his lungs by an enraged punk with UK SUBS emblazoned on his leather jacket. Brand New Age was painted in a wild scrawl beneath the group's name. Another constable pulled his truncheon and actually tried to make a fight of it. His head was taken messily away from his shoulders and slung into the thick of the mob for his efforts. His torso was dragged through the grass by two screaming heavy-metal warriors, blood leaving a snail trail amongst the buttercups and daisies. Another bobby was down on his knees begging for mercy. His helmet was almost reverently taken from his head, positioned under his chin, and filled with the blood from his own slashed throat by a hippie with a Charles Manson T-shirt and a rusty machete. The last survivor actually had his right leg on the stile and was just about to catapult himself over on to the path that led alongside the school when he was seized and dismembered like a human-sized fly, his legs and arms popped from their sockets and sent twirling away into the depths of the maddened crowd. Schoolchildren herded around the corpse, supervising the limb-pulling with relish as their deepest body-in-pieces fantasies were enacted by the enraged crowd.

Green grass was saturated with red, and still the band wasn't satisfied.

This was the sight that greeted Captain Yates's eyes as the Land Rover roared into Cirbury's car park. 'My God!' he croaked. The UNIT driver next to him gaped as he saw the torso of a policeman being held aloft by the insane crowd like a particularly gory Guy Fawkes dummy. After seeing that spectacle, there was no way he was going to be able to bring the speeding vehicle to a sedate halt. Instead, the Landrover barrelled into a double-decker bus with skulls and the names of punk bands painted all over it.

Yates was thrown forward by the collision, his outflung arms protecting him from the shattering windscreen glass. The driver was not so fortunate. The steering wheel was severed from its shaft on impact and the column driven deep into the gurgling trooper's chest.

Yates fell back in his seat, cuts crisscrossing his face. The bonnet of the Land Rover was steaming.

'Get out!' he roared to the soldiers in the back of the vehicle as he yanked at the passenger door. He made five yards before the explosion, swatted him on to his face, skidding him through the grit.

Two troopers helped him up, their faces shocked and scared. Yates gazed at them blankly while the world slowly settled into place once more. He wondered distractedly why UNIT was recruiting such pale-faced, callow boys into the task force, but then remembered he'd been one once himself. He was sure that, in the Brigadier's eyes, he still was. Then shock and absurd ruminations drained away and he was the trained man of action again as he shook himself free of the well-intentioned soldiers and unholstered his revolver.

'Right! Follow me!'

Action. At last.

He led the five troopers along the path that led from the car park, alongside the silent school and towards the field of stones. Through the gaps in the cedars that fringed the path he could see the mob surging around the mummer band again, and the music was still pumping out into the night air.

Yates could feel it peeling layers of sanity from inside his skull as he ran – or was that just his natural horror at everything he had witnessed today. The five soldiers jogging alongside him were silent, rifles cradled tightly, their boots crunching reassuringly on the gravel of the path.

They reached the stile and Yates didn't hesitate to vault over it, landing amongst the daisies in a defensive stance, revolver levelled. He was scanning the crowd for Jo, but the medley of heaving bodies was so confused he couldn't pick her out. He waited for the others to clear the stile, then set off at a jog towards the crowd, bearing slightly to the right so as to skirt the mob and lead the troopers around to confront the band. He was going to pull the plug on those bastards and it was going to be the most satisfying thing he ever did in his life.

Kane had been watching the proceedings from the edge of the field for some time. He saw the policemen torn apart with abstract amazement. He listened to the band playing and the amazement, the fear, the madness began to level out. He felt a calm steal over him, and he knew peace of mind for the first time in…

For the first time in years.

He gazed at the mummer standing next to the blonde woman, and all his paranoia, all his self-doubt vanished. When you've pissed and puked your way to the bottom of the pile, there's really nowhere left to go, no stone left which hasn't already been lifted and crawled under. Debauchery had betrayed him. It was never as good as it sounded. He had watched people first laugh with him, then laugh at him, then no longer laugh at all. He had been watching himself die without realising it. Now he stood beside a puddle of gore from a ruptured bobby and listened to the music call, and felt suddenly clean. The mummer had seen him, and beckoned him to join him near the big standing-stone behind the band.

Kane began trudging through the field to answer the summons. He ignored the soldiers who leapt over the stile a few hundred yards behind him. His eyes were fixed on the mummer, and for the first time in front of his fellow villagers he could hold his head up high. They parted to let him pass, and there was respect and awe on their faces.

Kane was no longer a bum.

There was the towering barman from his local, the Falcon,

extending a warm hand of friendship. Kane took it, a smug grin on his face. The vicar whose font he'd spat in the other day, here he was now, his dog collar spattered with blood and patting Kane on the back. Ha! My old friend the librarian – don't we go back a long way! Give me a hug you old trout! So many faces that had always despised him, now stepping forward to claim some acquaintanceship with him. And Kane lapping it up as he strode through the crowd, heading for the mummer, jeans crusty with urine, stubbled and wild-eyed, hair dishevelled; he was the sorriest sight you ever saw, and yet tonight he was the big man, apparently. Kane didn't stop to wonder why, he just let it come. Right at the front of the crowd… Cassandra: gorgeous, always aloof, now gazing at him with a lascivious glint in her eye, her cheekbones exquisitely hewn, hair a dark, shining mystery. And she fell into his arms.

'Kane, you're a sodding hero,' she said and kissed him sweetly.

Kane barked with savage laughter and glee.

Every dog has his day.

He crushed her lips with his, squeezing her against him as if he somehow knew he would never get the chance again, and was going to make up for all the lost time – all the pouts and scornful glances, in the pub, in the street; all the sarcastic put-downs that he had always known were hiding some obstinate passion. Time to collect, bitch.

And she tasted *good*.

The crowd roared with approval, and Kane finally lifted his head from her delicate beauty and pushed her firmly away, smacking his lips with the back of his hand as he strolled towards the mummer.

Yates led his troops around the crowd. Nobody tried to intercept them, confounding the captain's expectations after the mob's summary treatment of the token police force. As the UNIT men got nearer the furiously performing band, the hellish noise made Yates feel his head was about to pop open like a nut squeezed in a nutcracker. He halted, lifting up a hand to warn the soldiers. They were in a position to the right of the crowd, behind a standing stone that blocked them from full view of the mummer, who, though he was only twenty yards from them, was apparently not aware of their presence in the field,.

'OK,' he briefed the men, 'we're going to take out the band. You've seen what their influence has caused the crowd to do to those policemen; you don't need me to remind you of all the other atrocities that have taken place probably because of them. I'll handle the mummer.' He turned to a gangly private next to him, whose eyes were wide and scared. Yates sympathised with him; he felt unnerved himself. There was something horribly unnatural about the whole situation.

'Hooper: terminate the singer.'

The private immediately steadied his FN against the standing stone, sighting along the barrel. He fired a quick burst that was only just audible above the din coming from the band. The singer was performing a macabre jig, spiked codpiece thrusting out lewdly. The round caught him full in the chest and hurled him backwards, microphone spinning from his hand. He landed in a thistle patch and lay still. The rest of the band continued to play as if nothing had happened. The mummer turned slowly in their direction.

You're mine, you bastard. Yates aimed his revolver at the gaily coloured figure. The gun coughed in his hand, once, twice, three shots. The mummer jerked as each bullet smacked into him, but did not go down. Yates steadied his arm for a head shot, and delivered it. A rose of dry, ruptured flesh bloomed on the mummer's forehead and he grinned wide, wider. As he grinned, the singer sat up with a sudden movement, his shades still in place. He groped for the microphone and finding it, stood up and lurched towards the mike stand where he slotted the mouthpiece back into place with an almost disgruntled air.

The mummer's grin was impossibly wide now. He looked past the soldiers crouching behind the standing stone, and Yates followed his gaze.

The cattle truck was parked not far from them and now, as the UNIT captain watched, its back doors were opening.

'You've got to be joking!' he hissed incredulously as a group of figures began to descend the ramp. The five troopers stiffened, and one of them dropped his sub-machine-gun with an oath of horror.

Jo saw Yates hiding behind the stone and wondered for a moment how she knew him. She watched as the singer was shot down, his howling momentarily and rudely cut off. Then the word she was groping for popped into her mind just as Sin voiced it for her:

'Pig! It's that pig friend of yours!' the Chinese shouted over the roar of the band.

'No friend of mine. I told you –' Jo began, and then stopped. The mummer was buffeted by bullets from the 'pig's' gun. He was Captain Mike Yates of UNIT, and she was Josephine Grant of the same organisation, assistant to…

The patroniser. The bully. The know-it-all. Yes, she thought uncertainly, that's right. If he were here now, she'd… Sin's hold on her hand became tighter. The Chinese was watching her carefully. On impulse she leant forward and kissed Jo softly on the lips. Her other hand caressed her cheek. In front of them, the singer was back on his feet and continuing his horrible vocals as if he'd merely been heckled.

And Jo remembered all the indignation, all the anger, oh yes, all the hate…

The figures lurched down the ramp and advanced towards the troopers. Five of them, all wearing eighteenth-century clothing: tricorn hats, long dark, rotting overcoats with large brass-buttoned sleeves, leggings and boots with silver buckles. One was wearing the leather mask he must have adopted to perform his roadside chores, the eyeholes revealing dry sockets of bone within. Three of them still bore the remains of the nooses that had hung them around their necks, and all five were carrying long flintlock pistols. Their faces were eaten away by time and the worm; what flesh remained clung precariously to yellowed bone, like lymph peeling from a fresh tattoo. The fists that clutched the pistols were also bereft of skin, and glowed white in the moonlight.

One of the soldiers – the young private who had dropped his weapon – backed away, moaning.

'Private Councell!' Yates barked immediately. 'Stand fast!'

Private Hooper, who had been so ineffective in terminating the singer, spun to confront his superior officer. There was a wet sheen of horror on his face. 'This isn't happening! It *can't* be.'

Yates turned to the trooper and hope flared suddenly inside him. 'You're right, Hooper! This is just an illusion. The mummer's playing with our minds, that's all!' Just suggestive hypnosis, then; and of course Yates was fully aware of similar assaults from the not so distant past. The Keller machine, for one. 'Concentrate, men. Try to clear your minds. Like Hooper said: this isn't happening.'

The leading highwayman levelled his pistol. There was a flash of gunpowder and Hooper was lying on his back in the daisies, a golf ball-sized hole in his forehead.

Yates almost lost it then. Luckily, his training and experience kicked in. 'Fire at will,' he shouted to the four remaining troopers as he aimed his own revolver at the lead 'ghost' and squeezed the trigger.

The chatter of sub-machine-guns tore through the night. The highwaymen from beyond the grave tottered and jerked under the impact of the hail of bullets, and came on.

Yates was still groping for sane answers. Of course, the Keller machine had produced hallucinations that were incredibly real to its victims. They *believed* they were being eaten by rats or drowning, and their belief killed them. If he could somehow convince his men not to believe in these horrors they couldn't be hurt...

The UNIT trooper to his immediate right spun round in a perfect 180 degree turn, his FN dropping from his nerveless fingers, his throat opening up to release a torrent of blood where eighteenth-century shot had ploughed through twentieth-century carotid artery. Helplessly, Yates watched him fall.

Charmagne waited meekly beside the mummer for Kane to reach them. He seemed to be taking his time, enjoying the adulation. She could feel it herself, coming off the crowd, mixed in with the hate vibes. The adulation was confined to just the three of them, she understood that vaguely: the mummer, herself and Kane, and although she didn't fully realise why, a suspicion growing deep in her subconscious was slowly moving to the surface. The hate – and that was by far the stronger of the two emotions streaming from the crowd – was directed at the forces of repression beyond this select gathering. The Establishment, society, the monarchy, any system that inflicted rules and regulations which enforced poverty on one side and riches on another. Even the villagers, some of them comfortably affluent, were joining in the hate party – they'd long forgotten who they were supposed to be reviling. She registered the electric animosity and it made her feel indefinably strong. Over to her left, she could see the soldiers battling with the uncanny representatives of wealth-redistribution, and it moved her to smile. With all the hate directed at them from the maddened crowd and embodied in those walking cadavers, the troopers didn't stand a cat's chance in hell.

She wondered for a moment how she came to be standing in a field of ancient stones with a furious crowd in front of her and a man dressed as a seventeenth-century mummer next to her. She wondered, too, who she was. The answer to both questions didn't matter, so she let them go. A vague memory of stumbling around in endless dark troubled her, but gazing into the mummer's bizarre, bottomless eyes wiped the fear from her mind. The moon reassured her too – it was so serene and beautiful. Kane reached them, and though she had never seen him before she felt instinctively that she knew him, and that it was right he should be with them. She smiled, and he grinned wolfishly in return.

* * *

Kane reached for the blonde woman's hand. It was something he felt he should do. It was like finding a long-lost sister or a best friend he hadn't seen for years, although he was quite certain they had never met before. She was beautiful, and yet he felt no sexual desire for her. He stood beside her and faced the crowd. He beamed at the strange mummer man, who walked forward to take his free hand and then Charmagne's forming a little circle of three. There was a name floating distantly in his mind, and it carried a rag of fear with it. Rag? Yes, Ragman. What was that? It was gone. It was nothing. So was the fear.

The mummer smiled wildly at Charmagne. 'Orphan no more: you too are my descendant. You are both children of my loins and well matched: a yearning for truth and change in the fair one, a lust for despoiling in the foul one.' He swung his head so that the grin covered Kane, and then faced the journalist again. 'Unlike your distant blood kin who stands beside you, stinking of his own excesses, *your* forefathers wandered far from the birthplace of your *disgraceful* lineage – now 'tis time to come home.' His words were clear even over the roar of the band. 'You two shall live and spawn alone. In a *new* world filled with the children of the Great Leveller. In a kingdom of rags.'

Kane didn't really understand the words, and yet at the same time they made perfect sense. He smiled, to show he was with the dude spiritually. He looked at Charmagne and it didn't surprise or frighten him to see her eyes were grey as pebbles. From the way she was staring at him, something similar had probably happened to his.

And now he could really *feel* the throbbing of the stone behind them, stronger than all the others in the field pumped by the ley lines. The stone… the *lodestone*… he knew what it was, and again he did not know how, or why.

Like a grotesque wedding band celebrating the union of Kane and Charmagne, the resurrected punk mummers played on….

The travellers had taken possession of Stonehenge. They were in, through the gap the burning camper van had left, and now they were celebrating. It was half an hour to midnight, the summer solstice was imminent and they had beaten the army. They cheered and roared and flung rocks at the soldiers who didn't know whether to advance after them into the megalithic circle or remain where they were.

The Brigadier stood beside his command jeep and watched their confusion. His walkie-talkie was in his hand, but he didn't need it. He had enough men; he knew what to do. The folded orders were tucked away in his pocket and they could stay there – he didn't need them either.

He witnessed the frenzy of violence in front of him, saw his soldiers awaiting instructions as they attempted to re-form the cordon around the flaming hulk of the camper van.

'These filthy deviants are attacking the *queen* when they attack us!' he bellowed to Sergeant Benton, who stood indecisively next to him. 'They're trying to bring down everything our country stands for! Give the order to fire at will, man!'

Benton grinned happily and turned to Corporal Robinson. She had already heard and immediately trotted towards the cordon, unslinging her own FN with alacrity.

She pushed past two troopers and let off a burst of staccato fire before bothering to pass on the command. Two punks who were lobbing rocks in their direction went down like mown wheat. Sheer joy flashed across her face. 'Fire at will!' she bawled into the momentary silence that greeted the shooting. 'Kill the bastards. Kill *all* the stinking, idle bastards!' She was loosing off another round before she finished shouting. A tight knot of hippies and heavy-metal warriors danced a macabre jig of death as the FN round cut through them. Robinson let out a long tribal war scream as she kept the trigger depressed, hosing the scum with bullets:

'DIIIIIIIIIIIIIIIIIIIIIIIIIIIIIIIIIIIIIIIIIIIIIEEEEEEEEEEEE!!!!!!!!!!!!'

The travellers surged forward, into the swathe of gunfire, not caring, tyre irons, knives, rocks all held aloft and ready to use. The distance between the two forces closed. The UNIT soldiers who were still forming a cordon on the other side of the monument advanced between the trilithons, forming a pincer movement with the travellers in the middle, firing as they came, blasting the hippies and punks from behind.

The travellers tore into the soldiers ahead of them and the mummer's wishes reached fruition. Army and hippies, the law and the lawless, locked in combat: the ultimate clash.

Microcosm of a sliding society with the mummer as its gleeful patriarch.

Through a gap in the surging crowd Sin could see Nick, still sitting against a stone not far from the band. She laughed wildly. Got what you deserved, you bastard! That'll teach you to lose your heart to the heartless. Gonna wind up dead, son, that's what your mother should have told you when you started seeing me. Dead as coffin nails.

Don't look so bloody disapproving now, do you? She laughed again, and her heart was black.

The band played a thousand-mile-an-hour hate ballad just for her, and she was sure the singer had announced it as 'The Song of Sin and Her Fool', before the guitarist fired his manic riffs into the audience and the drummer released his own special kind of thunder.

Yates and his three surviving troopers backed away from the advancing highwaymen. The captain was almost out of ammo, and his men were on the point of breaking. He could see it in Private Councell's face. The soldier was shaking and not aiming his FN properly – and even when he did, the bullets had no effect on the ghosts from another age. The shots tore away patches of rotting cloth and sent chips of bone into the air but certainly didn't deter the corpses in their implacable march.

'Make for the trees!' Yates barked, firing his last round into the nearest cadaver. The bullets slapped away the tricorn hat leaving a grinning skull wrapped with white strands of hair bare to the elements, but did little else. The ghoul lurched closer and Yates could see a knot of worms twisting in one eye socket. The ancient flintlock lifted to point at him and he dodged wildly aside, pulling at Private Councell to follow him.

He was too late: the highwayman pulled the rotting noose from around its own neck and flipped it over Councell's. It pulled tight and the private collapsed to his knees choking, his FN dropping into the buttercups.

Yates paused, then dived for the weapon, rolling and coming up firing, all in one agile, practised movement. The round tore through the bony face, unfastening the robber's leather mask and drilling away its grinning teeth. The monster carried on choking Councell, ignoring the bullets even when the ferocity of the live round dug through its spine and lifted its head away entirely, blasting it into a thistle patch. The headless gallows thing simply tugged harder.

Yates' gritted his teeth and continued firing. Councell's face was purple, his hands digging at the rope biting into his neck. His tongue was flopping grotesquely. From the corner of one eye Yates saw Private Whitcombe go down, a hole in his chest smoking from a flintlock shot. When he saw Councell's head nod forward and his eyes lock on nothing, he ceased firing and ran. Ahead of him he could see the last surviving trooper dashing for the elm trees at the edge of the field. As he watched a hole puffed open in the soldier's back, catapulting him into a bed of nettles. Yates passed him at a zigzag run, expecting to feel hot agony in his own spine at any second.

They're only a mirage they're only a mirage they're...

He darted a frantic look over his shoulder.

The mirages were still coming.

Captain Yates, what a fraud. He's running away from ghosts. Always thought you were a bit wet, Mike. Even when I was flirting with you, you big girl's blouse.

Jo could see him dashing frantically towards the edge of the field. What a prat. If he'd had any nouse, he'd have torn his uniform off and joined them in their Hate Day celebrations. The solstice was imminent, and solstices always meant something weird, didn't they? Midnight would unleash the dogs of war assuredly. She would be dancing at their snapping heels.

She glanced at Sin. The Chinese girl looked gorgeous and lethal and Jo wanted to kiss her again. Sin released her hand while she groped for a cigarette, and then hunched forward to light it, and in the space where her head had been Jo could see right through the crowd, and over to where Nick sat slumped against a stone.

Nick was the voice of dissent, wasn't he? And that's what happened to people who didn't stand in line.

She frowned. That didn't make sense. They were all fighting for the right *not* to have to stand in line, weren't they? Why did she suddenly feel so confused and…

Alone?

The band had paused between songs. The guitarist's strings had snapped like spider threads and he was stoically fixing them, while the singer spat into the crowd impatiently and the mummer stood in a circle with his two chosen ones.

Jo remembered that she was supposed to hate and, for a very brief moment, wondered why.

The door of the police box opened.

The Doctor didn't look up at first. It would only be another phantom from his brain, here to torment him. He felt so very old and tired. Perhaps he was on the brink of regeneration.

Regeneration?

That was just another cheating memory. Another delusion. He was a mad old man dressed like Noel Coward, sitting hunched in a police box. That was it. No Daleks, no Cybermen. There never had been, and never would be. They were simply the products of a crazy, deluded mind. His own.

'Doctor?'

The visitor had spoken. Still he did not look up. It sounded like a young girl. He knew *who* it sounded like, but then she didn't exist either. She was like the Master and the autons. And, just like them, she'd come to terrorise this poor old man.

'Doctor, *please*…'

There was a broken sob in the plea that was so familiar. Don't look up – it'll only strengthen the delusion.

Don't look up.

'We need you, Doctor.' She sounded desperate, forlorn. Terrified.

He raised his head and looked at Jo.

She was standing over him inside the cramped confines of the police box. He blinked at her dazedly.

'Go away!' he snapped.

She knelt down before him, eyes wide and tearful.

'But we really *need* you. Everything's going horribly wrong.'

'Yes. Well, it usually does, doesn't it? And then I come along and fix it. Well, not this time, my dear.'

'Why not?' she sobbed. 'What's happened to you?'

'Perhaps I've woken up. Perhaps I don't want to play any more. Perhaps I just want to go home.' He thought for a minute. 'Wherever that is.'

'You've got to help us, just like you always do. You can't give up now. The world's gone bad. The monsters are here… Doctor, *the monsters are loose in England*.'

The Doctor smirked. 'Thinking parochially as ever, eh, Jo? England's not the centre of the universe you know. The fate of the cosmos does not hang on the fate of the home counties.'

'Wiltshire, actually, Doctor. And maybe, this time it does.'

He looked at her carefully. She seemed real, her tears and her anxiety, at least. 'Did *he* send you?'

'Who?'

'The one who calls himself the Great Leveller. The ragged fellow.'

Jo smiled. 'Then you remember. So you'll know you have to come.'

The Ragman. Perceptual vortex. The TARDIS. Gallifrey. Daleks. They *could* be real. There was just the slightest chance they could be. The thought filled him with hope.

'Jo?'

'Yes, Doctor?'

'We always win, don't we?'

She smiled again. 'Yes, Doctor.'

His hope faded. 'That's not very realistic, is it? Then it's just like I feared: a dream within a dream. And so are you.'

The telephone rang. He jerked his head towards it.

'You should answer that,' Jo said, wiping away her tears. 'It might be important.'

The Doctor let it ring. 'And it might be another dream. Another shade.'

Jo plucked the receiver from its cradle and passed it to him. The Doctor took it reluctantly.

'Hello,' he said carefully.

Jo vanished. The Doctor didn't even notice. 'Yes,' he said into the mouthpiece. 'If you're sure. Very well.' He pulled himself stiffly to his feet, hung up the receiver and pushed open the police-box door.

Outside it was dark, but he could see the faint outlines of moonlight around the back doors of the cattle truck. He pressed his hand against one. It wasn't locked. He was about to push them apart when they began to move outwards of their own accord, slowly, creaking with protest. He hesitated.

The guitarist had fixed his strings. The mummer gestured agitatedly at the band and the four undead punk minstrels launched into another atrocity ballad.

Jo blinked at them, and her confusion vanished.

At Stonehenge the law and the lawless tore into each other with renewed ferocity. The moon swung over the mayhem, and blood splashed on the sarsens.

* * *

Midnight. The witching hour, and now it was a new day. The mummer gazed across the sea of frenzied heads before him and released the hands of his two 'children'. He stepped slowly backwards, nearer to the lodestone, his birthstone. Not too close. He was only too aware that the shock waves he was divining could consume him now that the morphic fires were stoked to their fiercest intensity. He felt the pull, felt the waves of power rippling through him. His vision turned red: everything, the trees, the stones, the grass, the travellers, villagers – all red. The beasts of anarchy were about to be released upon the land. Already he could hear their snarling.

Yates ducked behind a dead elm as gunpowder ignited and bark flew from the trunk next to his face. The highwaymen were still shambling onwards, steadfastly reloading their ancient weapons with balls and ramrods, grinning their yellowed bony grins as they came. Yates found himself contemplating the surreal nature of the scene: five rotting corpses dressed in Dick Turpin outfits lumbering through buttercups in the moonlight with the bodies of modern-day UNIT troopers stretched out in death at their feet. He shook his head. He mustn't lose himself in the dream. They'd destroyed the Keller machine and its Pandora's box of phantoms. All he needed to do was destroy whatever was producing *these* horrors of the mind.

It was no good running. He had to confront this head-on. The mummer was the answer. And if he didn't respond to bullets, perhaps he'd respond to an honest to God grenade.

The trouble was the only one carrying grenades was Private Hooper, and he'd been the first to bite the thistles.

Yates took another look around the tree trunk. The shuffling highwayghosts were twenty yards away. If he ran fast and resumed his zigzag gait, he might be able to dodge them and their flintlocks and maybe reach Hooper's body unmolested. Maybe.

A branch exploded above his head as another eighteenth-century weapon discharged itself angrily.

And maybe it would have been a hell of a lot easier if he'd used his head earlier and ordered Hooper to use his grenades straight away. But then maybe that was why he had never made major. Hell, maybe he was being too hard on himself. Maybe there were too many maybes.

He leapt out from the cover of the trees and started his suicidal flight back across the field. If his actions surprised the ghost-killers, they showed no signs of it. They simply loaded their pistols unhurriedly, cocked them, and fired.

The back doors of the truck were opening. Jo sucked in her breath with expectation. The band's music filled her head, squeezing it with vice power. Her excitement was back. The thrill of the hate. And it was quite possible in that blasting storm of sound to hate *everyone*. And everything. She began to dance, wildly, crazily, still clutching Sin's hand. All around her the crowd was succumbing to the same urge. The songs told her of artifice falling and brutal honesty rising. She welcomed the beasts of anarchy with open arms, and yes, she too could hear them howl.

Wasn't it beautiful?

Chapter Twenty

Yates had made it past the first highway robber. The killer swerved to track him and the captain felt a noose flick past the skin of his face. He threw himself to one side as the barrel of a flintlock loomed before his vision and the powder exploded. He was running, dodging, throwing himself into somersaults, leaping up again. Another ghoul barred his way, the barrel swinging up, and Yates had never seen a muzzle so huge. It became the centre of his universe. Instead of ducking aside he hurled himself directly towards that huge dark circle.

He crashed into the bony robber and together they bounced into the grass. Yates rolled frantically, twisted the flintlock from the skeletal paw and thrust the long, rusting barrel between the fleshless jaws of his assailant. He pulled the brittle trigger and the CRACK of gunpowder igniting was the most honest and exciting sound of weaponry he had ever heard.

He was crouching astride the cadaver, smoking flintlock in his hand, and he had never felt so *vital*, so much like a soldier in all his life. It was truly exhilarating.

Then he looked up from the shattered skull beneath him and saw the mummer standing before his stone, arms rising up into the air, and he remembered Jo and that he had a job to do.

The highwaything was still wriggling beneath him, although most of its bony head was scattered amongst the daisies. Yates leapt away from it and recommenced his dash towards Hooper's body.

Five yards away, and he felt his left shoulder tugged violently while searing pain bit through him simultaneously. The roar of the flintlock that had inflicted the pain came an instant later, it seemed. He was slapped forward by the impact, rolling through a bed of nettles that stung his cheeks. He came to a rest lying right next to Hooper. The private's face was turned towards him, eyes bulging, mouth open, as if to say: *Get us out of this one, sir.*

Yates lay there for a moment clutching his shoulder and moaning. Sweat oozed down his face. It felt like a sharp pole had been rammed through his deltoid muscle. He wanted to just lie there and forget everything. All he could concentrate on was the pain.

Get up you wet bastard! You'll never make major like this. GET UP!

Yates gaped at Hooper. For a crazy second or two he was sure the private had spoken the words. Nope: just another delusion, Mikey-boy. It was his own voice, seeming so detached from him because of the pain. He struggled to sit up, and almost fainted as red agony ripped at his muscle like the claws of a panther. He screwed his eyes shut. When he opened them the highwaymen were closer.

I've got a job to do. I've got a job to do. If he kept repeating it like a mantra, he just might be able to get to his feet. Hooper's body jerked while the captain searched through his knapsack. Yates choked: he was sure the dead private was getting up to join him; then he realised it was flintlock shot that was buffeting the corpse.

Now he was on his feet, and although the world was swaying and blurring he had a grenade in each hand. And boy, was he going to use them.

The back doors were open.

Jo looked to the horizon beyond the sparse elms marking the boundary of the field, and she could see the towers of London, situated surreally on the range of hills that normally displayed the white horse. She stopped dancing and pointed for Sin to share the view, to witness the capital's tourist sites spiking up from the moonlit grass, as if she could not trust her own vision. The GPO tower, Big Ben, the Houses of Parliament and, there, the grim Tower itself, all jumbled together and surrounded by rolling Wiltshire countryside. Jo could see that the white horse was still there, under the buildings. It was champing and tossing under the burden, and look! the towers were falling down...

Falling down…

My fair…

The horse was no longer a chalk outline but a massive skeleton that reared up from the fabric of the hill and bucked with fury. Big Ben took a dive. A giant equine skull threw the tall clock into a pile of rubble that slid down the hillside. The Houses of Parliament collapsed in a slow cascade of rubble. Immense hooves kicked backwards and the GPO tower teetered and was no more.

'It's all falling to pieces…' Sin hissed in Jo's ear, '… gloriously.' And the band played a death knell at one hundred miles an hour, the singer chuckling and jigging on the spot.

The Tower of London was no more. The skeletal horse danced wildly across the spine of the hill, huge, empty eye sockets scanning the world for chaos, gaping bony mouth champing, champing, and then it was sinking back into the grass and soil and again becoming a chalk outline and nothing more.

'The beasts of anarchy,' sighed Jo.

'Come to play, baby,' Sin laughed. Jo joined in the laughter.

The mummer gestured at the rubble that littered the moonlit hills. Kane and Charmagne gazed at the spectacle, their eyes grey as stone, still holding hands.

The mummer was pointing in a different direction now, and suddenly the elm trees on the edge of the field were bearing strange fruit. Jo had to squint to make out the figures hanging from the branches in the darkness, but it was worth the effort.

Sin squealed with delight. 'I will die happy knowing I saw this day. And so will many more.'

Jo was grinning from ear to ear.

The entire royal family was turning slowly in the night breeze, dangling from nooses. There the princess, so fond of dancing on the grave of the deprived; there the queen, gurning sourly with rigor mortis. There other feckless princes, born to squander, born to leech, purple-faced, greeting their subjects with lolling tongues rather than regal waves of the hand.

'Parasites!' spat Sin. The band had turned to play to their new, albeit, dead audience. The power chords seemed to make the royal corpses twitch and spasm, as if they were jerking along to the rhythm of the damned.

Jo began to dance again, hand in hand with the lustrous-haired Sin. This was the final number of the night, they knew that instinctively. It was gone midnight and the Doctor had been right all along: the band *was* playing them all the way to hell.

And she'd never felt so good in all her life.

It was then the Doctor stepped down from the back of the cattle truck.

The first grenade tore one of the highwaymen messily in half. The top part of the torso rose eerily into the night sky before flumping down on top of one of the standing stones, where it lay, balanced precariously. The cocked hat rolled in the grass at Yates' feet. The flintlock landed next to some sheep droppings. The lower torso remained standing, dust streaming from the midsection.

Yates frowned at the gruesome sight, clutching the other grenade indecisively. Should he use it on the other corpses, or save it for the mummer? He threw a look over the field towards the band and the wildly cavorting crowd. No contest. Time to ice the mummer. He lurched away from the highwaymen, wincing at the pain from his ruined left shoulder. Take out the leader and the mirages would go too. That was the plan. It seemed like a very sensible one too.

Jo and Sin turned as if somehow sensing that the Doctor was there, behind them. The band, too, whirled away from their royal performance to face this new arrival.

When the mummer swung around there was a devilish snarl on his face.

The band stopped playing, their chords of violence no longer required: the crowd were loaded with enough ley-hate power.

Travellers and villagers alike stared as one at the frilly man who dared.

Who *dared*.

'Ragman…' the Doctor said.

It was hand-to-hand combat now. The filth and the fury. And which was which, and who was who? Throats were torn out, eyes gouged. Corporal Hannah Robinson snapped the neck of a hippie from behind, leapt over his body and on to the next. She could see Benton wrestling with a green-haired good-for-nothing, a savage grin plastered on his face. Behind her she could hear the roars of the Brigadier in full, demented battle cry.

'Take them all down!! By the gods, terminate the bloody lot of 'em!!'

She laughed like a berserker as she ran for a fat-bellied oaf in a straining Hawkwind T-shirt. 'Wanna Silver Machine, freak?' she spat, pulling her broad-bladed army knife from its belt and slamming it home through the gap-toothed bastard's neck. 'Take a ride on that beauty!'

This was sheer heaven. Or if it was hell, then her Sunday School teacher had got it *badly* wrong all those years ago.

Hell was a good-time place. She only regretted it had taken her so long to get here.

'What can you do, frilly man? The Beasts of Anarchy have already escaped.'

The mummer gestured at the hills surrounding the village and the field of stones. Huge, vague shapes capered and frolicked darkly against the slightly paler night skies. Ferocious howls reached the field faintly, and, just audible over the chaos, an insane, echoing piping, picking up where the band had finished off.

'More illusions and falsehoods?' the Doctor asked, stepping through the crowd that parted willingly enough. He felt the fierce, primal energy pulsing from the ley lines beneath his feet and concentrated in the lodestone behind the mummer; reeled from the resulting vibe of utter antipathy that sparked from the people.

'It's what they want to see; it's what they expect. Anarchy must have a form, Time Lord, even if it exists only in their heads.' The crowd was silent, still gazing blankly at the Doctor. He saw Jo as he passed, and put out a hand to touch her cheek. She flung it away from him and he moved on, approaching the gaily clothed mummer.

The band waited for further instruction, their instruments drooping. The Doctor paused before the singer, then abruptly plucked the wraparound sunglasses from the shaggy head. Maggots frothed from empty sockets, ghostly pale in the moonlight. The Doctor replaced the shades and walked past Charmagne, past Kane.

He reached the mummer. The piping continued, becoming louder as the cavorting creatures thundered down from the hills, prancing and dancing over the ruins of London as they came.

'Civilisation's end,' the mummer said.

'Reality-wound, to be exact,' the Doctor answered matter of factly. 'Bleeding from the open doors of your little perceptual vortex over there.'

'Vain one, I could pluck your spine through your velvet trappings and fling it to the crowd,' the mummer said, relishing his own words.

'You could,' replied the Doctor bravely. 'So why haven't you done so?'

'Perhaps I enjoy the theatricality of duelling with you, egotistical one. I trust your Time Lord friends called for you across the gulf of space, and rescued you from your mental wanderings? Be they frightened of what I shall bring to their homeworld in time? 'Tis well they are afraid. But first, there is you. Why have I not squashed you as yet? Perhaps I like to play fair. You are alone: slaughtering you alone would not be fair. Someone will be along to help you soon.'

his head briefly. He could see Yates
...ross the field. He put up a hand to warn the
...the UNIT man paused.

The Doctor turned his head briefly. He could see Yates staggering painfully across the field. He put up a hand to warn the captain away and the UNIT man paused.

'You want fairness, do you, Ragman? How can that be, when you're everything that's foul? Let's see you as you really are: drop the pretension that you claim to detest so much. Let your children see their real father.'

'You be wise, despite your appearance, frivolous one. You have guessed the nature of my seed children – both descended from the same unfortunate wench.' And here the mummer sniggered lasciviously. 'You want to see my true appearance. Why? It is not new to you.'

The Doctor could sense the anger of the crowd growing the more he taunted the mummer, and the electric hate in the air was making him feel faint. Yet he held his ground as beads of sweat appeared on his brow and his hearts began to race against each other as if to see which would be the first to burst.

'But it will be new to those to whom you lie,' he replied firmly.

'Lies?' the mummer hissed. 'I am here to *destroy* lies.'

'Then show them your real face, Great Pretender.' The Doctor placed his hands on his hips defiantly. He paused, then threw his final barb. 'Ah, but then, you can't, can you? Resuming your natural morphic form would make you too vulnerable to the pull of your birthstone. You might get sucked back into it. But, by that logic, you can't amplify those same forces to the degree needed to blanket the world in antipathy *unless* you retreat into your morphic state. Am I wrong?'

The mummer's response was merely a snarling laugh. As if unperturbed by the Doctor's intuitiveness, his body glowed a lurid green colour – and the hideous shape of the Ragman stood hunched and spindly before the crowd. The slow-worm hair lifted evilly, the grey head slowly surveyed the faces of his ragamuffin disciples. One thin arm rose and gestured to the hillsides where distorted black shapes still cavorted to the whistling of discordant pipes. The moon was hanging low over the horizon, and its face was the Ragman's, blood dripping from crooked jaws and falling to the fields below where the bones of civilisation lay scattered. With each drop that fell a baby screamed in agony, the sound seemingly drifting from far away, yet simultaneously clear and distinct as if from over the next hedge.

'Let it be,' the Ragman said. 'Your plutocratic society has crumbled away. Children of the shameful are dying upon birth. There will *be* no more children, but those of the Leveller.'

'You don't want a world changed for the better, Ragman. You just want a world run in *your* image. The ultimate vanity.' The Doctor turned to Kane and Charmagne. 'Look upon your "father", see the lies, the pretence. They are worse than any you've suffered in this society.' He strode forward and seized Kane by the shoulder. '*Look at him!*'

Kane turned slowly, looked at the Ragman, blinked. Blinked again. His eyes momentarily resumed their natural colour then flicked back to grey rock.

The Doctor grasped Charmagne's hand, swung her round to face the 'mummer' in his natural state. 'You're a tyrant: a selfish egomaniac embodying everything these people want to destroy,' the Doctor continued, waving an arm towards the travellers, the punks, the hippies, the Rastas. 'You're a morphic monstrosity; a mutation of cosmic spew and human indignities. You *are* scum, Ragman. Real scum from the end of time. And your time's surely run out, because I don't think your children want to play any more. They've had enough of your tyranny.'

The Doctor's eyes narrowed as the Ragman looked from Kane to Charmagne and the nest of worms coiled furiously on his bald rock-head. 'They're the only ones you're scared of, isn't that right, Ragman? Like most children, there comes a time when they grow older and want to disobey the rules – challenge authority! *Your* authority. Maybe they have a little of their father in them… maybe just enough to stop even you.'

Charmagne released Kane's hand and her eyes were almost human, albeit with a grey shade. She glared at the Ragman with reawoken horror. 'You're not my father,' she said quietly. The horror smouldered into rage. *'You're not my father!'* She lunged towards the Ragman.

The Ragman twitched his sharp-fingered hand towards one of the roadies standing at the fringe of the crowd. The biker was still clutching a pitchfork with which he had repeatedly stabbed the corpse of one of the policemen, as if to check the lawman really was dead or perhaps simply because he enjoyed doing it. Now he swiftly interposed himself between Charmagne and the alien, holding the tool warningly across his chest.

Charmagne thrust him aside with one hand. The roadie spilled at the Ragman's feet like a toy flung away by an impatient child. She grinned in her rage, feeling the newly acquired alien strength garnered from the lodestone. She swung the pitchfork up and rammed the tines through the alien's grey neck in one agile movement.

The crowd moaned.

Trickles of dust sprang from the wounds as Charmagne withdrew the pitchfork. The Ragman backed away a step, teetering slightly as he felt the pull from the stone behind him. His mouth worked vilely, and again he beckoned. This time a young woman stepped forward from the crowd and wordlessly approached Charmagne. The Doctor recognised her immediately.

Sin.

The Chinese girl stood in front of the Ragman, facing Charmagne defensively. The Doctor opened his mouth to call out to Nick's erstwhile lover – but the name froze on his lips because it was already too late.

Charmagne hardly noticed this new barrier to her fury. The pitchfork went back, then forward with brute, alien-spawned power. The long tines passed easily through Sin's chest, impaling her against the Ragman. Blood mingled with the dust pooling at their feet.

Sin's eyes opened wide. Wider. Her hands flew up to grasp the pitchfork sunk deep inside her. Now her eyes were filled not so much with pain, but with realisation, and loss, and the horror of true regret. Her mouth opened. Blood blossomed from her perfect, sensuous lips. Her head swung painfully to one side as she searched for something… someone. Maybe she found what she was looking for. Maybe she didn't.

She said one word, so quiet, surely no one could hear it. She said: 'Nick…' And then she died.

From the crowd a scream. Jo's.

The Ragman backed away one more step. Sin's body slumped to the grass.

Charmagne stared, without understanding, at what she had done.

Then the night lit up and the air screamed.

Yates had arrived.

His aim was not good, however, due to the impedimental effect of his wound and the grenade that was destined for the Ragman only reached as far as the band, still waiting immobile and silent. After the blast, the singer and the bass player picked themselves up as if they'd been hit with pillows rather than highly concentrated explosives. The bassist had lost his shades upon the impact, and one arm. He didn't look too bothered, but then he had no eyes to express much emotion. His instrument lay at his feet.

Yates collapsed on the grass, near-unconscious from pain.

The crowd was stirring. Bewildered cries arose. Faces were shocked and afraid. The roadies stumbled towards the band as if waking from a dream, not knowing what should come next. One of them seized the guitarist, shook him slightly. The Ragman laughed gutturally, dismissively. Immediately, the guitarist wilted and the roadie was holding an empty minstrel sleeve. Beneath the pile of deflated mummer clothes, filling the leather boots – dust, and nothing more. Dust and shades. The guitar stuck up out of the dust dune like a flag. Behind it, the drums bore drifts of grey particles, the stool supported tatters and nothing more. The bass player was gone, drifting in the night breeze, not even bones to mark his fall. The singer remained. He tottered forward, seized the roadie by the neck, barked with mad laughter, and tore his throat apart as effortlessly as if he was ripping open a crisp packet.

'Join the Unwashed,' he croaked, 'Join the Unforgiving…' His shades tumbled from his eye sockets as his face fell inwards. Then he was boots, codpiece and a heap of dust on the grass.

Dust and no more.

The Doctor witnessed the scene without making any moves. If he was surprised by the Ragman's callous dismissal of his resurrected punk mummers, he didn't show it. If the act was one of defiant perverse bravado, it didn't impress him. Nor did it seem to impress the crowd. A shout went up from a punk:

'Freak!'

Others rallied to the war cry until it became a furious chorus.

'FREAK!!!!!'

The hate was still there, but now it was being diverted, redirected towards the one who had led them to this false night of blood and terror. Punks and hippies, Rastas and bikers – villagers too – hurled themselves forward.

The Ragman let them come.

The Doctor was pushed roughly aside. 'Wait,' he tried to shout. 'This isn't the way.'

The crowd had hold of the Ragman. They bore him aloft like an ugly banner, and then they began to tear him. He was in the claws of a pack of animals, not a gathering of humans. They wanted blood.

They got dust.

Billows of the grey stuff. Clouds. The head was ripped away and dust fountained from the neck. Arms came away like action-man limbs with more jets of crumbling grit. The torso was flung aside and the crowd, momentarily appeased, fell silent. Jo stumbled through the crush, seeking the Doctor.

The distant piping ceased. The shadowy abominations stopped their dancing, disappeared altogether. The rubble of London was also gone. The white horse slumbered in mid-gallop under the serene moonlight.

Jo fell against the Doctor, sobbing pitifully – just as the Ragman's head commenced rolling through the grass, hopped on to the severed neck of the torso and opened its mouth in a sick grin. The severed limbs wriggled in a similar ambition to join the parent body. The Ragman rose before the crowd, complete. The slow-worms twisted with malevolent laziness.

'You would challenge me?' the being hissed. He waved one arm in a cutting gesture. Several travellers hit the grass like wheat before a scythe, and did not move again. *You would challenge ME?* His mouth opened wide in thwarted, insane fury.

Kane was gaping at the Ragman with open disgust. Hate blazed in his semigrey eyes. 'You're back,' he snarled, stepping forward. In his mind it was no longer the alien standing before him, but his old enemy. The one with the crawling jar. It had always been him. It would always be Simon.

'I thought I got rid of you…'

The Ragman's boulder-head swivelled, and the worms wilted on to the scalp like seaweed drooping after a retreating wave. Then the mummer was back, bright minstrel streamers, mummer's cap, straw-like spiky hair. But now the depthless eyes were wary, the grin not so self-assured.

'I led you, my child,' the mummer wheedled. 'You belong to me: look – it is your minstrel friend, your Pied Piper come to lead you to a better place.'

Kane wasn't listening. Hands out-thrust, he launched himself at the mummer, who reeled back from the mighty shove and flailed against the pulsing lodestone immediately behind him. The rock glowed hungrily in response, and an unearthly scream came from the mummer's shark-like mouth. The being struggled forward again, as if from the brink of a precipice. His scream became a gurgle, then a snarl.

Kane wasn't done. 'There ain't no better place, boy,' he said calmly, 'at least, not for the likes of me.' He grabbed the mummer's head and slammed it hard against the standing stone. Dust puffed from the cracked skull like spores squirting from a burst puffball.

The mummer's head drooped as if the alien were stunned, and then the being was the Ragman again, tatters wrapped around a gaunt, grey body. His true body, his most *vulnerable* body.

As if realising this, Kane shoved again. In a state of flux created by the Ragman's own orchestrations the rock opened greedily to receive its former prisoner. Kane turned his head briefly, looking back towards Cirbury as if ironically acknowledging all those who had always stood by him throughout his life – all the countless friends and supporters who were there for him now. He didn't see Cassandra begin to approach him, one hand outstreched. Then he shrugged stoically and threw his arms around the Ragman, propelling both of them inside the gaping red maw of the living rock.

A scream shrilled briefly, then was cut off like an echo shut away in a box. For ever.

The stone was just a stone again. A grey standing stone, in a field of grey standing stones.

Charmagne sat down on the grass, her eyes staring vacantly at the crowd, eyes that were dazed but absolutely blue.

Jo lifted her head away from the Doctor's frilly chest, and her eyes fell first of all upon Sin's body, and then upon Nick's hunched against a standing stone as if waiting for the sun.

'What have we done?' She thumped the Doctor's chest ineffectually. 'How did it come to *this*?'

The Doctor stroked her head but said nothing. There wasn't an awful lot he *could* say.

A grey, dismal dawn found Brigadier Alaistair Lethbridge-Stewart striding through the battlefield that was Stonehenge. Probably for the first time in his life, he was wondering why he had become a soldier.

Bodies were strewn everywhere. Between the bluestones, on top of each other, draped over UNIT jeeps.

Everywhere.

UNIT troopers, hippies, punks – the numbers of the dead were roughly equal on both sides. The living staggered away from the site of so much hate and fury, eyes locked and strange.

Dazed and confused.

The Brigadier paused in the centre of the ancient monument, surveying the carnage. At his feet lay Corporal Hannah Robinson, eyes wide and scared, mouth frozen in a hate rictus. Her hands were fastened tightly around the throat of the chief roadie, whose hands in turn were clasped around a knife buried deep in the corporal's chest. The Brigadier heard a scuffle of boots and glanced up.

Benton stood dishevelled and bleary beside him. The Brigadier found he could not meet his sergeant's eyes, and dropped his glance. Another first. Benton stumbled away, his right sleeve ripped and soaked with blood.

The lawless survivors – hippies and punks, Rastas, bikers, outlaws and outsiders – staggered away from the stone circle, and towards an uncertain future.

Cassandra found herself unable to leave the standing stone. Her right hand played softly over its uneven surface, as if trying to trace an outline. An outline of a face.

'He's still there,' she said to nobody. 'I can *see him*.'

Jo was bandaging Captain Yates's shoulder, but paused to look up. She wondered who the strange dark-haired beauty was, and what she thought she could see in the lodestone. It was just a rock.

Nothing to see.

'He was so full of hate,' Cassandra said, stroking the rock more passionately.

'The summer of hate's all over now.'

Cassandra turned, tears tracking down her cheeks. The Doctor smiled kindly at her, then addressed the travellers who were still milling around the field, shocked and horrified and above all very, very confused.

'You can all go home now,' he said.

The travellers stared stupidly back at him.

The Doctor rubbed his chin, realising what he had just said. Jo joined him, putting an arm around his waist, seeking comfort in her loneliness. He smiled sadly at her…

'I know exactly how they feel,' he said.

Overhead, storm clouds were gathering blackly. The first few drops were already beginning to fall.

On the distant hillside, the white horse waited patiently for the rain.

Acknowledgements

To Mum and Dad for putting up with me when I was bad, for NOT disowning me when I was 12, and for everything really. It can't be fun to pick up your son from a police cell, Dad, but you were great about it. But am I still good for nothing, Mum? Two books out doesn't change that, surely? Lazy Bones sitting in the sun...

To Tash: Sorry. For everything. But your mum always said I was no good. Thanks for standing by me.

To Justin Richards for his incredible enthusiasm and great suggestions.

To Aleanna Mason for the brilliant cover design inspiration.

To Johnny R for the attitude, and to Sidney for showing me the mayhem.

To the Anti-Nowhere League for being an uncontrollable Beast of a band, and for giving me beer when I was young and alone. Jesus giving water to Ben Hur ...? Okay, perhaps not.

To the Damned, of course, for 20 years of anarchy, chaos and destruction, and for finally writing new songs.

To Syd for showing me how to Flame, and for taking me on Interstellar Overdrive too many times. Come back, come back...

To the real Dead Boys: Sid (again), Stiv, Malcolm, and my old mate Jason. (Ten years ago, but not forgotten.)

To all my friends – in Wotton or Bristol or wherever – odd sods all of 'em. Bless Ya.

About the Author

Having visited real stone age tribes in Irian Jaya, New Guinea, and lived with treehouse-dwelling former cannibals (they stopped eating human flesh five years before!), Mick Lewis could be said to have travelled back in time without the aid of a TARDIS. He intends going back to what the missionaries have called 'the hell of the south coast' shortly, this time to visit the dreaded village of Korfar, whose inhabitants *still* practise cannibalism and who greet every approach by missionaries with storms of arrows. As well as clearly having a death wish, Mick is obviously drawn to the dark side of things – his first novel *The Bloody Man* centred on the legendary 17th century cannibal Sawney bean (in whose supposedly haunted cave on the east coast of Scotland he stayed alone one night for research) and he was recently ignominiously sacked from his job as a gruesome actor at the York Dungeon for being too scary and making too many kids (and adults) cry!